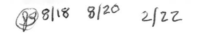

8/18   8/20   2/22

THE VIEW FROM THE LIGHTHOUSE

MIRACLES *of*
MARBLE COVE

THE VIEW FROM THE LIGHTHOUSE

MELODY CARLSON

New York, New York

Acknowledgments

Every attempt has been made to credit the sources of copyrighted material used in this book. If any such acknowledgment has been inadvertently omitted or miscredited, receipt of such information would be appreciated.

"Baking with Shelley" originally appeared as "Someone's in the Kitchen with Graham & Audrey" in *Angels on Earth* magazine. Copyright © 2008 by Guideposts. All rights reserved.

"From the Guideposts Archive" originally appeared as "His Mysterious Ways" by Cathy Slack as told to Skip Westphal in *Guideposts* magazine. Copyright © 1987 by Guideposts. All rights reserved.

Cover and interior design by Müllerhaus
Typeset by Aptara

Printed and bound in the United States of America
10 9 8 7 6 5 4 3 2 1

CHAPTER ONE

A second chance.

That's what the lighthouse on the bluff meant to Diane Spencer. At least, that's what she hoped it would mean.

She stood beside her car in the gravel viewpoint, gazing across the cliff and down at the lighthouse. Tall and white, classic and majestic, it stood securely anchored to the rocks. A testament to strength and protection. The sea wind rocked Diane backward as if the gust had been thrown at her by the sea that crashed on the rocks below her in a muted roar. The cry of the seagulls and the musky scent of the ocean took her back to her childhood. Back to before she needed a second chance.

With a sigh and a private promise to return here before the day was over, Diane got back into her car and drove toward town.

Marble Cove. She couldn't keep the smile off her face. The buildings, the church, the wharf glimpsed down narrow streets—it all looked the same as she remembered. She half-expected to hear her mother's laugh from the passenger seat.

Or Eric's.

The thought dampened her joy. But as she parked on a quiet side street, the joy resurfaced, and she had to resist the urge to pinch herself. She could hardly believe she was really here. This was it!

As always, the old iron lampposts along the street were adorned with hanging flowerpots. The pretty baskets—filled with geraniums, lobelia, pansies, and ivy—swayed gently in a soft sea breeze. This breeze also carried the pungent aroma of coffee beans being roasted nearby. Diane smiled. The Cove on Main Street must still be in business. How many mornings she and Eric had gone there to . . .

She sighed. Whoever invented the word *bittersweet* knew what she was talking about.

Diane looked down the familiar street, watching an elderly couple peer into the window of the shoe shop. They looked like regulars. Was it possible—was she really about to join them as a full-time resident of Marble Cove?

She locked her car, placed the strap of her oversized bag over her shoulder, and walked toward Main Street, taking in the friendly cobblestones and old-fashioned storefronts. She spotted a quaint bookstore she recognized. The Crow's Nest sat on the street corner, its exterior designed to resemble a ship. The windows were portholes and the rounded doors were appointed with brass trim. Inside, she knew its shelves were filled with wonderful books, both old and new, and there was a reading loft upstairs. On how many occasions had she and Eric totally lost track of time in there?

Diane paused outside of The Mercantile, admiring the variety of flags displayed in the front window. She knew she could find almost anything in that well-stocked store—from rubber boots to vegetable steamers to party goods. Part of its charm was that some of the merchandise didn't exactly change very often. She peered through the window down a long narrow aisle and saw all sorts of interesting treasures, some of which had been there for decades. Diane sighed happily. Between the sunshine and the cheerful shops, everything in this town felt absolutely perfect.

Except for one thing.

She found herself standing outside the plate-glass door of the real estate office. Could she do this? Should she? It wasn't at all how she had imagined this moment. But ... that's how things were. Nothing to do but move forward. Diane took in a deep breath, pushed open the door, and went inside the office.

A massive wooden beam crossed the ceiling of the office from left to right. Wooden slats, as if from the deck of an old sailing vessel, composed the ceiling itself. Red brick walls on two sides and white plaster walls on the others. Patricia Finley, who still reminded Diane of a college coed more than a real estate agent, sat at a wide white desk cluttered with an array of vertical files in metal racks. Behind her chair stood a tall white plastic bookshelf clogged with wide three-ring binders. If she had any lights on, Diane couldn't see them, but the space was flooded with lovely morning light through the doors and tall windows.

"Hello, Diane!" Patricia stood and vigorously shook her hand. "So wonderful to see you again. Did you have a good drive over?"

Diane took a seat on the other side of the desk. "Yes, it was lovely. But only after I decided to abandon my effort to trail the moving van. It got stuck in the slow lane of the morning commuters—they were going about thirty miles an hour."

Patricia's right eyebrow dropped. "Why were you *following* them?"

"I suppose I was being paranoid, imagining the movers making off with my things." She chuckled at her own silliness. "You see, I did a news story a few years ago about a moving company scam. You arrange for a reliable company to move your furniture; then the movers show up early and, unbeknownst to you, they have a phony van. They empty your house and you never see your belongings again."

"Oh my goodness!" Patricia looked concerned, like maybe the fraternity had cancelled out on the mixer this Friday night. "But you're sure your movers are on the up and up, right?"

Diane made an embarrassed smile. "I actually pulled over and called the moving company just to double-check on them. They were completely legit."

Patricia laughed as she picked up a manila envelope from a desk. She flipped through, looking at photos. "Let's see. Oh yes. Your wonderful new home. So, are you excited about taking occupancy today?"

"I could hardly sleep last night," Diane said. "Of course, it didn't help that I've been staying with my daughter, and she just got a new cat that likes to prowl all night. Plus her apartment is in a noisy neighborhood."

"Well," Patricia said, closing the file and folding her hands atop it. "Your new neighborhood is very quiet. You should sleep like a baby tonight."

"I can't wait."

"The keys and everything are in here." Patricia handed her a manila envelope. "I can go over there with you for a final walk-through if you like."

"No, that's okay." Diane waved her hand. "I feel like I know the cottage by heart." She chuckled. "I actually drew out a floor plan based on the measurements you e-mailed me."

"Really?" Patricia cocked her head to one side.

"To figure out furniture placement. I had to decide what would fit and what to get rid of." Diane shook her head. "Going from 2,700 square feet to about a third of that is a challenge."

"I wish I'd known you wanted to figure that sort of thing," Patricia said. "I could've sent you our little software utility that lets you see it all in 3-D."

Diane shook her head. "I probably would've drawn it out by hand anyway."

"Well, it's an adorable cottage. Even after your sale officially closed, I had several more inquiries. So consider yourself lucky you jumped on it as quickly as you did."

"Thank you." Diane tucked the envelope into her bag. "I feel very fortunate." She shook Patricia's hand. "I so appreciate your help with everything. And I hope you'll drop by and see me after I get settled in."

"I'd love to." Just then the phone rang. "Have a great day!" Patricia waved and Diane called out good-bye.

Then, feeling like a kid on Christmas morning, Diane went back outside and looked up and down the cobblestone street. It was official—*she was a citizen of Marble Cove!*

She stood there, torn as to whether she should go directly to her adorable little cottage just a few blocks away, stand right there and break into a delirious happy dance, or head to the Cove to get a latte and perhaps a bite to eat.

She elected to simply stand there on the sidewalk on Main Street, smiling so wide her cheeks strained. She knew she looked ridiculous—but she just didn't care.

Diane felt slightly lightheaded, which reminded her of what could happen if her blood sugar was low. So she opted to get something to eat.

It had been more than two years since she'd been at the Cove, a delightful coffee shop with the best poppy-seed muffins she'd ever tasted. But on her way there, she stopped in front of what used to be the five-and-dime store—a cheesy little shop that Diane had often brought Justin and Jessica to as children. Yet now the sign was gone, and as she peered in the window, she realized the space was completely cleared out.

"Hello?" A short gray-haired woman emerged from the building with a package in her arms, peering curiously at Diane. "Something I can help you with?"

"Oh no ..." Diane smiled at her. "I just thought the five-and-dime was here."

"Well, there's a new Walmart over by Tussacusset," she said crisply. "Most folks can find what they need over there."

"Thanks, but that's not what I meant. I'm moving to town today, and I suppose I'm getting reacquainted with things." Diane remembered how some Maine residents could be a bit dubious of newcomers. "Anyway, I noticed something had changed, and I was just curious."

"Oh well, then." The woman smiled. "I'm relatively new too. We moved here back in the seventies."

Diane laughed. "You call that new?"

"You do know that this *is* Maine?"

Diane nodded. "Yes, I'm aware of that."

"Anyone who's not third or fourth generation is considered new." She frowned slightly. "Never mind that my great-grandparents were born not far from here. The fact that I was born in Vermont makes me an *outsider*." She laughed and then nodded to the vacant building behind her. "As for your curiosity, this is going to become an art gallery one of these days, although it seems to be taking forever. I'm calling it Shearwater Gallery."

"Shearwater? Like the bird?"

She smiled. "That's right. And I'm the owner." She slipped her package beneath her elbow and stuck out her hand. "I'm Margaret Hoskins. Welcome to Marble Cove."

"Thank you. I'm Diane Spencer, and I'm pleased to meet you."

Margaret frowned. "Diane Spencer? Like Lady Di, eh?"

"I used to get that a lot." Diane made a tolerant smile.

"Well, as I said, *welcome*. And, if you like art—primarily nature subjects—I hope you'll stop by Shearwater. Not today, of course, but when we're open, with luck in time for the tourist season."

"Thank you. I'll be sure to do that." Diane tipped her head toward the coffee shop next door. "Right now I'm heading to the Cove."

"Well, so am I," Margaret told her. "Care for some company?"

"I'd love it."

Inside, the Cove was dark. Diane knew it had once been a fisherman's pub, and she thought the worn pine floors and wood-paneled walls probably hadn't changed much over the years.

The two women had barely entered the coffee shop when they were greeted by a thin young woman with raven-black hair. "Hey there, Margaret," she called out. "Ya want your regulah?"

"Thanks, Brenna," Margaret said. "Brenna, this is Diane Spencer. Diane's just moved to town." She turned to Diane. "I believe you said today was your first day here, right?"

"I've vacationed here for years, but today I become a full-time resident." Diane vaguely wondered about the moving van's progress, although they had promised to call her cell phone when they arrived.

"Welcome," Brenna said. "Now, what can I get for ya?"

Diane ordered a latte before peering through the curved glass pastry cabinet. "Do you still have poppy-seed muffins?"

"Not today. But the bluebear-rah ones ah good."

"That sounds fine," Diane said. She smiled at the girl's quaint way of pronouncing *blueberry*. Brenna sounded as though she'd been born and raised in Maine—probably a descendent of many generations.

With her order in hand, Diane followed Margaret through the dimly lit room. Margaret waved, calling out cheery greetings to the other patrons sitting around the small wooden tables. Margaret had a youthful energy about her, and despite her sturdy stout stature, displayed a definite spring in her step.

Margaret guided them to an available table. "Now, tell me, Diane, what brings you to Marble Cove?"

Well, it would have to come out sooner or later. Diane steeled herself and began.

"I grew up coming here on vacation. When Eric and I married, we continued the tradition with our kids. We dreamed about moving here." She had to stop and take a drink before she could continue. Margaret watched her cautiously.

"Two years ago," Diane said, "we'd been planning a weekend trip out here to meet Patricia Finley. She's a real estate agent here. We'd been talking with her on the phone, and she told us she'd found the 'perfect beach bungalow' for us, so we were coming out to see it. The night before we were supposed to leave, Eric had to go to a faculty meeting at the Barker Center. He was a literature professor at Boston College. On his way, he suffered a heart attack."

Margaret gasped. She put her hand on Diane's.

Diane couldn't let herself cry. "By the time the paramedics arrived, Eric was gone." She concentrated on her muffin. "For the next two years, I felt certain that our dream of living in Marble Cove had died with him. But now," she said, trying to sound chipper, "here I am."

Margaret patted her hand. "I'm so sorry, dear."

"No," Diane said, "it's a dream come true." She looked down at her coffee cup. "Except that I'm alone. I hadn't planned on that."

"You're not alone, dear," Margaret said. "Marble Cove is full of delightful people—friends you've yet to meet."

Diane smiled. "Thank you. I do believe that."

"Now, you haven't mentioned a career, and you seem too young to be retired. So what do you plan on doing for income now that you're one of us?"

Typical Maine practicality. Diane almost laughed. "No, I'm not retired. I used to write for a newspaper. But after Eric died, I went into something of a slump. I kept working, but I quickly realized I needed a change. I wanted to shake things up, try something new, reinvent myself." She chuckled. "I know it will sound cliché, but I decided that I want to write a novel."

Margaret's eyebrows went up. "A fellow artist! That's wonderful!"

"At my age?" Diane grimaced. "You don't think it's too late?"

Margaret laughed. "I don't know how old you are, but I'd guess you're in your forties—that hardly seems too old to become a novelist."

"Thank you, but I'm fifty-four."

Margaret waved her hand in a dismissive way. "Women nowadays—everyone knows they aren't aging like they used to. But, even so, I scarcely think fifty-four is too old to write a book. In fact, I believe I was about your age when I took up painting."

"And you're already opening a gallery?"

"I try." Margaret sighed. "Some people might not agree with my assessment that I'm an artist. I've only been at it for a dozen years, and I've still got lots to learn. But I also feel that I'm just hitting my stride. Thus came the idea of the gallery. Actually, it was Allan's idea—he's my better half. Anyway, my point is that if I, at my age, can take on something like opening an art gallery to display my own works, surely you can take on the writing of a book."

"I really appreciate your optimism. A number of my acquaintances have questioned my sanity. Even some well-meaning friends thought it would be impossible to make this transition: to quit my job, sell my home, move to Marble Cove, and write a novel."

"Some people are intimidated by dreams."

"Maybe so. It sounds silly, but as a child, when I came here with my parents, I would imagine myself living here. I would pen these hokey mystery stories in my little notebook.

Every single one was set in or near the lighthouse." She chuckled. "I think I was in love with it."

Margaret's brows arched high. "The Orlean Point Lighthouse?"

Diane laughed. "Yes, I suppose I was a hopeless romantic. But it always seemed so mysterious and wonderful to me. I felt the lighthouse had some secrets to tell."

"That's very interesting."

"Why's that?"

"I have a similar feeling about the Orlean Light."

"Really?" Diane studied her new friend.

"Allan thinks I'm obsessed with it. I've painted dozens of pictures of it. Finally Allan talked me into painting more wildlife, and I've tried to move on, but I'm still drawn to it."

"That *is* interesting."

The people at the table beside Diane and Margaret got up and headed for the door. Diane noticed several parties waiting for a table near Brenna's hostess stand. Over the pervasive aroma of coffee, she detected what smelled like a new batch of chocolate cookies. She thought she could come here every day and be happy. Well, now she could.

"So you're going to be a real novelist and write stories about the lighthouse?"

Diane grinned. "Does that sound terribly foolish?"

"Not at all."

"Anyway, here I am." Diane held up her hands. "And really, it seems slightly miraculous that I'm doing this. Despite the sluggish real estate market, my house sold quickly, and the same week that sale closed, a sweet little cottage came up for sale right in town and—"

"You don't mean the Benson house?"

Diane thought for a moment. "Yes, the family selling the house was named Benson."

"On Newport Avenue?" Margaret's eyes grew large.

"Yes, that's right."

"Well—can you believe it? You bought the house next door to mine!"

Diane laughed. "Well, hello, neighbor!" She lifted her coffee mug like a toast.

Margaret grinned as they clinked the mugs together. "Wha'd'ya know?"

"So tell me a bit about the neighborhood. Are you happy you're in it?"

"Why, of course!"

As Diane listened to how wonderful the neighborhood was, she finished the last of her muffin and latte. "You're making me very anxious to see my little cottage now," she admitted. "I only did one walk-through, and that was on a rainy night in April. But even so, I knew it was just what I wanted, so I didn't hesitate. I've been very anxious to see it by the light of day."

"Well, of course, you are." Margaret stood and picked up her package. "Now I need to get this over to the post office, and you need to get on your merry way. So let's not waste another minute. It's been such a pleasure to meet you. And now that I know we're neighbors, well, I expect we'll have plenty of opportunities to get better acquainted."

"Yes!" Diane wanted to give her new neighbor a hug but wasn't sure about Maine manners and decided to restrain herself ... for now. "I'll see you later," she called as they parted ways.

Then, hurrying back to her car, she felt decidedly giddy as she started the engine. She had done it. After all those years of dreaming and planning and hoping, she had finally made it to Marble Cove.

CHAPTER TWO

Diane stood staring at her new home, trying to soak it all in. All she could think was that the one-story cottage was perfect.

Perfect from the driftwood gray shingles to the milky white window trim and ocean-blue shutters. And the russet-red door was so inviting, she couldn't wait to go in. Oh, the front yard was a bit neglected, the flowerbeds overgrown, but the overall general effect was charmingly quaint. A writer's cottage! She was just about to go down the brick path to the front porch when she heard someone behind her.

"Whatta'ya doing here?" demanded a child's voice.

Diane looked down to see a little boy dressed like a superhero staring up at her with a suspicious expression. "Hello," she said with a smile. "Who are you?"

"I *said*—whatta'ya doing here?" He placed his little fists on his hips, glaring at her as though he planned to zap her with his superpowers.

"I'm sorry!" A young blond woman hurried to cross the quiet street with a baby in her arms. She looked flustered. "We just got out of the car, and I didn't even see him come over here." She frowned down at the freckle-faced lad. "Aiden, you know you're not to cross the street by yourself."

"I'm not Aiden." He scowled at her. "I'm Spiderman." He pointed his finger at Diane now. "Whatta'ya doing here?"

"Aiden!" The woman shook her head.

Diane laughed. "It's okay. Spiderman is just keeping the neighborhood safe. And as the newest neighbor here, I appreciate that." She leaned over and looked in Aiden's blue eyes. "My name is Diane Spencer. I just bought this house, and I'm moving in today." She stuck out her hand.

"Oh?" He glanced at his mom and then shyly put his hand out.

She firmly shook it. "It's a pleasure to meet you, Spiderman."

"My name's Aiden," he said quietly.

"Aka Spiderman." She grinned.

"Ak … huh?"

"That means *also known as* Spiderman," Diane told him. He still looked confused.

"I'm Shelley Bauer," the young woman said. "We live across the street." She held up the golden-haired little one in her arms. "And this is Emma. Welcome to the neighborhood. It'll be nice having someone in this house again."

"Thank you. I'm looking forward to settling in." Diane tickled the baby's chin. "And I just met Margaret Hoskins today too."

"Margaret is a real sweet lady." Shelley tipped her head to where Aiden had squatted down on the sidewalk, petting a black-and-white cat that was taking a sunbath. "That's one of the Hoskins' cats." She chuckled. "Aiden is always trying to sneak them into our house."

They chatted a bit longer before Emma began to squirm.

"Oh," Shelley said, "she's getting hungry. I probably spent too much time when I made a trip to the store," she said as she jiggled the baby. "That's what I get for trying to use grocery coupons."

Diane ran her hand over the baby's downy head. "And were you shopping with your little ones in tow?"

Shelley nodded with a weary sigh. "Yeah, it was pure madness."

"I remember those days. Taking small kids to the grocery store is like walking into the battlefield unarmed. Nothing prepares you for it." Diane laughed.

"And by the time I get these two fed, unload the car, put things away—we are all going down for a nap."

"I don't wanna nap!" Aiden wailed.

"Oh dear." Diane put a hand on Shelley's shoulder. "Hang in there. And next time you need to go to the grocery store, consider leaving the kids with me. I mean, once I'm settled in. I'd love to play grandma."

"Thanks." Shelley smiled but looked uncertain. "I appreciate it."

Now Diane remembered how Mainers could initially be reticent, and she wondered if she'd crossed the line. Also, what intelligent mother would hand her children, no matter how unruly, to strangers? "Or maybe you can all just come over for tea and cookies sometime soon."

"*Cookies?*" Aiden's eyes widened with interest.

Emma cried louder and squirmed.

"That sounds nice," Shelley said over the baby's wails. "But we better get moving." With Emma cradled in one arm, Shelley grabbed Aiden's hand.

"But I want cookies!" he yelled.

"Great to meet you, Diane," Shelley called as she struggled to get them all across the street. "See ya!"

"Hang in there," Diane called back, wincing at the sounds of both children crying and fussing now. She felt slightly guilty but knew it wasn't her fault.

She also knew it wouldn't be long before those worn-out kids would be napping. She hoped Shelley would be too. Because one thing Diane did remember about those early childhood years was that the louder they screamed, the harder they fell—into their beds. Naps, she thought, were God's saving grace for young mothers.

She turned back to her house now, smiling happily to see that it was still sweet and welcoming—and all hers. Digging in her purse, she found the envelope and fished out the keys. She walked up the herringbone brick path and onto the small front porch, imagining how her pair of white shaker rockers would look sitting there. And she'd have to get a large planter, fill it with geraniums, and place it in the corner. With great anticipation, she put her key in the keyhole and listened as it clicked the lock open. Let the fun begin!

She pushed the door open and walked into her house. But the first thing that greeted her was *the smell*—and it wasn't a cheerful aroma of cookies baking or even the pungent scent of garlic and onions sizzling in olive oil. No, this smell was foul and stale and reminded her of something dead.

Leaving the door wide open, she ran over to open a window, which appeared to be stuck with paint, and then to another one, which was equally stuck. Finally she dashed through the house, holding her breath, and opened the back door, hoping a cross breeze might waft through and freshen the air a bit. She ducked out the back door and stepped onto the shaky little back porch. It occurred to her then that her sweet dream cottage might come with a few nightmares.

Undaunted, she used this opportunity to stroll around the house, taking in the backyard. Though it was overgrown with weeds and was even more neglected than the front yard, the good-sized fruit trees and a nice selection of hardy perennials showed potential. She ventured on around the side of the house and saw that the sweet white picket fence was a little wobbly. Finally she went to the front porch again.

Diane stood there trying to think. What would cause a smell like that? A backed-up sewage pipe perhaps? Rotten food left in the refrigerator? She hoped there wasn't a dead animal in there. The image of a family pet that had been left behind, forgotten, trapped in the fridge ... made her cringe. She was tempted to call Patricia and ask for help, but she reminded herself she was in Maine now. People here were independent, self-sufficient, take-control sorts. How would it look if on her first day here she was calling the Realtor and crying for help?

She stood on the porch and thought hard, making a plan. On her mad dash through the house, she'd seen nothing terribly out of the ordinary. Perhaps it was a bit more run down than she remembered, but she'd seen nothing that might've caused such a foul odor. She decided to make her way back toward the bedroom and bathroom this time to see if the smell was stronger back there.

Bracing herself, she dashed in again, this time checking other parts of the house. She'd run in, check a corner or room, and run back out to clear her lungs. On her third run-through she realized the smell was strongest in the kitchen. And either she was getting used to the smell or the air was refreshing itself a bit, because as she sniffed around, opening the fridge—no dead mouse, thankfully—checking the sink drain, she wasn't nearly as sickened as she had been originally.

Finally she opened the cabinet doors beneath the sink. And there, in a plastic trash bin was the source of the offensive smell. Just some old trash that no one had thrown out. Probably the remains of the Bensons' last meal. Holding her breath, she grabbed the bin. Carefully, not wanting anything to spill out, she carried it out the back door and across the yard, where she set it down a safe distance away— and downwind. She'd deal with it later. Whew! That was a relief.

Feeling greatly encouraged, she returned to her house and even managed to open a few of the windows. Though she was glad the movers hadn't arrived yet, she was now getting worried. What could possibly be taking them so long? She remembered she'd left her cell phone charging in the car.

When she went outside and grabbed her phone, she discovered several irate messages from the moving company, saying they'd taken the wrong highway and needed directions. Why didn't they have a GPS or just a regular map? She called their number.

"No worries," the guy who answered assured her. "We're only twenty, maybe, thirty, minutes out now. Larry just got confused. We'll be there around one."

"Oh, good." Diane closed her phone and wondered if the air quality in the house had improved much. She knew she had some scented candles ... somewhere in that moving van. Probably packed in the bottom of a box in the deepest recesses of the truck.

"Hello there!"

Diane turned at the voice.

Margaret was waving from the front porch of the celadon-green house next door.

"Oh, hi!" Diane called as she went over to the fence line. "My moving van got lost. But that's probably a good thing since it needs some airing out in there." She explained about the forgotten trash beneath the sink. "I'm just glad it wasn't something serious. I do hope the smell will clear out before the furniture arrives."

"I have just the ticket." Margaret disappeared into her house. A couple of minutes later, Margaret emerged with a pump bottle of some kind. "This is a completely natural product. Made from grapefruit peels. It's the best air freshener ever."

"Grapefruit," Diane nodded. "Sounds good to me. You want to come in?"

"You bet."

They walked through Diane's house with Margaret spraying liberally and Diane feeling increasingly hopeful.

"Now," Margaret said, "while the air circulates a bit, you come on over to my house for some lunch. That is, if you like black bean soup."

Diane grinned. "You are my kind of neighbor, Margaret."

"I was going to bring some soup over to you," she said as they went next door, "but I think you need a break." She opened the door to her house. "Come on in."

Diane looked around the room. Well-worn leather couch and chairs, colorful pillows, knitted throws, a couple of Navajo rugs, interesting wooden furnishings, a bookcase that went from floor to ceiling surrounding the fireplace, and several cats.

"Excuse our mess," Margaret said in an offhand way as she tossed some newspapers into a basket on the hearth. "None of us are too much into housekeeping."

"This simply looks inviting to me."

"Allan?" Margaret called. "Come in here and meet our new neighbor."

A balding man about the height of Margaret came into the room, brushing something from his hands and smiling self-consciously as Margaret introduced them. "Excuse the dust," he told her. "Just sawdust."

"Are you building something?"

"Allan is a talented carpenter." Margaret pointed to the coffee and end tables. "Those are his."

"I noticed them when I came in," Diane said. "They are beautiful. All that inlaid wood and the smooth shapes—it must be a lot of work."

"Each piece is one-of-a-kind," Margaret told her. "A work of art."

"Oh, I wouldn't say that." Allan waved his hand and sat down in a dark green recliner.

"They look like art to me," Diane said. "Do you plan to sell them in the gallery?"

"I do," Margaret said. "But Allan is dragging his heels. Now if you'll excuse me, I'll run and put lunch together."

"Can I help?" Diane asked.

"No, you get acquainted with Allan."

Allan invited her to sit, and she filled him in on where she was from and why she'd moved here. As she finished, she wondered how many times she'd have to tell her story and if there was a way to make it more interesting—or less depressing. "How about you?" she asked. "Have you always been a furniture maker?"

"No. Margaret and I used to have an accounting firm. Just pursued our hobbies on the side." He chuckled. "I think it was a form of mental health. Then, about ten years ago, our hobbies started to take over. We sold the business and have been doing pretty much as we please since then. The way I got hooked on furniture was by making frames for Margaret's art. The more I handled these different kinds of woods, the more I realized I loved woodworking and wanted to do bigger things. It's all been kind of a discovering process."

She smiled. "Sounds delightful to me. And what a wonderful place to do it, here in Marble Cove. It's no wonder you feel inspired. I confess I'm feeling inspired myself. One of the reasons I've moved here is to try to write a novel. I've always wanted to, though it still feels a little strange saying it out loud. But hearing about you and Margaret is encouraging."

"Sometimes you get to that place where you realize there's more to life than making money ... and you're willing to take a risk and do something you love." He smiled. "I'm not saying life's perfect. It's certainly not. But it's a lot less stressful than it used to be." A fat striped cat jumped into his lap. "This is Lizzy." He stroked the cat's head. "Our daughter loves cats. We have three now, and we keep telling Adelaide no more, but if she finds a stray ... well, it's not easy."

"Does your daughter live with you?"

He nodded, still stroking the cat. "Adelaide is our special girl. She came to us late in life, and she has mild Down syndrome. She'll be twenty-five next winter. She's volunteering at the community center today. They have a program there that she enjoys where local companies match their volunteer hours with funds to send to a charity of their choice. If they meet their goal, they have a big bash at the end of the summer."

"Come on, you two," Margaret called from the kitchen. "Time to eat."

"Down you go, Lizzy." Allan stood, dropping the cat to the floor. "I better go wash up, or Margaret will box my ears."

Diane smiled at him. Such a sweet fellow. Already she felt she knew him. She went into the kitchen, where a charming table was arrayed with bright-colored dishes, placemats, and napkins. "What a fun table setting!"

"Nothing really matches," Margaret said from the kitchen. "But as you can probably guess, I love color. I suppose that was what drew me to painting. I wanted an excuse to play with color." She put a yellow bowl of sour cream on the table. "Have a seat. I already dished up the soup. And the rye bread is homemade."

"You bake bread too?" Diane shook her head.

"Actually, Allan is the baker," she said quietly. "He doesn't like me to tell anyone about his culinary talents, mainly because he uses a bread-maker."

"Even so." Diane looked at the thick slices of dark bread. "I had a bread-maker and I never produced anything that looked as good as this."

"*Mmm.*" Allan smacked his lips. "I'm starving."

"Just so you're not too impressed," Margaret said as Diane sat down. "We don't always sit down to a pretty table at lunchtime."

"That's true." Allan put a napkin in his lap. "Sometimes she just throws the food out into the garage for me to eat off the floor."

Margaret made a face at him.

Diane laughed. "You two are making me feel so at home." She dipped her spoon into the soup.

"Well, we've been hoping someone would buy the Benson place for something beyond a vacation home," Margaret said. "The cottage was vacant most of the time when they owned it. And the house across the street from us is a vacation house as well. So having a full-time neighbor next door is a huge relief."

"Yes," Allan said. "We're happy to welcome you to the neighborhood."

"And I must say this lunch is delicious," Diane told them. "If the gallery doesn't work for you, you might want to consider a restaurant."

This made them laugh.

"I'm afraid cooking is not my strong suit," Diane said. "After my kids were in school, I went to work full-time, and I suppose I used that as an excuse to shy away from the kitchen. Not that I never cooked, but I tried to avoid it if I could. Then after the kids were gone, we ate out a lot."

"Well, you'll be challenged to eat out a lot here," Margaret said. "There are fewer than a dozen restaurants to choose from, and half of those are fish and chips or pizza."

"Maybe I'll learn to cook." Diane looked at the ceiling. "I can't believe I just said that."

"If you do, I'll share produce from my garden with you," Margaret offered.

"That sounds wonderful."

"Watch out, Diane," Allan said with a twinkle in his eye. "Margaret's always trying to foist her produce on to any unsuspecting neighbor. Come August, you could be up to your eyeballs in zucchini squash."

"Well, if I do unload some zucchinis on you," Margaret said with a wink, "I'll give you some good recipes too."

The lunch passed pleasantly with them chatting like old friends. They were just finishing up when Allan pointed to the front window. "Is that your moving van?"

Diane went to look. The big truck came to a stop next door. "Yes—finally!"

"Well, you run along," Margaret said. "And let us know if you need any help."

Diane thanked them both and then hurried back to her house, where the truck was just parking. Two men hopped out of the cab and opened the sliding door at the back of the eighteen-wheeler. Diane thought her furnishings looked slightly lost and out of place in the back of the big truck. But seeing it all, here at the house ... it suddenly felt very real—as well as a bit scary. She was really doing this.

CHAPTER THREE

Diane's blueprint for furniture placement helped in getting everything unloaded from the moving van. But once the muscle boys were gone, Diane realized she'd have to do some rearranging on her own. She also knew she'd need to do some painting and a few repairs and upgrades to make the place really comfortable. But she'd expected as much. The main thing was that her belongings were unloaded, and she was going to be able to sleep in her own bed tonight. That was, if she could locate the boxes containing her bedding.

However, before the sun went down, she needed to do something very important—something she'd been waiting to do all day. Diane *had* to take a walk on the beach. It was something she'd been looking forward to for weeks—that first walk on the beach as a permanent resident of Marble Cove. And she planned to walk all the way to the lighthouse. She knew the sun wouldn't set until eight, so if she started out soon, she'd have plenty of time to get there. Despite how safe she felt here, the idea of walking on the beach alone and after dark was a bit unsettling.

She'd noticed some clouds rolling in and the wind picking up, so she pulled on her polar fleece jacket and her new pair of Bogs. She'd ordered the waterproof boots online and couldn't wait to try them out. A perfectly clean and dry promenade walk ran along a long strip of the beach, but she wanted the freedom to wander down by the water's edge, perhaps find some shells. And she wanted to keep her feet warm.

She slipped her cell phone in her pocket, only to be safe, and was only stepping off her porch when she saw an elderly woman cross the street and walk purposefully down the sidewalk toward her.

The old woman had an expectant look on her face, and in her hands was something wrapped in a blue and white gingham towel. "Wait!" she called out. "Don't go yet."

Diane pointed to herself. "Me?"

"Yes!" The woman smiled broadly as her plaid woolen jacket flapped in the breeze. "Oh, I'm so glad I caught you." She ceremoniously handed the towel-wrapped baking dish to Diane. "Welcome to the neighborhood. I am Mrs. Peabody." She pointed to the lavender two-story Victorian house across the street and smiled. "That's my house over there."

"Hello, Mrs. Peabody. I'm Diane Spencer. This is move-in day for me."

"Oh yes, I know all about it. You were a newspaper reporter and your dearly departed husband, may he rest in peace, was a professor ..." She rattled on with a clipped Maine accent that replaced the *er* sounds with *ah* sounds.

But the most amazing thing was how she spouted out information like a walking Wikipedia. Mrs. Peabody had missed a few details, but most of her facts were curiously spot-on. So much so that if this little old lady didn't have such a sweet round face framed in a wreath of curly white hair, Diane might've suspected the old girl was a stalker ... or an FBI agent.

"Well, you've certainly done your research." Diane studied the small, neatly dressed woman.

Mrs. Peabody wore what looked like a Pendleton jacket from the 1950s over a straight woolen skirt. She appeared to be in her eighties, with a mind as sharp as a tack.

Mrs. Peabody made a sheepish smile. "Oh, you'll have to excuse me, dear, but I like to stay on top of what's going on in the neighborhood. And your Realtor, Patricia Finley, happens to be my great niece. We meet for coffee sometimes."

Now that rang a bell. Diane did recall Patricia mentioning an elderly aunt on Newport Avenue. She'd jokingly called her Mrs. Busybody.

Mrs. Peabody pointed to the warm baking dish in Diane's hands. "That's some macaroni and cheese. I thought you might not have had time to go to the grocery store. First, set your oven to 350 degrees and let it bake for about twenty minutes, and it should be just right."

"Thank you." Diane smiled. "I love macaroni and cheese."

"Oh, good—good." Mrs. Peabody nodded happily. "I thought to myself, what would my new neighbor like, and then I said to myself, *Doesn't everyone like macaroni and cheese?* I know my grandchildren always did. Every time they came to my house they expected macaroni and cheese and strawberry Jell-O with bananas and chocolate cream pie. I make the best chocolate cream pie—and that's no exaggeration. I used to win the blue ribbon at the fair every year. But I finally got too old for that. Now I grow roses. Do you like roses?" She paused for a breath.

"Yes, I do."

"Well, then, I'll have to give you some cuttings for your yard. I know the Bensons' backyard is in wrack and ruin these days. Poor old George got too old to keep it up nice anymore. Of course, they were just vacation folks. But back when they first got the place, every time they arrived here, George would get out the mower and the edger and hedge trimmers, and he would go straight to work. And I'd say to myself, *Doesn't that man know it's supposed to be a vacation house?* But no, no, there he'd be, a-working himself half to death. Why, you'd think he'd hire one of the local boys to do it for him. I even suggested that very thing once. Well, George didn't like that one bit. I suppose he thought I was interfering. But I'd a-thought he'd understand how I had to look at his unkempt yard the whole year long while he and Gladys were away. Oh my, look at those clouds. It's sure a lowry day." She paused, as if temporarily winded.

"Well, thank you again, Mrs. Peabody." Diane tipped her head toward her cottage. "I better get this into the oven straight away. I was about to take a walk on the beach, and it will be so lovely to come home to dinner all ready to eat. You have no idea how much I appreciate your kindness." Diane kept her chatter coming nonstop as she slowly backed away.

Her goal was to keep Mrs. Peabody from initiating another long monologue. "I'll see you around, then," Diane called. "Thanks again!" She waved and turned and hurried away. She didn't mean to appear unfriendly; she simply wanted to get to the beach before nightfall.

With the casserole safely in the oven, Diane peeked out the window to be sure Mrs. Peabody couldn't intercept her for another chat. The coast was clear, so she ducked out the door and headed straight for the beach.

It was still slightly unbelievable to realize she actually owned a Marble Cove cottage—and it was less than two blocks from the ocean! Just the idea made her feet feel light as she hurried toward the sea.

The sound of the ocean had been playing in her ears all day, rumbling and steady, enticing her to come out and say hello. She didn't think she'd ever tire of that sound, and she hoped never to grow deafened to it like some locals claimed would happen. Her eyes drank in the varying shades of blue in the sea and sky as she walked down the promenade. Breakers rolled over in flashes of white foam. Seabirds squawked overhead. Several other walkers were out. Not as many as there would be during tourist season, but enough to make her feel comfortable about being out here on her own.

After a bit, she ventured from the promenade and out onto the sandy beach. Strolling along the edge of the surf, she kept a lookout for shells or maybe a piece of sea glass. She'd been collecting sea glass since childhood and had a big jar she hoped to one day fill.

She took in a deep breath, relishing the feel of the southerly breeze in her face. It was all so perfect—so wonderful— she almost wished she had someone to share it with. And naturally, that reminded her of Eric. How many times had they walked this beach together? And she had never once guessed that someday she would be walking here without him ... that he would be gone.

Ironically, she had actually imagined the opposite at one time. She had fully expected it would be Eric walking this beach without her, and surely by now. As if it were yesterday, she recalled the conversation they'd had about five years ago.

"I want you to remarry after I'm gone," she had firmly told him as they walked along this very stretch of sand. Keeping her gaze directly forward so he couldn't see her eyes, she had continued. "You're the kind of man who needs someone alongside him. You need a good woman." Then she'd forced a laugh. "And I'm sure there will be a long lineup of them."

"Oh, Diane." He'd used that tone that meant he didn't want to talk about this.

"We have to face facts," she'd persisted. "The treatments haven't worked—there's nothing left to do. When I'm gone, you'll need someone. I understand this."

Then he had stopped walking, pulled her toward him, wrapped her in his arms, and they had held on to each other—right here—and cried. Like children, they'd stood there sobbing and clinging to each other until finally nothing was left ... no more tears, no more emotions, just the two of them holding on.

Then Eric had taken in a deep breath and adjusted Diane's pale blue L.L.Bean hat—which she'd used to hide her bald head—and he'd taken her face into his hands, gazed deeply into her eyes and tenderly kissed her. "Diane," he'd said in a raspy voice, "*I love you.* And I know this with certainty: You are the only woman I will ever need. I am a one-woman man."

She sighed as she continued to walk. It turned out he'd been right.

The old lighthouse came into sight now. She didn't know how long ago the Orlean Point Lighthouse had been decommissioned, but it had to have been before she was born, because she'd never seen it work. She knew that the stately white structure was still a beloved landmark in Marble Cove.

What was it about this structure that made it feel like more than just a lighthouse? It seemed like a spiritual icon to her. Whether it was symbolic of hope or faith or second chances was unclear, but she always felt encouraged to see the dignified tower—rock solid and unchanging. Although no light flashed from it, she liked to imagine what it would look like to see a long golden beam cutting through the fog or the dark of night. It must've been quite a sight back in its day.

She walked on, admiring the lighthouse as she approached it. She was just coming up to the rocky section of beach, the area where her children used to love exploring the tide pools, when motion caught her eye.

Looking to her right, she spotted a yellow dog running over the rocks away from her. But as she looked closer, the dog appeared to be limping, and then it stopped and turned to look at her. She glanced up and down the beach now, expecting to see an owner nearby. But most of the walkers seemed to be heading back toward town.

"Hello," she called out to the dog. "Are you lost?"

The dog stood there, watching her with its tail straight down, almost as if frightened. She didn't know dog breeds, but it looked big and lovable, and it was about thirty yards from her now. She called out again, but the dog turned and started limping away.

Although she called and called, the dog seemed determined to move toward the craggy rocks. She wondered if it had fallen from one of the cliffs, perhaps from one of the few homes up there. Diane wanted to help the animal, but she knew she couldn't safely follow it through this rocky area, and even if she reached it, what would she do? It looked too big to carry. It was possible that its owner was around, maybe even looking for it. So feeling slightly foolish but sincere, she asked God to watch out for that yellow dog ... to get it safely home.

Diane resumed walking up the path leading to the lighthouse. Feeling slightly awed and tremendously happy, she paused and looked up at it. Here she was—just her and the Orlean Point Light. She'd made it.

"Here you still are," she said to the lighthouse. "Standing as straight and tall as ever." She reached out and patted the smooth, hard, white surface. "Good old boy. I came back, just like I promised I would." She looked up to the glass-windowed area that had once housed the giant lamp. "What I wouldn't give to see you light up sometime." She chuckled, thinking it was fortunate no one was around to hear her conversing with the lighthouse. "I just came out here to tell you I'm a full-timer now. I expect I'll be seeing a lot of you. And you might even become a character in my novel."

Diane noticed that the sky was getting darker and fog was rolling in. "Well, Orlean, since you can't light my way home, and I didn't think to bring a flashlight, I guess I'll have to say adieu." She patted it again. "But don't worry, I'll be back tomorrow."

She was about to turn when a flash caught her eye. She paused and squinted, peering up at the lighthouse through the dusky light. Was it possible? Had she really seen a light coming from the top of the tower? She stared for several minutes, willing the flash of light to come again. But nothing. Just the sound of the crashing of waves upon the rocks.

"Did you do that just for me?"

A rumble in her stomach reminded Diane of the casserole in her oven. Whether the light had been real or a product of her imagination, her hunger was authentic. So she turned away, imagining the tales she might concoct based on a mysterious light from a decommissioned lighthouse.

Soon thoughts of the lighthouse were replaced with the desire to see her new home again. Oh, it was good to be here in Marble Cove—good to be alive. And it was good to know that hot macaroni and cheese awaited her at her sweet little cottage. At home.

CHAPTER FOUR

Diane peeked into the oven—the cheese was bubbling. She turned off the heat and looked around for something to use as a potholder. She wished she'd been more specific when marking boxes. All of the "kitchen" boxes had been brought into the kitchen, but which box had the kitchen linens in it?

After opening several, she found the one with tea towels and potholders and was able to remove the sizzling casserole from the oven. The oven door creaked loudly as she closed it.

Her plan was to replace the dated appliances and maybe even the cabinets, unless they were sturdier than they looked on the outside. But the plastic countertops really had to go. For that reason she didn't feel too concerned when she set the hot dish with only a towel beneath it on the Formica. Now, if she could just find the dishes and silverware.

Eventually she sat down in the living room to eat, using a large cardboard box that was filled with pillows and throws as a table. The cheesy casserole was delightful—just like her own mother used to make—and Diane knew she'd have to think of a special way to thank Mrs. Peabody.

After dinner, Diane went through the bedroom boxes until she found enough linens to make her bed for the night. She hadn't brought the king-size bed she and Eric had shared. It would've overwhelmed this small room, and she certainly didn't need something that big. Instead, she'd opted for a relatively new queen-size bed that used to be in their guest room.

From now on, her "guest room" would be limited to a sofa-bed that shared the room she planned to use as her writing studio. If Justin and Jessica ever came to visit at the same time (which she suspected would be rare since Justin was deployed overseas), one of them would have to sleep on the living room couch. But at least the deep-seated sofa and its down-filled pillows were comfortable.

This creamy white sofa and matching easy chair and ottoman were some of the recent purchases she'd made specifically for the cottage. Their old leather sectional would have been far too large for the small living room, so she'd sold it along with many other pieces at a three-day estate sale that Jessica had helped her with.

Hoping to create an atmosphere that was reflective of the seaside location, Diane had opted for light ocean-like colors—oyster white, sandy beige, sea-glass green, and pale aqua. She'd been collecting bits and pieces over the years, stashing them away in a spare bedroom closet, hoping for the day when the seaside retreat became a reality. Her plan was to create a cross between shabby chic and comfortable contemporary. She just hoped it was possible.

With her bedroom somewhat situated, Diane walked from room to room in the small house, making a list of the things she'd like to do before she unpacked. Fortunately the pinewood floors running throughout the house were in good shape. A bit worn perhaps, but nicely worn. However, the dark and dingy walls were in need of paint, and although Diane had painted more than a few walls in her life, she thought perhaps she wanted help this time.

She'd already collected a number of paint samples, all in seaside colors. She hoped good interior painters wouldn't be hard to come by in Marble Cove. Also, she realized as she noticed a dripping shower nozzle, she would need a handyman to see to some small repairs as well as some updating here and there. Maybe her new neighbors would have some recommendations. Certainly, Mrs. Peabody would have an opinion.

Finally, exhausted, Diane settled into her new bedroom. She pushed the boxes against one wall, creating an open trail to the doorway. She also made sure to plug in the bathroom night-light, a seashell one that Jessica had just given her last night. "So you don't go stumbling around in the dark," Jessica had wisely said.

After years of always being too cold at night, Diane had taken to cracking open a window this past couple of years. It was something that came along with being middle-aged. "Power surges," she'd explained to Jessica once. "Someday you will understand." But as she forced the sticky window open, she realized this was one more thing to put on her handyman list. Fortunately, she'd budgeted for these little home improvements.

It was past ten when she sank down into the pillow-top mattress. With a new lighter-than-air eiderdown comforter and the smoothest cotton sheets she'd ever felt, Diane felt certain she would sleep like a baby tonight. Often she had to read herself to sleep ... sometimes staying awake into the wee hours of the morning. But hearing the sound of the surf through the open window—that peacefully rumbling, never-ending mariner's lullaby—she suspected she would soon be asleep.

★   ★   ★

The next morning, Diane awoke to the haunting sound of a foghorn. Lying there in the gray early dawn, she just listened as the low mellow tone repeated itself again and again. She didn't know much about music, but she thought it was probably playing in a minor key. Then she wondered how far apart the sounds occurred. Counting in her head for several minutes, she decided the foghorn repeated about every thirty seconds. For some reason she found this immensely comforting.

The house was cold when she got up. It hadn't occurred to her to turn on any heat last night, nor to close the window at some point in the night. She looked outside the front window. A dense blanket of fog draped over the neighborhood. But instead of feeling disappointed, like she often did as a child while visiting at the sea, she experienced a sense of heightened anticipation, wondering what this day would hold.

She muscled the window shut and turned on the forced air furnace, listening as it rumbled to life. Then, looking more closely at the stone fireplace in the living room, she realized that what she really wanted was a fire. A cheerful, crackling fire. And, unless she'd imagined it, she'd seen a lean-to wood shed on the side of the house. She started to go out the door still wearing her pajamas but thought better of it. She was new in the neighborhood, and she didn't want to shock anyone. So she changed into her most comfortable jeans and a Boston College sweatshirt, slipped on her clogs, and went outside.

She'd just gathered several pieces of wood and was heading for the porch when she heard someone calling out to her. Looking across the street, she saw Shelley, the young mom, waving as she picked up the newspaper.

"How's the moving in going?" Shelley called out.

Diane set the wood on the porch and then turned around and smiled. "Great! Thanks!"

"Dan told me to tell you to holler if you need help with anything."

Diane nodded, walking toward her. Unless she was mistaken, Dan was Shelley's husband. "Is Dan very handy at unsticking windows?"

"Oh, sure." Newspaper in hand, Shelley crossed the street toward Diane. "Want me to send him over to give you a hand?" She lowered her voice. "He's not working today."

"Oh?" Diane had to think hard to remember what day it was. Wasn't it still early in the week?

"He wouldn't want me to mention it, but they're going through some changes at the shipping company where he's employed. He usually works all the time. In fact, I'm always complaining about being on my own with the kids so much. But this new boss laid off a bunch of the guys—he said for just a few days." She glanced back across the street. "But I can tell Dan's pretty worried."

"Would he really want to help me?"

"Sure. Like I said, he's really handy. He grew up in this big family where they did everything for themselves. I mean like real pioneers." She chuckled. "Remember that old TV show *The Waltons*? I used to watch reruns of it when I was a kid. I'm always telling Dan that's just like his family. All the kids had to help out with chores and building and stuff. But as a result, Dan can fix just about anything."

"I've already got a fairly long to-do list."

"Then let Dan have at it." Shelley nodded eagerly.

"Really? Yesterday with the kids you seemed a little ... I don't know. You're sure you don't want him around to help?"

"I think it would be good for him to help you, Diane. And I have a little friend of Aiden's coming over for a playdate this morning. Dan probably won't enjoy that much, and I can't cancel at this late notice."

"I'd love to have Dan's help, and I'll gladly pay him."

Shelley frowned. "No, no ... I don't think so. Dan can't take money from a neighbor."

Diane folded her arms across her chest and firmly shook her head. "By the same token, I couldn't take free labor from a neighbor."

Shelley's mouth twisted to one side as if she were thinking.

"You tell Dan that if he wants to work for me, I'm happy to *hire* him," Diane stated. "Otherwise, I'll have to ask around and see if I can find someone—"

"No, that's okay," Shelley said quickly. "Let me tell Dan first."

"Good." Diane smiled. "Does he like to paint? Walls, I mean?"

"He's an excellent painter."

"Does he have tools?"

"Oh yeah. Dan adores tools. And he has a great little workshop in the garage. Between tag sales and what his parents have given him for birthday and Christmas presents, Dan's acquired a pretty nice collection."

"Tell him to come on over if he wants to work."

"Thanks, Diane." Shelley looked relieved. "I'll do that."

Diane walked back to her house. She picked up the firewood and took it inside. The furnace was working, but she decided it did still need a little help.

She had just gotten the fire started when she heard a knock on the door. "Coming," she called as she hurried to answer it.

"I'm Dan Bauer," a tall, sandy-haired young man told her. "Shelley said you could use—" He stopped talking and pushed right past her and burst into the living room.

"*What?*" Shocked, she turned to see that smoke was pouring from the fireplace.

"The flue!" he yelled as he knelt next to the fireplace, shoving the burning wood aside and reaching right inside the chimney.

"Oh dear!" Diane stared in horror. "Be careful!"

There was a clang of metal and Dan stood back up, looking down at his blackened hands and forearms. "The damper was closed, ma'am."

"I see that now. Are you okay? You didn't get burned, did you?"

"Nah, I'm okay. But maybe I could wash off my hands."

"Of course." She shook her head as she followed him into the kitchen. "I feel like such a fool. I can't believe I didn't think to open the damper."

"Ah, so didn't I," he said as he scrubbed his hands.

She cocked her head. "I'm sorry?"

"*Hmm*? Oh, 'So didn't I.' We say it here in Maine. It means, like, 'I did the same thing once.'"

"Oh!" She tore off a couple of paper towels for him. "Well, thank you for opening it. I can't imagine what a mess that would've made."

He smiled as he dried his hands and she could see a bit of Aiden in him. Or maybe it was the other way around. "So, anyway, Shelley said you could use a hand around here."

"That seems rather obvious." She told him a bit of what she wanted to do and then walked him around, pointing out some of the specific tasks as he made a list.

"Which do you want done first?" he asked after the tour.

"Well, if the painting was done, I could put my things away. That would be nice."

"Have you got the paint?"

She frowned. "No. But I did pick out the colors."

He nodded. "Well, that's usually the hardest part, anyway. Do you have a preference in paint brands?"

"Not really. Just as long as it's good and has low VOC."

He nodded. "I like the sound of that."

She showed him the paint chips she'd picked out. "I want this sandy tone on the living room walls. And this pale aqua in the kitchen and bathroom. The sea-glass green in the bedrooms. And all the trim can be this color." She pointed to the oyster shell white.

"Uh-huh." He looked around the kitchen. "You got something I can write on?"

She handed him her notepad and a pen.

"I'll just write down what you need and then, if you want, I'll go to the paint store and get it. I should be able to get started here in an hour or so. Does that work for you?"

She nodded eagerly. "Should we talk about your wages?"

He shrugged. "Whatever you feel is fair, ma'am."

"Please, call me Diane."

"Sure."

"So ... about the paint store," she said. "Should I give you a check or—"

"Nah, I got an account there. I'll just bring you the receipt."

"Oh, great." She smiled. "I feel lucky to have you."

He looked uncertain. "You might not feel too lucky once I start painting."

"Oh?" Now she was worried. "Why?"

"I mean because I'll probably get in your way. This is a pretty small place."

Diane laughed. "Oh well. How about if I try to stay out of your way while you're painting today?"

He looked more hopeful.

"And I'll move some things around and gather the boxes together, so it'll be easier for you to work. Will you pick up plastic drop cloths and whatever else you might need at the paint store?"

"I'll get what it takes to get 'er done."

When Dan left for the paint store, Diane busied herself with getting the house ready for him. She couldn't believe how quickly this was moving. She hated to rejoice over Dan's temporary layoff, but if he could paint as well as Shelley said, she would happily make this worth his time.

Chapter Five

Dan set the boxes of paint on a drop cloth in the middle of the living room floor. "You want me to start in here?"

"I was thinking you'd start in the spare bedroom," Diane said. "I want to get that room set up first. It's going to be my workspace, and I figure I can keep myself busy in there while you're painting the other rooms."

"Sounds good." He started unfolding another drop cloth. "What kind of work do you do?"

"Actually, I'm planning to write a novel."

He looked impressed. "You're a writer?"

"Sort of. I used to write for a newspaper. But this will be my first attempt at a book."

"Good for you. It's cool seeing someone following her dreams."

"It certainly took me a long enough time."

He headed down the hall with the drop cloth over his arm. "Better late than never, eh?"

She chuckled. "Absolutely."

While he worked on the spare bedroom, she did what she could to get the other rooms ready for painting:

removing light switch and outlet covers, masking around the baseboards and windows, putting down more plastic drop cloths. Her plan was to have him paint her bedroom next. And at the rate he seemed to be going in the spare room, she thought he could easily get the bedroom done today as well.

★   ★   ★

By the end of the day, Diane had made good progress on getting her office set up, and Dan had finished her bedroom and started in on the living room.

"I'm only laid off until Monday," he said as he was getting ready to go home. "But if it's okay with you, I'll keep working for you until then."

"It's more than okay, Dan. I couldn't be more pleased with your work. Really, you're a very good painter."

His face broke into a wide smile. "Thank you." He glanced at the door. "Well, I guess Shelley might be glad to see me coming home by now. Although it's earlier than usual."

"I'm sure she will."

As soon as Dan left, Diane felt the need for another walk to the lighthouse. She pulled on her polar fleece jacket and Bogs again. But before she headed out for the beach, she grabbed a granola bar and shoved it in her pocket. She wasn't technically hypoglycemic, but she'd been borderline for long enough that she tried to keep her blood sugar level in mind.

The fog was still thick in the neighborhood when she stepped outside. But by the time she reached the shoreline it was beginning to clear, making for a lovely evening. There were very few walkers on the promenade, but maybe folks assumed the beach was still as socked-in as town. As she walked, she realized that the air temperature had warmed considerably, and she didn't really need her jacket. Taking it off, she tied the sleeves around her waist and quickened her pace. She wanted to make it to the lighthouse and back and still have time for a quick run to the grocery store before dark.

She was just going past the tide pool area when a movement caught her eye. Something was splashing down in one of the tide pools. Thinking it might be a seal playing, or maybe injured, she ventured closer to take a peek. To her surprise, it appeared to be the same dog she'd seen yesterday, and it seemed to be struggling as if trapped in the deep tide pool.

Diane cautiously approached, wondering what she could possibly do to help the poor animal. "Easy there," she said gently as she came near. She walked around the edge of a tide pool to get closer, careful not to fall in herself. Looking up with desperate golden eyes, the dripping wet dog seemed to be begging for help. With her heart pounding, she tried to position herself near the dog, wondering how she might rescue the animal. She looked at the deep tide pools and jagged rocks and knew this was dangerous. But she also knew she couldn't leave this poor animal stranded.

"I'm going to help you," she calmly told the dog. "But I need to figure this out first."

The dog continued to paw at the sharp rocky edges of the tide pool, and she could tell by the bright red color of the seawater that the dog's paws were bleeding.

"It's going to be okay." She knelt on the sharp rocks. She stroked the dog's wet head, trying to soothe it. The big yellow dog had no collar, nothing to hold on to and pull it out with.

Finally it occurred to her that she might use her jacket to make a sling. If she could somehow slip it around the animal, she might be able to pull it out. Balancing herself on the rocks, she untied her jacket, zipped it up and put it into the water. But despite several attempts, she was unable to get it securely around the dog. The animal looked up at her with the saddest eyes she'd ever seen and let out a little whimper.

"It'll be okay," she said again. She looked down into the tide pool and considered climbing in. Except that it was a deep one, and she wasn't sure she'd be able to climb back out. "We'll figure this out," she told the dog as she clutched the fur of its neck, trying to buoy it in the water.

She wished she'd thought to bring her phone along so she could call for help. The tide was starting to come in now. If she left to go find help, there was a slight chance the water might rise enough to allow the dog to swim to shore. There was also a chance he might not make it with the tide coming in.

"God, help me," she said aloud as she made another attempt to slip her jacket around the dog. "Help me to help this poor animal." Reaching down into the water, she managed to slip the other sleeve around the dog's middle and was even able to grab the sleeve on the dog's other side without falling in. She now had the dog in her makeshift sling.

Using both hands to hold tightly to the soggy sleeves, she slowly stood, balancing herself as a small wave washed up around her ankles. "Here we go." She pulled up on the sleeves, lifting the dog in the water. "We can do this."

With all her strength she pulled up again, hoisting the dog out of the tide pool. Now, praying as she walked along the precarious rocky edge, she headed for higher ground. Her arms ached, but the sand was getting closer and it seemed the dog was trying to help by walking.

Finally out of the rocks and on the sand, Diane collapsed with the wet dog in her lap. "We made it!" She looked down at those golden eyes. She let go of the jacket sleeves and stroked the dog's wet head. "You're going to be okay."

The dog licked her hand as if to thank her.

Running her hand down the dog's soggy back, she could tell the animal was too thin. She pulled the granola bar from her pocket and opened it. She took a small bite and gave the rest to the dog. It ate eagerly and then licked her hand again.

"We have to get you home," she said as she slowly stood. "Can you walk?"

The dog stood on unsteady legs, and she could see that something was wrong with the left back leg. She decided to try the sling idea again. She wrung the seawater out of the jacket and then wrapped it across the dog's middle, pulling it around and actually zipping it this time. Then, taking the sleeves in her hands, she lifted the dog and began to walk. The dog was too heavy for her to completely carry, but it did what it could to help, supporting its weight when it could. She could tell the animal was in pain, not only from its back leg, but its bloody paws as well.

Every minute or so, she would put the dog down and catch her breath. Her arms ached and it was slow going, but she reminded herself it was harder on the dog than it was on her.

"Hello!" called a woman's voice from behind her.

Diane stopped and turned to see Margaret hurrying to catch up with her. "Am I glad to see you!" Diane said.

"What on earth happened to you?" Margaret asked with concern. "You look half drowned. And where did you get that dog?"

Diane explained the rescue and how the dog was injured. Without saying a word, Margaret took one of the jacket sleeves from her, and together they transported the wounded animal down the promenade.

"This is so much easier with two of us," Diane said with relief. "I told myself I'd bring a flashlight, and I didn't. I didn't even bring my cell phone, though I don't know who I would've called. I don't suppose 911 people do animal rescues."

"I'm not sure they don't," Margaret said. "I read a story about them rescuing a deer from a swimming pool."

Diane rubbed her shoulder, which was starting to cramp a little. "I know the dog is in bad shape. And I think the poor thing is half starved."

Margaret looked down at it and shook her head sadly. "Well, he's a boy and a golden retriever. Those are usually someone's beloved pet."

"I wondered if he could've fallen from one of the houses up on the cliff."

Margaret looked up at the houses on the ridge. "That would explain the injuries."

"But surely someone would've come looking for him." Diane was relieved to see they were nearly to the turn-off spot on the promenade now. In a few excruciating minutes she'd be home. "What do you think I should do? Is there a vet in Marble Cove?"

"Dr. Spangler," Margaret said. "Let's go to your house so you can get out of those wet things, and I'll give him a call. They have a twenty-four-hour answering service. I know this for a fact because one night Oreo came home half dead from a bad cat fight, and Adelaide would not go to bed unless we took him to the vet first."

"I hope the vet will be willing to take him tonight," Diane said. "I could try to care for him myself, but I wouldn't even know where to begin. Besides that, my house is turned upside down with painting. You know Dan and Shelley Bauer on our street? Dan's doing some handyman work for me."

"You mean he's not working for the shipping company anymore?"

"He's just laid off for a few days. Maybe I shouldn't have said anything. Shelley was acting like it was kind of hush-hush."

Margaret laughed. "Nothing is hush-hush in Marble Cove. It's a small town, Diane."

"Oh ... right."

"But I won't say anything."

They turned onto Newport Avenue now. The dog wasn't even trying to help anymore. In fact, it looked completely limp. "Do you think he's sleeping?" Diane asked quietly.

"Probably exhausted. Let's get him in the house," Margaret said as they went up the porch steps.

"Yes. I want to get him warm." Diane was shivering as she unlocked the front door.

"You need to get warm too."

They carried the dog inside and gently laid him on the floor. Diane opened a box and removed a woven throw, which she placed over him.

"Now you go take a hot shower," Margaret commanded. "I'll tend to the dog and call the vet."

Diane did as told, letting the hot water wash over her until she finally felt warm again. Then she quickly dressed in a gray velour jogging set and Uggs and came back out to check on the dog and Margaret.

"Dr. Spangler is going to meet us at his office," Margaret said. "We'll use my van to transport the patient."

"Is the patient okay?"

"He seems to be sleeping soundly."

Using the makeshift sling, they carried the dog over to the Hoskins' house. After loading him into the back of Margaret's minivan, they were soon on their way.

"Thanks for helping," Diane said as Margaret drove. "I feel bad to take you away from your family—and at dinnertime."

"Oh, I already fixed dinner. Allan and Adelaide like to eat early. I'll get mine when I get back."

Diane glanced to the back of the minivan, curious as to how the dog was doing. She hoped he wouldn't wake up and start struggling, but all seemed quiet back there. "Do you think he's going to make it? I mean, I was thinking that his injuries could be pretty bad—especially if he fell down the cliff."

"Dr. Spangler will figure things out," Margaret assured her.

"I know it probably seems a bit childish ..." Diane felt a lump in her throat as she turned back around. "But I really do care about this dog. For some reason it feels so important to me that he survive this."

"It's because you're invested in him," Margaret told her. "It's only natural that you should care."

"Yes, I suppose so. Plus, he's been through so much, and I guess that reminds me of ... me."

"You mean about your husband?"

"Well, yes, but ..." Should she open up to this woman? Well, was she wanting a new beginning or not? For some reason this experience had triggered something deep within her. "Margaret, I haven't told you this yet, but I'm a cancer survivor."

Perhaps it was just nerves or raw emotions, or perhaps it was something about Margaret's kind gaze, but for the next five minutes as they drove through town, Diane told her story.

"I don't usually talk about it much," she said at the end, "but I honestly feel like I escaped death. None of the treatments worked, and it was against all odds that I'd be alive today. Yet, here I am." She sighed. "I was given a second chance. I just hope the dog gets a second chance too." Suddenly Diane felt self-conscious and a bit silly. "I don't know why I'm going on like this," she said. "It probably sounds ridiculous."

Margaret parked in front of the vet clinic. "No, it doesn't sound the least bit ridiculous. Not to me, anyway. In fact, I can relate to your story—probably a lot more than you could possibly know."

As they got out and went around to the back of the van, Diane wondered if Margaret might be a cancer survivor too. For some reason, that wouldn't surprise Diane much. From the start, she'd felt that her friendship with this older woman was going to be special.

CHAPTER SIX

The dog seemed barely conscious as the two women eased him from the back of the van, carrying him as they had before in the makeshift jacket-sling.

"Hello there," hailed a male voice. Diane looked over her shoulder to see a slender gray-haired man in a navy windbreaker waving from an open side door. "Bring the dog back here."

"Diane," Margaret said as they went into the kennels area, "this is Dr. Spangler. Dr. Spangler, Diane Spencer."

Dr. Spangler shook Diane's hand. "Nice to meet you, Diane."

"Nice to meet you too," Diane said. "Thank you for meeting us like this. I hope we didn't disturb your dinner."

"No problem. I'm used to these things." He helped them hoist the dog onto a stainless steel examining table and began to remove the polar fleece jacket.

The dog's eyes were open now, and he let out a low whimper.

"This jacket was a good idea," Dr. Spangler said as he set the damp jacket aside and began to look more closely at the dog. "Looks like you've had a rough time of it, boy."

He felt around on the dog's body, probably looking for broken bones. "My assistant is coming in," he told them as he listened with a stethoscope. "I don't usually treat large dogs without help."

"Do you think he'll require surgery?" Margaret asked.

"I'm not sure yet, but it's a possibility."

"He's not my dog," Diane said. "I just found him in trouble, with no one else around. But I'm willing to cover the expenses—I mean, to keep him alive—I mean, if you think it's in his best interest. I just think he's such a sweet dog." And now she was crying.

"Don't worry about that yet," Dr. Spangler told her. "The dog might have an ID chip, and an owner might be involved."

Just then the assistant, a young woman, came into the examining room and Margaret led Diane out to the waiting area, where she handed her a tissue.

Diane's hands were shaking as she blew her nose. Suddenly she remembered that she hadn't eaten in quite some time. "Oh, Margaret, I think my blood sugar is too low."

"You're diabetic, dear?"

"No," she said, looking at her hands, which were trembling. "Hypoglycemic ... s-sort of. But I need some carbs. A cookie or bread or French fries or something."

"Right," Margaret said, standing. "I'll tell Dr. Spangler that we're going to run out and grab a bite to eat. I'm rather hungry myself."

*   *   *

Fifteen minutes later they were seated in a cozy booth near the fireplace at Captain Calhoun's Crab and Lobster House.

Diane sipped lemonade and was feeling a little more together. The waiter set a gigantic lobster roll before her.

"This is just what the doctor ordered," she said. "I had a granola bar with me on my walk, but I ended up feeding it to the dog! That probably wasn't the smartest move, but I felt so sorry for him."

Margaret laughed. "You sound like a dog lover to me."

Diane worked to spread butter on a roll. "Oh, I loved dogs as a child, but I married a man with allergies. So pet ownership was impossible for our family. When Jessica, that's my daughter, moved out, she got a kitten straight away." She bit into the lobster roll and nearly swooned, it tasted so good. "They should call this 'heaven on a roll,'" she said as she wiped her mouth with a napkin.

Midway through the meal, Diane remembered Margaret's earlier comment. Suddenly she was very curious. "You said you could relate to my cancer survival story ..." She waited, forking into her coleslaw and wondering if she'd stepped over some line.

Margaret refilled her thick stoneware mug with tea from the little metal pot. "I too am a survivor."

"Really?" Diane nodded. "Cancer too?"

"No. I actually think it would be more difficult to survive cancer. But my story is interesting in its own way." She stirred some honey into her tea with a thoughtful expression.

"And after seeing you help that dog this evening ... well, it all came rushing back at me."

Now Diane was really curious. "Do you want to talk about it?"

"Not many people know of the story. Well, other than those who were there that day. I suppose they've mentioned it to some others. But I've only told Allan. I wouldn't want Adelaide to hear of it. Poor thing, it would frighten her and she'd never want me to go out on the beach again."

A jolt of alarm went through Diane. "Something happened on the beach?" Surely their lovely beach wasn't dangerous. "Shark?"

"No, no. Nothing like that," Margaret said. "It was my own fault. I really should've known better. You see, I love to swim in the ocean. I know, I know, it's not the safest place to swim. But something about the chill of the water, forcing one's way through the waves ... well, it just awakens my senses, and I feel alive again when I get out."

"I guess I can understand that," Diane said. "I used to swim in the ocean as a child. I suppose I've turned chicken in my old age."

"Oh, you're not old." Margaret frowned. "I swam at your age, and I still swim from time to time. I plan to swim this summer."

"Well, maybe I will join you. I used to swim three times a week at the fitness club." Diane polished off the last roll. "So tell me, what happened?"

"It was a nice sunny afternoon, the kind of day when you feel that nothing can go wrong. I knew there were some good-size waves out there, but nothing I hadn't swam in before. I was happily swimming out, feeling on top of the world and probably not paying the closest of attention, because *wham-bam,* just like that, I was toppled over."

She paused to take a sip of tea. "I wasn't really frightened at first. Oh, the wave was tossing and turning me, and I suppose I swallowed a bit of seawater. But I told myself to just swim out of it." She paused again, looking directly at Diane. "But I couldn't. It was as if I was trapped in the water, or the motion of the wave. I had absolutely no control. No matter how I tried, I could not find my way to the surface."

She shook her head. "I've read a bit about such things since that time. Sometimes swimmers get sucked down far enough that they don't know up from down. You'd think you would naturally float up, but if the wind's been knocked out of you and there's any kind of undertow, which may have been the case that day ... well, it's useless."

"Oh my!" Diane stared at this mild-mannered woman and tried to imagine her in distress. "You must've been terrified."

She nodded. "I was. And although I didn't actually see my life flash before my eyes, I did see Allan and Adelaide, and I felt so bad that I would be leaving them alone. Allan tries to help with Adelaide, but the truth is she is very dependent on me. They both are." She pressed her lips together and looked down at her tea.

"So, tell me, what happened?" Diane demanded. "I know you survived, but how did you survive? Inquiring minds want to know!"

Margaret looked up with a fraction of a smile. "It's actually rather mysterious. The last thing I remember was feeling the water pulling me down and how sad I felt that I was leaving my loved ones in the lurch. After that ... nothing. When I finally came to, I was on the beach. Sopping wet and out of breath, but very much alive. I sat up and looked around and no one was there. It was the oddest thing."

Diane puzzled at it, looking for a solution. "I wonder how you got out of the ocean. Do you think that maybe when you stopped struggling, your body actually was thrown upward by the wave?"

Margaret laughed. "Funny you should say that. I honestly remember thinking that the ocean must've decided it didn't want me—and that I'd been spat back up. Because, really, it made no sense. A couple came running over to see if I was all right, but they hadn't actually seen what had happened."

"Maybe the sea did spit you out."

"Maybe," Margaret said, spinning the ice in her glass. "Except there were some clues in the sand."

"What sort of clues?"

"It appeared that someone else had been there. Judging from how the sand was disrupted, it looked as if I'd been dragged out of the water and laid down. Most mysterious of all, a set of footprints led away into the rocks."

"Who?" Diane asked.

"That, my dear, is the mystery. I haven't the slightest idea. I was too worn out from my ordeal to attempt to follow the footprints. They did appear to be rather large, so I assumed it was a man. Later on, I heard a report that the people in one of the houses up there on the cliff had seen someone rescued from the surf. The story was that a swimmer was in trouble and a man swam out there and rescued her. Naturally, I knew it was me, but I was too embarrassed to let on. Besides, as I mentioned, I didn't want Adelaide to hear of it. So you must promise me you won't repeat my story."

"You can trust me." But even as she said it, Diane wondered if she could use the story in a book, with changed names and places, of course. She knew she'd clear it with Margaret first.

"Speaking of near drownings," Margaret said, "would you like me to check on the dog? Dr. Spangler gave me his cell phone number and said to call back in an hour."

"Yes, I'd like to know how the poor old boy is doing."

Diane waited as Margaret talked to the vet, but she couldn't make much from Margaret's responses of "Uh-huh," "Yes" and "I see."

Margaret closed her phone. "The patient is doing well. He is even wagging his tail."

"Oh, I'm so glad!" Diane felt tears of joy filling her eyes, and this time she knew it wasn't from low blood sugar. "Have his owners been found?"

"No. Dr. Spangler said he doesn't appear to have a chip and he seems malnourished and dehydrated. He's got an

IV in him now. He set the broken bone in the left rear leg; apparently it was a clean break. The assistant is just finishing putting a fiberglass cast on it. They want to keep him overnight just to stabilize him. And they are trying to locate his owner."

"Oh, good."

"So we are free to go home now."

Diane waved to the waiter for the bill, insisting she buy since Margaret had been such a godsend to help her out.

"I'm just glad I came along when I did," Margaret told her as they went out to the minivan. "I often walk out to the lighthouse later in the day. But not *every* day. I almost didn't go today because of the fog."

"I'm very thankful you did."

"And I'm thankful that I could share my survival story with you," Margaret said.

They climbed in the van and headed back toward their neighborhood in comfortable silence. When they turned onto Newport Avenue, Margaret patted Diane's hand. "I'm equally thankful that I can trust you not to repeat it to anyone." She chuckled. "Perhaps we'll have our own little secret survivors club, Diane. Just you and me."

"And the dog too?"

Margaret laughed heartily as she pulled up at Diane's curb. "Yes, of course, that old dog too, bless his heart. We'll give him an honorary membership."

"I doubt he'll spill the beans."

Diane got out and the women said their good-byes.

Back in her living room, Diane surveyed her house, which looked like a war zone. Between the clumped furniture, piles of boxes, painting tools, and drop cloths, it was just not too inviting. Even so, she felt glad to be home. She spent the next couple of hours putting her freshly painted bedroom into order. Or at least partially in order.

Locating the boxes with the extra touches—artwork and lamps and accents—would take a few days. But the current improvement was remarkable. The walls were now a soothing shade of celadon green that looked cool and peaceful with her creamy white duvet cover. Once again, she had no doubts she would sleep well.

★　　★　　★

In fact, she slept so well she was surprised to hear someone knocking at her front door at just a few minutes past seven in the morning.

She threw on a robe and stumbled to the door. "Just a minute."

It was Dan. "I wanted to get an early start today because I promised Shelley I'd only work until two. Then I'll babysit the kids for an hour or two—just while they're napping. That way, she can go out and do whatever she likes."

"That's very generous of you." Diane tried to clear the sleepy fog from her brain. "But, um ... if you and Shelley are willing, I'd love to sit with the kids. And that way you could keep working." Now she felt a bit guilty. "Although

I suppose that's a little selfish on my part. You'd probably rather be with your children."

"No, that's a good idea. And they'll just be sleeping, anyway. How about if I call Shelley after a while? I don't want to wake the baby up yet. I'll call in an hour or so and see what Shelley thinks of your offer."

As it turned out, Shelley was open to the idea, but she wanted to wait until the kids were down for their naps. Then she'd call Diane to come over and sit with them while they were sleeping. Dan put his phone away and picked up the paint roller.

"That's great," Diane told him.

"It's great, except that now Shelley's all hyped up, thinking she needs to clean house." Dan slowly ran the paint roller up the wall by the window and down again.

"She doesn't need to clean house for my sake," Diane said firmly. "That's nonsense."

"You don't know my Shelley." Dan shook his head as he dipped the roller in the sand-colored paint. "She'd rather die than be caught with a messy house."

"Well, I can remember having that same feeling as a young mother. But it's so silly. I think I'll go have a little chat with Shelley. Any chance I can get a cup of coffee over there?"

"Oh yeah. Shelley always makes a big pot in the morning. It keeps her going all day."

"Good." Diane reached for her fisherman knit cardigan and headed out the door. She didn't want to step on any toes, and she sure didn't want to get a reputation as a busybody—she'd rather leave that title to Mrs. Peabody—but still …

Diane glanced over at the tall lavender Victorian home. It actually looked a little spooky in the roiling morning fog. It would probably make for an interesting spot on Halloween night. High up, just below the roofline, was a widow's walk with a wrought-iron railing. She hadn't noticed that architectural detail before. As she crossed the street, she vaguely wondered if Mrs. Peabody was a widow ... or if she ever went up there and walked around. Still so much to learn about her new neighborhood.

CHAPTER SEVEN

As Diane approached the Bauers' home, the front door opened and a stout middle-aged woman holding a box marched purposefully to the SUV parked in the driveway. Shelley appeared in the doorway with Emma propped on her hip.

"It won't be any trouble at all for me to re-price everything with the right stickers," the woman called over her shoulder.

Diane noticed Shelley's chin raise a notch. She was wondering if she should postpone her unexpected visit when the woman noticed her.

"Hello," the woman said with a nod. She had opened the car door and grabbed the steering wheel to heave her short frame into the front seat.

"Hi there," Diane said.

The woman slammed the door shut and honked a good-bye as she waved to Shelley. Shelley grabbed Emma's arm and waved.

"Sorry to pop in like—"

"You weren't supposed to come until this afternoon, and not until I called." Shelley ran her free hand through her uncombed hair. "Dan said that—"

"I can go," Diane said, motioning toward her house. "Dan said you had coffee over here, but we'll catch up later." Diane offered a reassuring smile, trying not to look at the stain on the front of Shelley's Celtics sweatshirt.

Shelley blinked and backed up. "No, it's fine. I actually just put a pot on. Come on in."

"I'm sorry to pop in right after you saw off your last visitor."

"Dan's mother." The way Shelley said this made it sound as if it were an unwelcome visitor.

Diane decided not to pursue this as she leaned over to where Emma had just been situated in a playpen near the kitchen. "Hello there," Diane said cheerfully. "You look like a happy girl today." With rosy cheeks, Emma intently chewed on the teething toy, her chin wet from drooling.

"I'm eating Cheerios," Aiden sang out from his booster seat in the kitchen. He still had on pajamas, footy ones with red and blue race cars on them. "Want some?"

"Thanks." Diane smiled at him. "But I just came for coffee."

"I want coffee too," he whined at his mother.

"No way." Shelley handed Diane a mug with a lighthouse on it. "You have to get a whole lot older first."

"I'm older," he protested loudly. "You said I'm older than Emma. I want coffee!"

"You know what my mother used to tell me about drinking coffee?" Diane leaned over to look into his big blue eyes.

He peered up with interest. "What?"

"My mother said that kids who drink coffee never grow up to be big and tall." She stood up straight now. "Like your daddy. He's big and tall, isn't he?"

Aiden nodded with a serious expression. "Daddy doesn't like coffee."

"See, there you go."

"Do you take anything in your coffee?" Shelley asked.

"No, just black. This is perfect," Diane told her, taking the cup. "Thanks."

"Want to sit?" Shelley nodded to a kitchen chair.

"Sure, if you have a minute, I thought we could talk a bit about this afternoon." She wasn't sure how much to say, just in case Aiden wasn't comfortable with the idea of being left alone with a neighbor.

Shelley sat down across from Diane. Her expression was a mixture of curiosity and tiredness. "Okay."

"First of all, I don't want to think that you're doing some special clean-athon just because the neighbor is coming over."

Shelley frowned. "What did Dan tell you?"

"Just the truth." Diane looked around the kitchen and shrugged. "Everything looks perfectly fine and normal to me. In fact, it looks a whole lot better than my house at the moment. And now that I've seen it, there's hardly any reason to go to any extra effort in cleaning things up. Right?"

"I suppose you're right."

Diane smiled. "Good."

Shelley let out a long sigh. "Thank you."

"By the way, Dan is doing a brilliant job at my house."

"Really?" Shelley's eyes lit up.

"Absolutely. I'll bet that if he wanted to—I mean, if he wasn't working in shipping—he could go into professional painting."

Shelley sadly shook her head. "Except that even the professional painters are having a hard time finding jobs these days. My friend's husband is a painter, and he seems to be out of work half the time lately."

"Oh."

"But it's nice how it worked out for him to help you. He seems to enjoy it."

"So you're really okay with me, uh, coming over later?" Diane glanced at Aiden.

Shelley looked down at her coffee cup. "It's just that I hardly ever leave them with anyone. Not even their grandparents."

"Why not?"

"It's a long story." Shelley shrugged, glancing at Aiden. "Looks like you're almost done."

"Can I get down?" Aiden asked.

Shelley looked at his nearly empty bowl. "Just eat those last two pieces of banana."

"Okay." He shoved them both into his mouth and started to get down.

"Slow down there, cowboy," Diane told him. "I always made my kids finish chewing their food before they went running around."

"That's right." Shelley held up an index finger. "No food in the mouth while playing."

Aiden dramatically chewed and then finally swallowed. "There!" He opened his mouth to show her.

She wrinkled her nose. "Thanks. Now you are free to go and play."

"Aiden," Shelley said with a playful tone, "close your mouth or the flies will blow your liver."

He snapped his mouth shut. "Can I watch Sesame Street?"

Shelley pointed at the kitchen clock, where every numeral was represented with a lighthouse. "Yes, but it won't be on for a few minutes. You go and get dressed first. Then you can turn on the TV in the family room."

"Oh-*kay!*" he shouted happily, running down the hallway and letting out a whoop.

Diane looked at her with wide eyes. "The flies will do what to his liver?"

"Blow," Shelley said. "I don't actually know what blow your liver means, but it's what my mom always said to make me shut my mouth when I'd leave it hanging open."

"Gotcha."

They heard Aiden laughing at the TV.

"Energetic, isn't he?" Diane asked.

Shelley nodded. "He keeps me busy."

"So I am curious, Shelley. Why are you so uncomfortable about leaving your kids with anyone?"

"I've been trying to do some playdates with Aiden and his buddy Jeremy. Just an hour long so far. But I really don't feel good about leaving both of the kids. Definitely not for any length of time."

"Not even with their grandparents?"

Shelley let out a little groan. "Especially not with their grandparents. If my mom lived nearby, I might leave them with her now and then. But with Dan's parents ... well ..."

"I thought Dan was from a big family. I would think his parents would be very good with kids." Diane studied the mug in her hand; it had a picture of a lighthouse on it—not the Orlean Light, but similar.

"I know they are. It's just that his mom is equally good at finding fault with me. Particularly with my parenting and homemaking skills. Dan's mom has no problem telling me— in painful detail—every single thing I'm doing wrong. She'll try to say it nicely. But it's easy to see through her little 'suggestions.'"

"You're sure she's not just trying to help?"

"She probably thinks she's being very helpful. But pointing out everything that's wrong does not feel helpful to me. And, it's not like I'm oblivious. Good grief, I know I'm doing plenty wrong. Sometimes I feel I'm barely keeping my nose above water. Sure, Aiden might have dirty fingernails sometimes, and Emma gets an occasional case of diaper rash, like when she's had orange juice, which she's sensitive to. I just don't want to hear about it every single time. *You know?*"

Diane smiled. "I do know. My mother-in-law used to be kind of a pain too."

"Really?"

Diane nodded, taking a sip of coffee. "Oh yeah."

"And Dan doesn't realize it, but he can be like that sometimes too. He's always got a better way of doing almost everything. Or at least he thinks he has. But at least he's starting to get that I don't want that kind of help. Unfortunately, his mom is a little more stubborn. I just wish she'd respect that these are *my* kids, this is *my* house, and I want to do things *my* own way."

"And you should."

Shelley looked uneasy. "I can't believe I just vented like that to you, Diane. I'm sorry."

"Don't be sorry. I think you needed to get that off your chest, and I don't mind listening. In fact, it's probably good for me to hear that. Both my kids are grown, and I could end up being a mother-in-law someday. I hope I'll remember to tread carefully."

"You'll probably make a terrific mother-in-law." Shelley sighed. "Thanks for putting up with my little temper tantrum."

"I don't think you were having a temper tantrum as much as you were trying to establish your boundaries."

"That's right. I do want boundaries."

Diane felt guilty now. She knew she'd forced her way into Shelley's world this morning. "And, please, forgive me if I stepped over the line by coming over like I did—uninvited. Having worked in the newspaper world for so many years, I suppose I can be a little pushy sometimes."

"No, no, you're fine, Diane. I'm glad you came to visit. Now I won't feel nearly so desperate to get everything perfectly cleaned today. But I will tidy up some." She waved her hand across the kitchen table, which was littered with random dirty breakfast dishes, cereal boxes, and clutter. "You've already had a sneak peek into my kiddy kingdom. Isn't it delightful?"

"Just remember, I've been there, done that. I remember how it felt trying to keep it all together, trying to get everything just right." Diane finished the last of her coffee. "And you know what?"

"What?"

"Looking back, I can see that I should've lightened up a little."

"Lightened up? How?"

"Sometimes I got so caught up in being the perfect little wife and mommy that I'm sure I missed out on some of the more important things."

Shelley looked really interested. "What kind of things?"

"Just everyday things ..." Diane thought back. "Like smelling my children's hair after a bath, kissing my husband good morning, feeling the sunshine on my face, listening to the rain on the roof, you know ... smelling the roses in the midst of changing diapers." She laughed. "Does that make any sense?"

Shelley nodded. "It makes sense. I don't want to be so obsessed with clean fingernails that I miss something important."

"Good for you." Diane took her empty coffee cup over to the sink. "Maybe you just need a little more time for yourself. If you're like I was, you're probably the last person on your to-do list. But you need to remember that you're important too."

Shelley looked dubious. "That sounds good. But with so much to do ..." She pointed to the kitchen floor, which had felt sticky and gritty beneath Diane's shoes, with some spilled Cheerios here and there. "Can you believe I mopped that just two days ago?"

Diane shook her head. "Just remember that this is a very short era of your life. Trust me, these kids are going to grow up a whole lot faster than you can even imagine. There will always be floors to mop and dishes to wash, but kids grow up and move on." She sighed, feeling a bit teary-eyed. "I know it doesn't seem like it right now, but it'll happen. It happens to everyone."

Shelley came over and opened her arms. "I just want to hug you, neighbor."

Diane gave a weak smile. "No complaints from me."

"Thank you, Diane," Shelley said as they hugged. "I really needed to hear that this morning."

"Well, it's true." Diane went over to the playpen now. "Before you know it, these days of diaper rash and Sesame Street will be gone."

"And you still want to babysit today?"

"You bet I do. I'll be waiting for your call." Diane made a goofy face for little Emma. "Two-ish, right?"

Shelley nodded and then bent down to pick up the baby, snuggling her face down into Emma's chubby neck.

"And I do hope you're going to go out to do something fun today. You are, aren't you?"

Shelley made a guilty smile. "I planned to run an errand or two. But I'll make sure to squeeze some fun in there."

"Good. See you then."

As Diane walked through the fog back across the street, she thought of the injured dog from last night. She figured the veterinarian clinic would be open now. She sat on one of the rockers on the porch and pulled out her cell phone. When the receptionist answered, Diane explained about the dog. "He's not actually mine," she said, "but I'd like to hear how he's doing."

"You mean Rocky," the woman said cheerfully. "He's a real sweetheart."

"Rocky?" Diane was confused. "The dog I found on the beach?"

"Yes. The one with the broken leg. He's doing much better this morning."

"So his name is Rocky?" Diane felt a stab of disappointment. "That must mean you located his owner."

"No. We just nicknamed him Rocky for convenience sake. Dr. Spangler mentioned you'd found him in the rocks on the beach, and he seemed like a fighter, so we're calling him Rocky. Dr. Spangler wants to talk to you about him."

"Oh, okay."

After a bit, Dr. Spangler got on the line and explained that Rocky was improving. "But it looks like he's either been on his own for a while or else he'd been in a pretty bad home."

"What do you mean?"

"Besides being malnourished, his coat is badly matted, and the break in his leg doesn't seem the result of a fall."

"I'm not sure I understand."

"Well, it could be from any of a variety of events: being struck by a car, falling from a pickup truck, and so forth. But my guess is that someone hit the dog."

"Oh no!"

"So even if his owners do show up to get him, I'm not inclined to hand him over without doing some investigating first."

"So what's to become of him?"

"We can keep him here for a while until he gets stronger, but if things shake out as I think they will, he'll eventually need a new home."

"How about with me?" she said without really thinking about it.

"That would be fine. Although I'm not sure how you'll feel if his original owners should show up and try to claim him. However, with no ID, it's hard to know. My receptionist has done some searching to see if anyone's reported a lost dog that fits Rocky's description. So far nothing's turned up. I'd estimate he's about three years old, and he seems to have a good disposition. I think he'd make someone a fine pet."

Diane felt her hopes rising again. "I'm willing to cover all his medical expenses ... especially if I can keep him," she said eagerly, hoping that might increase her chances of acquiring him. "I'd really love to have a dog."

"I'm sure Rocky would love a good home. And his leg should heal up just fine. But he does need some serious TLC."

"I can do that!"

"Then, unless something unexpected comes up, I'd say the dog is yours, Diane."

As crazy as it seemed, she felt like she'd just won the lottery. "That's great! I can't wait to get him." She looked in the front window of her house. Dan was just moving his painting things out of the living room. "I'm having some painting done inside my house right now, and I'd need to get some doggy things to get everything set for, uh, Rocky." She giggled. "I guess that's a good name for him. Do you think it would be okay if he stayed at the clinic for a couple of days?"

"I was going to suggest it. I'd like to keep an eye on him for a while. We have a kennel here, and we'll keep him on a careful diet to build up his strength without making him sick to his stomach. If you don't mind, I'll make sure he's up-to-date on shots and whatnot before he goes home with you."

"Yes, please do."

By the time she hung up, Diane felt like dancing. She was getting a dog! Rocky was going to be hers.

CHAPTER EIGHT

Throughout that day, Dan continued making good progress in Diane's cottage. He was just finishing up painting the bathroom as Diane was ready to head across the street to watch his kids.

"Did you decide on those kitchen cabinets yet?" he asked as he was moving his stepladder.

"I like your idea of painting them," Diane said. "They seem sturdy enough, and with a fresh coat of creamy white paint and new hardware, I think I could live with them quite happily."

"Great." Dan smiled. "And you want the same color as the trim, right? I can call the paint store and order it."

"Perfect."

He nodded. "Okay, then. I should be able to get it all done before Monday. That is, if you don't mind my finishing it up on Sunday."

She felt uncertain now. "It's okay with me. But I hate to see you wear yourself out, Dan. And working on Sunday ..."

"It's no problem. And I'd really like to get 'er done before I go back to work."

"Are you sure Shelley won't mind?"

"Shelley knows we can use the money." He dipped his brush in the paint. "Shipping isn't the most secure profession, if you know what I mean."

"Right." She nodded. "Well, I'd better get over there so Shelley can have some time off."

"Diane, you know about the shipping and fishing industry in Maine, don't you?"

The rascally sparkle in his eye put her on guard. "No ..."

"Sure. They say that in Maine if you give a man a fish, he can eat for a day. But if you *teach* a man to fish, he'll doze off in his boat and come home sunburned."

"Oh, you scoundrel!" she said, grinning. "I'm leaving now."

"See ya!"

As she walked across the street, Diane wondered if this was such a good thing. She didn't like thinking she was keeping Dan from his family on a Sunday. Still, she knew that was probably between Dan and Shelley.

Shelley looked a little uncertain as she let Diane into the house. "Aiden usually sleeps for a couple of hours, but Emma might wake up. And if she does, she'll be hungry. I'm still weaning her to the bottle, but she doesn't like it and she might fuss." Shelley showed Diane where the bottles of formula were already made, explaining how long to put them in hot water. "I used to microwave them, but my mother-in-law said not to." She rattled off more things, including twice showing her where the emergency phone numbers were.

"Shelley," Diane said quietly but firmly. "Dan is right across the street. And the children are sleeping. Everything will be all right. You are wasting precious time right now."

Shelley grimaced. "I suppose you're right."

With a hand on her shoulder, Diane guided Shelley to the front door. "Really, we'll be okay. Just go and have some fun."

"I'll be back by four," Shelley said.

"I know you will, sweetie."

Finally Shelley stepped outside and closed the door behind her.

With Shelley out of the house, Diane sat down with the book she'd brought along to read. But feeling antsy, she decided to look around to see if there was something she could help with. As she surveyed the house, she was surprised at how many images of lighthouses she found: prints on the wall, the rug by the front door, even the artwork on the cookie jar. Shelley obviously had an affection for lighthouses. It probably made it easy for Shelley's friends and family when her birthday came along.

Finally, Diane decided that the kitchen floor really could use a good cleaning. But would this be stepping over a line? Diane stood there staring at the lighthouse calendar on the fridge and thinking that she didn't want to offend Shelley. And yet ... Diane tried to remember how she might've felt if someone had stepped in and helped her when her children were small. Finally, she decided it would all depend on how it was done. If Diane could convince Shelley that she was simply feeling restless and wanted something to do to pass the time, perhaps it would be all right. Besides, that was the truth.

She located the broom, mop, and cleaning liquids and soon had the linoleum floor shining. She decided she didn't want to stop there. So, keeping a careful eye on the clock, she continued to give the kitchen a thorough scrubbing. She even went out into Shelley's backyard and picked a small bunch of flowers, which she arranged in a vase she'd found under the sink.

She was just putting the bouquet on the kitchen table when she heard Emma fussing. She ran some hot water in the Pyrex container before grabbing a bottle of formula from the fridge and sticking it in.

She went into Emma's room and smiled down at the baby in her crib. "Hello, little angel."

Emma gave her a curious look and then started to wail.

Diane picked up the baby, jiggling her in her arms and talking soothingly. "I'll bet you're hungry," she said as she walked her into the kitchen to get the bottle.

Finally, they settled in a rocking chair in the living room, and after several false starts, Emma decided to eat. Humming quietly, Diane remembered when Jessica was this size. In some ways, it felt like yesterday. In other ways, it was another lifetime.

After Emma finished the bottle, Diane took her back to her room for a diaper change. She had used cloth diapers for both her children. For some reason she had felt they were superior to disposable back then. But she knew that kind of reasoning was a bit out of touch nowadays. And after hearing Shelley's comments about her mother-in-law, Diane knew she would always be careful to keep any "helpful" mothering tips to herself.

She had just settled Emma into her playpen when she heard the front door opening—and it wasn't even four yet.

It was Shelley. She came in carrying a couple of grocery bags.

"You're early," Diane said.

"I had to make the store, but I got done sooner than I expected. How's it going?" Shelley asked anxiously.

"Just fine. Emma's had her bottle and a diaper change. Aiden's not even awake yet."

Shelley took the groceries to the kitchen, but there she stopped. "What happened here?"

"I hope you don't mind," Diane said quickly. "But I was antsy and wanted to pass the time. I've been dying to do some cleaning at my house, but until the painting's done, I feel like my hands are tied. It's like I just had to clean up something, you know? Had to get it out of my system. I hope you don't mind. I really didn't want to step over your boundaries."

Shelley turned to Diane with a big smile. "I'll forgive you this time. But if you ever want to watch my kids again, you'll have to swear not to do any more housecleaning."

Diane winced. "I have to swear?"

Shelley chuckled. "Well, no. I don't allow swearing in my house." She walked over to the sink. "Wow, I don't think I've ever seen this sink look so white. How did you do that?"

"Just a little bleach, a bit of elbow grease and a rub of olive oil. It's easy."

"You're kidding?" Shelley looked stunned.

Diane shrugged. "It's a little trick I used to use when I had a sink like this."

Shelley nodded. "That's good to know."

"And one reason I felt it was okay to do some cleaning in here is that I remembered how sometimes it was only at naptime I was able to get some of these chores done. Dan and I kind of took that time from you today, so it only seemed fair."

Shelley laughed. "Okay, okay, I do appreciate your doing this for me, Diane." She pointed to the vase on the kitchen table. "And those are lovely."

"I hope you didn't mind my taking them from your yard."

Shelley looked skeptical. "Those are from my yard?"

Diane nodded. "Every one."

"Who knew?" Shelley went over to the playpen, where Emma was starting to fuss.

"And now I'm going to let you get on with your life," Diane said. "But only if you promise to let me watch your kids again. You can see that nothing bad happened, right?"

Shelley nodded with an uncertain but hopeful look. "Yes, I think you're making a believer out of me."

As Diane left, she heard Aiden calling out for his mommy. Feeling relieved that she didn't have to explain to him why Mommy wasn't there, Diane slipped out the door and back over to her house.

Dan was still painting the kitchen walls. "How did that go?"

"Oh, fine," Diane said.

"The kids weren't too much trouble?"

"What? Of course not. Aiden just slept, and it's been a long time since I've given a baby a bottle. It was nice."

He sighed. "That's great. Thank you."

"No problem." She put her keys on the kitchen counter.

"So ... were you thinking of going out? I mean, into town?"

Diane hadn't been thinking anything of the sort. "Do you just want to get me out of your hair?"

He grinned sheepishly. "Well ... I *was* thinking you could swing by and pick up the cabinet paint for me so I could keep working here."

Diane watched him painting the pale aqua onto the wall behind the stove, admiring how much cleaner and beachier that color was compared to the dull mustard yellow it had previously been. Of course, now the russet-painted cabinets looked dark and gloomy. And the gold countertop, a chipped Formica straight out of the seventies, was very unappealing.

"Okay," she said, grabbing her keys again and getting her purse. "I have some errands to run anyway."

★   ★   ★

As she drove to town, Diane realized that, as much as she appreciated Dan's help, she was eager to have her little house to herself—so she could get it all set up. But she knew she needed to be patient. She really was grateful for Dan's work, and when it came time to pay him, she knew he'd probably be grateful as well.

She picked up the cabinet paint at the paint store before going to the hardware store for some things. She'd made a rather lengthy list, everything from new light-switch plate covers to garbage bags to a planting pot for geraniums.

Next she went to an appliance store Dan had told her about, just off of Main Street. It looked small and unimpressive from the front, but when she went inside, she saw they actually had a good selection of quality brands.

She'd already measured for appliances, deciding that all of them needed updating. So, with the help of Marge, a knowledgeable appliance salesperson, Diane made her selections in less than an hour.

"I think you'll be glad you went with stainless steel," Marge told Diane as she was writing them up. "Much better for resale value."

"I don't ever want to sell," Diane said.

Marge shrugged. "You never know."

Diane nodded as she wrote out a check. "Maybe not, but I plan to spend the rest of my days in my little cottage."

Marge handed her the receipt. "I do hope you'll be right." Now she explained when the appliances would be delivered and their policy for removing the old ones. "You can consign them to Webster's, if you want."

"Webster's?"

"The secondhand store. Or you can donate them to the Habitat for Humanity store, if you like. You don't need to decide now. Just let the delivery guys know when they come."

Diane folded the receipt into her purse. "Marge, is there anyone you'd recommend for installing new countertops?"

"Depends on what you want. If you want something extra fancy, like granite slab, I can't be of much help. But I do have a brother-in-law who's a good tile man. And he even installs stone tiles like granite or soapstone or slate." She reached into a drawer and pulled out a business card. "If you tell him you heard about him from me, he'll give you a 10 percent discount."

Diane thanked her, tucked the card in her purse, and headed across the street.

She'd noticed a shop called the Pet Place, and she hoped they might have some of the supplies she'd need when she brought Rocky home.

To her delight, this shop had all kinds of things for dogs, cats, and various small animals. She felt like a kid in a candy store as she checked out the vast display of colorful collars and leashes and even doggy clothes. Who knew they made rubber boots for dogs?

"Can I help you?" a young man asked.

Diane held up her hands. "I don't even know where to begin." Then she explained about the dog she planned to adopt. "It's kind of crazy," she admitted. "I'm new in town and haven't even settled into my house. And here I am planning to bring home a dog."

"First of all, welcome to town," he told her. "I'm Lee Waters."

"Thank you, Lee. I'm Diane Spencer." She turned to the display of dog supplies. "So, what do I need?"

He rubbed his chin. "To start with, I'd say a good collar and some ID." He showed her what he felt was a sturdy collar. "There's even a pocket in it where you can hide Rocky's information. Even if a dog has a chip, it's a good idea to have something on him as well. Especially with a rehomed dog who might get lost."

Diane picked up a red collar. "How do I know what size?"

So he asked her about the breed and helped her pick out an appropriate one. Then he suggested a leash and showed her the new dog beds they'd just gotten in, pointing out that the coverings were washable. He also showed her dog dishes, chew toys, and grooming items.

Diane was reminded of how she'd felt as an expectant mother preparing for the arrival of a baby. Finally, with quite an accumulation of canine goodies, Lee helped her carry everything out to her car.

"I suppose I should've asked," she said as she closed her trunk, "about your return policy." She frowned. "In case something goes wrong and I don't get the dog."

"No problem," he said. "As long as you've got your receipt and nothing's been used, you can bring it all back. But I'll bet that won't happen."

She nodded. "Yes, I'm sure you're right." She hoped he was right. She wanted this dog more than ever now.

CHAPTER NINE

Margaret came over as Diane was unloading her car. "Have you heard how the dog is doing?" she asked with concern. "Is he going to be okay?"

"Yes, he's doing fine." Diane grinned as she pulled out an aqua-blue-and-beige dog bed and held it up for Margaret to see. "Dr. Spangler said I can bring him home on Monday."

"My, but that's pretty." Margaret caressed the soft fabric. "This is going to be one pampered pup."

"I hope I didn't overdo it, but the salesman at the Pet Place was quite helpful."

"It wasn't Lee Waters, was it?"

Diane looked at her. "You know Lee?"

"Lee's a good boy. Did you know he owns that shop?"

"No. He just acted like a helpful salesperson. But he did know all about dogs and what they need. Isn't he a bit young to be an entrepreneur?"

"Well, his mother, Evelyn Waters, helped him out there. Did Lee tell you that Evelyn's the mayor of Marble Cove?"

"No." Diane reached for the bag containing the food and water bowls. They were pale-blue and white ceramic and she knew they'd look perfect in her kitchen. "Look at these, Margaret."

Margaret chuckled. "Very nice. Do they come with a silver spoon to feed him with?"

Diane felt herself blushing. "Do you think I'm nuts?"

Margaret laughed. "Not at all. I just think the dog is about to land in a fine feathered nest. He's a lucky boy."

"They named him Rocky," Diane told her. "It seems he may have been abused and neglected, poor thing. I plan to spoil him rotten."

"And he'll probably reward you with his undying affection and loyalty."

Diane smiled. "I like the sound of that."

Margaret helped her carry the things into the house, taking time to check out the progress of the painting project. "Lovely colors you've picked," she told Diane as they stood in the pale aqua bathroom. Most of the painting in there was finished except for the vanity and a linen shelf, which would be painted creamy white, the same as the kitchen cabinets.

"Thanks," Diane said. "Since you're a real artist, I'll take that as a compliment." She showed Margaret her office. It was mostly together.

"What an inspiring room this is," Margaret told her. "I should think you'll be able to write a wonderful book in here."

"I have a feeling I won't be able to sit down and focus on writing until I get my cottage put together," Diane said. "Cluttered spaces tend to shut me down mentally."

Margaret went back into the living room. "All the shades you selected go so nicely together. It's all so ocean-like. Reminiscent of a soft summer day on the seashore, so peaceful and calm."

"Peaceful and calm?" Diane shook her head as she surveyed a lopsided pile of cardboard boxes and the clumps of furnishings still draped in paint-speckled plastic tarps. "I can only hope that someday it will all feel that way."

Margaret laughed. "Rome wasn't built in a day."

"You're right." Diane set the dog bed down on top of a large box. "Speaking of patience, I was thinking about your art gallery. You said you wanted it open in time for tourist season. Does that mean you'll be in business by Memorial Day?"

"That was my original plan." Margaret looked frustrated. "But as I said, Rome wasn't built in a day. Everything seems to be taking longer than I anticipated, and with Memorial Day just a couple of weeks away ... I don't know if I'll make it."

"Is there anything I can help you with?"

"I don't think so." Margaret sighed. "My problem isn't just in getting the gallery set up, because that's almost done. I also need to get more paintings finished so I'll have something to show."

Diane nodded. "That's something only you can do."

"I'm tempted to just go ahead and open the gallery on Memorial Day weekend. I've got a few other artists to show as well. But I'm afraid the walls will seem a bit barren."

Diane considered this. "You know, it might just be me, but I like an art gallery that's not too full. It can be overwhelming when almost every space is filled. It's like I can hardly think. I think it's rather elegant to have space between works. Shows them off better."

Margaret slowly nodded. "Less is more. Negative space. I like it."

"Exactly." Diane thought about the clutter in Margaret's house. It might be cozy and comfortable for the Hoskins' household, but Diane couldn't imagine an art gallery looking like that.

"Thank you, Diane." Margaret was going for the door now. "What you've said has inspired me."

"That's great."

Margaret paused with a hand on the doorknob. "And your offer to help, was that sincere?"

"Of course." Diane felt a little nervous now, wondering what she'd gotten herself into. Here she was, not even a week in town, and she was already babysitting for Shelley, adopting a new dog, and offering to help in Margaret's gallery. What if she was taking on too much? Somewhere in there she was supposed to be writing a novel.

"Do you think you could walk through my gallery with me and make suggestions?" Margaret asked hopefully. "I might be an artist, but I'm not terribly good with arranging things if they aren't on a canvas. You're from the city, and I expect you've been to a lot of galleries."

"Well, Eric and did I love going to galleries," Diane said.

"So if you have time, would you want to give me a little consultation?"

"I would love to!"

Margaret looked relieved. "Thank you!"

⋆   ⋆   ⋆

By Sunday afternoon, Diane was ready to have the painting project come to an end. She wanted to putter and play, and she wanted to transform her little bungalow from a storage unit into a home. Today, Dan was working on the kitchen, finishing up on the cabinets and trim. To distract herself from her own impatience, she wrote a nice thank-you card for Mrs. Peabody and took the baking dish back to her.

"Come in, come in," Mrs. Peabody said happily. "I'll make us some tea."

Diane thought of making an excuse, but already Mrs. Peabody was pulling her into the foyer.

"I have oatmeal and raisin cookies," she said in a tempting voice. "I made them yesterday."

Diane smiled. "I love oatmeal and raisin cookies."

"Then you go and sit yourself down in the parlor, and I'll be right back."

"Can I help you in the kitchen?"

"No, no, of course not, dear. I never let anyone in my kitchen except me."

As she went into the shadowy parlor, Diane wondered why Mrs. Peabody banned people from her kitchen. Maybe it was a mess. As she sat on a blue velvet sofa, she could tell that housekeeping was not Mrs. Peabody's strong suit. Everything in here seemed covered in dust—make that layers of dust. Diane knew that Mrs. Peabody was getting up there in years, so perhaps cleaning was difficult for her.

The furnishings in this room reminded Diane of an old movie set. Most of them were antiques, probably around a hundred years old, Diane guessed, and with their ornate carved woods and tassels and fringes, they were all very Victorian. Diane suppressed the urge to sneeze. Oh, for a HEPA-filtered vacuum cleaner in here.

"Here we are," Mrs. Peabody set a tarnished silver tray on the dusty table and sighed. "It's so lovely to have company. I get terribly lonely in this big old house of mine. Sometimes I wonder why I even stay here. Except that this home has been in my family for generations and I can't imagine anyone outside of the family getting their hands on it. Unfortunately, my children don't seem to appreciate the history. They live in modern houses with all the trappings and trimmings." She poured tea into a delicate tea cup. "They think I'm antiquated and old-fashioned." She chuckled as she filled the second cup. "I suppose I am. Sugar?"

"No, thank you. I like mine black."

Mrs. Peabody held the cookie dish toward her now. "Go on."

Diane tried not to think about the probable sanitary conditions of Mrs. Peabody's kitchen. She forced a smile, picked up a cookie and cautiously sniffed it. "It smells delicious."

"Here, take a napkin," Mrs. Peabody said. "I know they look like they're for Christmas, but they work just the same as the plain ones."

Diane took a Santa Claus napkin and smiled. "Very cheerful."

"I don't like to waste anything." Mrs. Peabody pointed to an ornately carved breakfront cabinet that was stuffed with all kinds of things. "My daughter says I'm a packrat, but I keep reminding her that old things have value. Someday when I'm gone and she's in here going through my things, she will see that." She nodded. "Then she'll be sorry." She peered at Diane. "Is it like that with you and your mother?"

"Well, both my parents have passed on. But my mother was different. I suppose she had the opposite problem. She got rid of everything."

Mrs. Peabody looked shocked. "Everything?"

"Yes. She didn't like clutter and had the habit of giving things away—even the things I wished she'd held on to." Diane shrugged. "But I suppose, in the long run, she did me a favor."

Mrs. Peabody's wrinkled forehead creased even more deeply. "How, pray tell, would that be a favor?"

"You've seen the tiny cottage I just moved into. I wouldn't have room for lots of things."

"*Hmph*. One simply *makes* room."

"I suspect you don't have that problem in this great big house. There must be lots of storage here." Diane tried not to feel sorry for Mrs. Peabody's daughter, the one who would have to come and sort it all out. Surely it would take months.

"Oh my, yes. I do have plenty of nooks and crannies to put things in. Then I forget where I've placed them." She tapped the side of her head. "I think it's called old age."

Diane smiled. "That happens to me too."

"I remember being in this house as a child," Mrs. Peabody said wistfully. "My grandparents lived here then, and my grandmother had such fine taste. Most everything in this room was selected by her. My grandfather's shipping business was doing rather well back then. And this house—why, it was the hub of activity in Marble Cove. My grandmother hosted teas and suppers and picnics. She was quite the social butterfly, and I wanted to grow up to be exactly like her."

"Did you?"

"I don't know. I doubt that I ever had the style she had. Oh, her closet was something to behold. Full of beautiful dresses with ruffles and lace. And she had jewelry and furs and hats. Oh my. Back in her day, she was considered to be quite fashionable. I used to love playing dress-up when I came to visit."

She reached for another cookie. "But my mother, well, she was not a bit like Grandmother. Sometimes I wonder why my father married her, she was so unlike his mother." She chuckled. "Or perhaps that is why he married her. My mother was a good woman, but she thought fancy clothes were a sinful waste of money. Mother was very sensible and frugal. And, of course, we did have the Great Depression to contend with."

Diane listened as Mrs. Peabody rambled on about various neighbors and history and events. It was like being tossed random pieces of a jigsaw puzzle with no idea of what the final picture should look like. Diane recognized some of the names as current neighbors, but mostly she felt lost.

"For instance, Mr. Wheeland's daughter Beverly..." Mrs. Peabody lowered her voice as if she thought there were spies in the house. "I feel absolutely certain that young woman has quite a story to tell." She shook her head with pursed lips. "But do you think I can get a word out of her?" She looked to the ceiling with a hopeless expression. "I simply do not understand why some people are so standoffish, keeping everything to themselves. Don't you believe that, as neighbors, we should be involved and interested in one another?" She peered curiously at Diane. "Isn't that what good neighbors do?"

"I ... I suppose so."

As if that were her green light, Mrs. Peabody continued rambling, and although some of the information was interesting, Diane eventually excused herself. "Dan Bauer, our neighbor, is doing some painting at my house," she explained as Mrs. Peabody saw her to the door. "He's probably just about finished up by now, so I need to go home and pay him."

"I do thank you for coming by," Mrs. Peabody said. "Please come again. It is so lovely to have visitors."

"Thank you," Diane said. "The tea and cookies were delightful." She waved and hurriedly exited the porch, going down the walk before Mrs. Peabody had a chance to start listing the ingredients in the oatmeal and raisin cookies.

Taking a deep breath of the fresh air, Diane wondered if Mrs. Peabody's lack of visitors was due to the stale dusty house or the nonstop chatter. Possibly a bit of both.

She found Dan working in the kitchen. It was close to three now. "Looks like you're almost done."

He nodded to the back wall where the trim around the door and a window awaited paint. "I still have quite a bit to go."

"I can do that," she said. "In fact, I can finish up all the remaining trim. I'm actually not half bad as a painter. It's just that I knew this whole house would be far too much for me." She laughed. "I'd probably still be painting by next Christmas. And I'd rather spend my time writing."

He climbed down from the stepladder, looking at her curiously. "You're sure you want me to quit? I don't mind finishing up."

"Let's consider it done," she said with a smile. "And while you're cleaning up, I'll go write you a check. Then you can go home and play with your kids."

He brightened. "That does sound good."

She went to her office, the one space that was almost completely together—and the space that inspired her to actually sit down and write prose. Instead, she sat at her tidy desk and wrote Dan a check. As she wrote the amount, she knew it was more than any of the other local painters would've expected for four days' work, but she didn't care. It was worth it. And the Bauers needed it.

"Here you go," she said as he gathered his tools into an empty bucket. "This is for what you've done, but if you have any extra time in the next week or two, I have some other odd jobs that need doing."

He blinked at the check. "Oh, Diane, this is way too much. I can't—"

"No arguing." She held up her hands. "First of all, you have no idea how grateful I am that you could jump in and do this so quickly. That's worth more to me than you can possibly imagine. Also, I'm from the city, where everything costs more, so I'm paying you based on what I'd pay someone there. And, really, that's all there is to it."

He slowly shook his head. "Guess I should think about moving to the city and taking up painting there."

She laughed. "No, please, don't do that. I like having you and Shelley for neighbors. Besides, don't be fooled: you might make more money working in the city, but it costs a lot more to live there too."

He nodded and tucked the check into his shirt pocket. "I wouldn't last a week in a big city anyway. I'm just a country boy at heart."

She walked him to the door. "Good-bye, Dan. And thank you."

"Thank *you*, Diane."

Diane shut the door behind him and looked around the living room and kitchen. "All right, you," she said to the house. "You're mine now."

She went to work arranging furniture in place in the living room. After several tries, she decided to set the couch parallel to the fireplace with chairs flanking either side. The effect was cozy and inviting—and would be even better with the fire going. Then, for the first time since she'd been in the bungalow, she set up her stereo system and plugged it in. With a Miles Davis CD quietly playing jazz, she started opening boxes and putting her house into order.

Finally bringing order out of chaos was satisfying, and as she hung pictures, set out pillows and even lit some candles, Diane began to not only appreciate the cohesiveness of the ocean-inspired color palette she'd chosen, but to realize that it made her feel happy.

It was after seven when Diane remembered she hadn't gone on her beach walk today. She looked out the front window. Fog rolled into the neighborhood. Its curling pale fingers made it look thick and foreboding. Would this be what Mainers called a lowry day, or did that have to be from real thunderclouds? She turned to her inviting living room, which was nearly done, and decided a fire in the fireplace made more sense than venturing out there by herself in the damp chilly air. Maybe she was nesting.

Chapter Ten

On Monday morning, with the new collar and leash all ready, Diane drove over to the vet clinic to pick up Rocky. She felt nearly as anxious as when she'd been about to deliver a baby. Oh, that was probably an exaggeration in her mind, but it was similar.

She all but skipped to the receptionist's desk. "I'm here to take Rocky home. How is he?"

"He's ready to go home," the girl said. She told Diane how much the bill was.

Diane pulled out her checkbook. "I've never had a dog," she said as she wrote a check. "I wonder if there's anything I need to know."

The girl smiled. "Just love him. And don't feed him too much. And let him out when he needs to go. Take him for walks so he gets his exercise. That's about it, really."

Diane nodded, slipping the copy of Rocky's medical papers into her purse. "That sounds simple enough."

"I'll go and get him."

After a bit, she came back with Rocky. Although it looked like someone had brushed him, he still looked slightly out of sorts with the blue cast on his back leg.

"Is he okay to walk?" Diane asked.

"Sure. He'll probably limp at first, but in time he'll put more weight on it."

Diane knelt down and ran a hand over his silky head. He wagged his tail eagerly. "It's great to see you, boy. It looks like someone cleaned you up."

"We did some grooming, but you'll see he's still got some mats. You can't really bathe him until the cast comes off."

"I got a product at the Pet Place," Diane said, "that's kind of a dry shampoo. Lee Waters recommended it."

The girl nodded. "That's a good idea. All right, you're ready to go. Oh, Dr. Spangler said you don't need to bring Rocky back in until the end of the month, unless he has a problem." She went over to a shelf of dog food and pointed at a bag. "And you might want to consider feeding him this brand. Just until he gets up to his proper weight."

"Okay." Diane nodded eagerly. "I want him to be healthy."

The girl also recommended some chewable doggy vitamins. Diane had just finished paying for these things when an old man came in with a small dog. The man was distraught over a possible poisoning, so Diane thanked the receptionist and, loaded down with the dog food and vitamins, managed to hold on to Rocky's leash and lead him outside.

"This is all new to me," she told Rocky as she opened the back of her car, waiting for him to get in. But he just stood there with a slightly confused expression—at least that's what she thought it was. "Can you get in?" She set down the dog products and patted the back seat. "Come on, boy." Still, he just stood there. Should she lift him? Go ask for help? Make a sling of her jacket?

She put the food and vitamins in the other seat and patted the one closest to Rocky again. "Come on, Rocky, can you get in?" She leaned over and attempted to hoist up his hind haunches, but he wasn't budging. She was afraid to hurt his bad leg.

"I know." She fished around in the bag until she found the doggy vitamins. She opened the canister and held one by Rocky's nose like bait. "Come on, boy. Come and get it. The girl said you'd love these and not even know they were healthy."

To her surprise, he actually looked interested in the treat. Rocky lurched his front legs up.

"That's it!" Slowly, Diane lured him up and into the car. "Good boy!" When he was all the way in, she gave him the vitamin and patted his head. "Now we can go home."

As she drove, she figured she'd just learned something about owning a dog: Treats made for good bribes. Maybe dogs really weren't much different from children.

Fortunately, unloading Rocky from the car was easier. He seemed eager to get out. He sniffed around the yard a bit, limping as he went. The late morning sun cast pleasant dappled shadows about the yard.

Diane finally led him into the house. "This is going to be your new home." She showed him his dishes in the kitchen, one of which she'd already filled with fresh water. Next she showed him his bed in the living room and a couple of the chew toys.

He sniffed around her house for a bit, walking clumsily, with his cast clumping on the wooden floor. Eventually he returned to the bed and, to her relief, got in and made himself comfortable. Feeling like a new mom with a baby who was about to settle in for his first nap, Diane sat on the sofa near his bed and simply watched him.

This companionship felt comforting and yet a bit unnerving too. She really wasn't sure what she needed to do. Did one simply go about one's business? Or did one attempt to make the doggy feel more at home? Finally, remembering his food was still in the car, she decided to attempt leaving him on his own for a few minutes. Really, what was the worst he could do? Chew on something?

As she was carrying the dog food toward the porch, she heard a voice quietly call out. Diane glanced toward Margaret's house and spotted a young woman with honey-colored hair watching her with interest.

"Hello," Diane called back. "Were you talking to me?"

The woman nodded with wide eyes. "My mama says you got a dog."

Diane set the bag of food down and went a bit closer. She saw in the woman's face the distinctive features of Down syndrome. "You must be Adelaide." She smiled. "I'm Diane."

"I know. Where is your dog?"

"He's in the house. Would you like to meet him?"

Now Adelaide looked uncertain.

"Should you ask your mom if it's okay?"

"My mama isn't here."

"Then your dad?"

Adelaide nodded. "Yeah. I'll ask my dad." And just like that, she sprinted to the front door and disappeared. Diane waited a couple of minutes, and Adelaide returned with a big grin. "Daddy says you are my friend too."

Diane smiled. "That's right. I *am* your friend too. I had lunch with your mom and dad the other day, but you were at the community center."

"I like the community center."

Diane opened her front door. "Come on in and meet Rocky."

"Rocky?" Adelaide giggled. "Your dog's name is Rocky?"

"That's right." Rocky came over to them now, wagging his tail with interest.

"You are a big dog." Adelaide tentatively reached down to pet his back. "Your fur is soft. Not like Oreo." She looked at Diane. "Have you felt Oreo? He is *really* soft."

"I don't think I've met Oreo yet."

Adelaide squatted on the floor now, giving Rocky a thorough petting, which he seemed to enjoy. "I didn't think I liked dogs. Not as much as cats. But you are a nice dog."

"I think he's nice too." Diane set the bag of food in the kitchen.

"You got a hurt leg." Adelaide looked sadly at the blue cast. "I hope you get better soon."

As Diane opened the bag of food, she decided she definitely liked Adelaide. What a sweet girl. "I wonder if I should feed him," she said to Adelaide.

"Is he hungry?"

"I don't know," Diane said. "I just got him this morning. I forgot to ask if he'd eaten or not."

"If you put food in his dish," Adelaide explained slowly, "and if he eats it, he is hungry."

Diane chuckled. "Yes, that sounds like good advice. You probably know more about pets than I do since you have cats."

"Yes." Adelaide nodded with a serious expression. "It is my job to take good care of my cats. I give them food and water and I keep their kitty-litter boxes clean. And I brush their fur too."

"That's a lot to do."

"Yes."

Diane filled Rocky's bowl with food, and it seemed Adelaide was right: He was hungry, because he did eat it. Diane wished everything in life was as simple and straightforward as that.

"It's time for me to go home now," Adelaide told Diane.

"How do you know?"

Adelaide pointed to the clock on the stove. "Both hands up. That means lunch time."

Diane nodded. "Right you are."

"Good-bye, Rocky," Adelaide said. "Good-bye, lady."

Diane smiled. "Good-bye, Adelaide. You come over again, all right?"

"All right." Then, before Adelaide left, she turned and looked at the living room. "This is a pretty room. I like it."

"Thank you. I just put it together yesterday. You and Rocky are the first ones to see it."

Adelaide grinned and left.

Diane turned her stereo on, and with a lively selection of golden oldies playing, set to work putting her kitchen in order. Because the cabinets, beneath many layers of paint, had originally been painted a pale yellow and the insides were in good shape, she'd opted not to have Dan paint the interior. But they still needed a good wash and some shelf paper.

As she scrubbed a stubborn spot, she was reminded of having done this before. It was shortly after she and Eric had married, and they were living in student housing. The cabinets in her first tiny kitchen had been in terrible shape. Diane had spent hours getting them clean enough to contain the pretty dishes they'd received as wedding presents. That was more than thirty years ago.

She was just putting down some sticky shelf paper when Rocky began to bark. She'd forgotten about the watchdog aspect of owning a pet, but she realized immediately that she kind of liked it. "It's okay," she told him as she went to see who was at the door. "Probably a neighbor."

It was Shelley Bauer.

"Hi, Diane," Shelley said quickly. "I probably shouldn't have dashed over here." She held up her wireless baby monitor. "But the kids are asleep, and I was just dying to see how your house looks all painted. Is it okay that I popped in?"

Diane laughed and pulled her in. "Of course. Didn't I do the same thing to you?"

Shelley looked down at Rocky. "Who is this?"

Diane quickly explained and then looked at the baby monitor. "Does that thing really work all the way over here?"

"It's supposed to." Shelley nervously glanced out the window toward her house. "But I better make it quick just the same."

So Diane gave her the whirlwind tour, and as they stood on the porch with the door open, Shelley seemed even more impressed than Adelaide had been. "Oh, Diane, it's so beautiful."

"Thanks to your husband."

Shelley just nodded.

"I really appreciated his help."

"I think he appreciated it too." Now Shelley frowned.

"Is something wrong?"

"No ... not really."

"Oh ... ?"

"I guess I'm a little peeved at my husband."

"Is it because he spent so much time at my house? I'm sorry. I should've—"

"No. It's because he spent almost everything you paid him on a gigantic flat screen TV and Blu-Ray player."

Diane grimaced. "Oh."

"We could've used that money to catch up on bills."

"Oh." Diane wished she could think of something besides *oh* to say.

"I know it's not your problem. And I shouldn't unload on you like this. But I've just been so upset."

"I'm sorry, Shelley."

"Yes, well, it's not your fault." She shook her head. "But honestly, I don't know what he was thinking."

Diane shuffled her feet. "Well, men sometimes think differently than women."

"Don't I know that." Shelley looked over at her house. "I should go."

"Come back with the children next time," Diane told her. "And stay longer."

Shelley looked around the living room with a worried expression. "With the kids? But it's so pretty and perfect looking. Do you really—"

"Trust me, it's all a lot tougher than it looks."

"But that white furniture?"

"Washable. Very washable. I wouldn't have gotten it otherwise." She nodded to Rocky, who was sitting by the door. "If my house can handle a dog, it can surely handle your little ones."

Shelley smiled. "Okay. I'll take you up on that offer then." She waved and dashed back across the street.

Diane sighed as she closed the front door. He'd spent his hard-earned painting wages on a big screen TV? "Oh, Dan, Dan, Dan." Still, Diane knew from experience that these missteps sometimes happened in a marriage …

and usually they were forgiven, and even forgotten after enough time passed. She hoped that would be true for Shelley and Dan too. However, Diane didn't envy them. With young children, financial stress, in-law problems, and job insecurity, the Bauers probably felt they were in the pressure cooker. Maybe that's why Dan had wanted to buy something fun.

CHAPTER ELEVEN

Diane wasn't sure it was a smart idea to attempt to walk Rocky on the beach on just his second day home from the vet, but he seemed excited when she hooked on the leash. She promised herself that if he started to slow down or show signs of pain, they'd turn around and slowly come back.

"Hello there, neighbor," Margaret called as Diane and Rocky stepped off of the porch. Margaret was unloading what looked like a painting from the back of her minivan.

"We're going to attempt a walk," Diane said.

"Want some company?"

"Sure!"

"Let me drop my things and grab a sweater."

Soon they were heading for the beach, walking slowly to accommodate Rocky, although he wagged his tail as he hobbled along.

"I was thinking about your story," Diane told Margaret as they reached the promenade. "How you nearly drowned that day."

Margaret just nodded. Buttoning her sweater, she looked out over the water.

"But you said you still go swimming in the ocean."

"I do."

"By yourself?"

"That's right. Although I'm much more careful about swimming in high seas or when there's an undertow."

"That's good to know." Diane glanced at the older woman uneasily. She wanted to give her some kind of a warning and yet that seemed a little silly. Margaret was several years her senior, and she obviously knew what she was doing.

"I never mention this to Allan or Adelaide," Margaret said. "I wouldn't want to worry them. And I know what you're thinking, Diane."

"You do?"

Margaret chuckled. "You think I'm an old fool for swimming in the ocean after I nearly drowned. But like I told you, swimming makes me feel alive and happy. And if I can't feel alive while I'm still alive, well, what is the point in being alive?"

"Yes, I suppose you're right. But maybe we could be swimming buddies, Margaret. If you plan on taking a swim, perhaps you could invite me along."

"You know, when I found you in the midst of rescuing Rocky last week, I'd been thinking about taking a swim that afternoon, but then I changed my mind."

"For my sake—and Rocky's—I'm glad you weren't out there swimming. I don't think I could've gotten him all the way home without your help."

"But do you know what made me change my mind?"

"Were the waves high that day? I can't really recall."

"No, the ocean was fairly calm. I was just looking for a place to sit down and take off my shoes when I noticed something odd at the lighthouse."

"Really? What did you see?"

"A light."

"A light?" Diane frowned. "You mean coming from the lighthouse?"

"That's what it looked like to me. And, of course, I know that's impossible since the light's been decommissioned for years, and I doubt the lantern even works. But that is exactly what it looked like, Diane. Very odd indeed."

"That is so strange." Diane peered down the beach toward the Orlean Point Lighthouse. "Margaret, I thought I also saw the light flash on the day I moved to Marble Cove. It must've been the same flash you saw. We couldn't both have imagined it, could we?"

"You really saw it too?"

"Yes."

"Oh my, that's so comforting. I thought I was losing my mind. Though I have no idea what the source of the light could've been." Margaret gazed at the lighthouse and shook her head. "Anyway, instead of swimming, I hurried on down to the lighthouse to get a closer look. In my rush, I didn't even notice poor Rocky. I suppose he was struggling down in the tide pools and I went right past."

"It's understandable that you missed him. I barely noticed him myself. So when you got down there, was the light actually working?"

"No. Not at all. I walked all around, trying to figure it out. It was completely deserted, as usual, and there was absolutely no rhyme or reason for a light. I began to wonder if I'd imagined the whole thing."

"Very curious."

"But do you know what hit me just now?"

"I have no idea."

"Being distracted by that odd flash of light, whatever its source was, made me go all the way down to the lighthouse. And that caused me to come back up the beach ... just in time to help you. In a way, that mysterious light brought me to your aid right when you needed me."

Diane grinned at Margaret. "So are you saying the lighthouse helped rescue Rocky?"

Margaret laughed. "That might be going a bit far, but it's how it seemed."

Diane nodded. "And as a writer, I must say it makes for a good story." She looked down at Rocky. "I think he's starting to slow down, I wonder if I should give him a rest."

"Maybe so." Margaret pointed to a bench next to the promenade.

Rocky seemed relieved to rest. As they sat there, Margaret told Diane about how much Adelaide had enjoyed her visit.

"She's a delight," Diane said. "She's welcome to visit me anytime. Rocky really liked her too."

"I feel guilty sometimes ..." Margaret let out a long sigh.

"Guilty?"

"Sometimes I feel I need to get away from her—to concentrate. Oh, I love her dearly; don't get me wrong.

But sometimes, if I'm trying to paint at home, well, it can be distracting. That's why I was painting at the gallery today."

"Oh ..." Diane ran her fingers through Rocky's coat. "I can understand that."

"Then I feel guilty about chasing after this dream, trying to start Shearwater Gallery, as if it's causing me to neglect my own child."

"But you need to have your own life too, Margaret."

She nodded. "I know that. In fact, when I nearly drowned that day, it all seemed crystal clear."

"How so?"

"I realized I needed to live my life more fully. I needed to take some risks and chase some dreams. It was quite an *aha* moment." She chuckled.

"I felt like that too," Diane said, "after surviving the cancer. Like I'd been given a second chance, like I didn't want to waste it."

Margaret reached over and clasped Diane's hand, giving it a warm squeeze. "It's encouraging to know that."

"So let's keep chasing our dreams then."

As if on cue, Rocky stood up and wagged his tail.

Diane laughed. "And I suppose I should turn back so I don't wear this guy out." She looked down the beach toward the lighthouse. "But you feel free to keep going, Margaret."

"I'm still curious about the flash of light I saw last week. The flash we both saw. And this is the first time I've been out here since then. Maybe I'll go down and check it out again."

"Let me know if you discover anything."

Margaret promised she would; then after assuring Diane that she was carrying her cell phone, the two parted ways.

Diane walked slowly, gazing out over the horizon to see that the wave action was calmer today. A small flock of pelicans went swooping past in a choreographed line, diving low near the water's surface. The line seemed to disappear beneath the height of a smooth rounded swell, but after a few seconds rose up again. Just like a dance.

By the time Diane reached home, she could tell Rocky was tired. He went straight for his bed and lay down. Before long his tail began thumping contentedly on the pine floor, as if to say he was happy to be home again.

Diane put on the teakettle, and while it was heating, she examined the samples of tiles she'd picked up at the tile store earlier.

She felt fairly certain she wanted to go with the soapstone tiles. She knew they would show wear more than the others, but her kitchen already seemed to have a veneer of wear upon it. For the backsplash she was going with a mixture of soapstone and glass in ocean tones of pale blue and green. Now all she needed to do was drop off her choices with Marge at the appliance store, and Marge would get them to her brother-in-law.

Diane made a short grocery list as she drank her tea. Then, seeing that Rocky was sound asleep and noting that it was just midafternoon, she loaded her tile choices and grocery list into a shopping bag and headed outside to walk to town. It was delightful being able to walk to town and gather groceries or whatever she needed, packing them home in a reusable shopping bag. This slower pace was surprisingly invigorating and Diane imagined herself walking everywhere, looking forward to when Rocky could accompany her.

On her way home—after dropping off the tile samples and gathering some fresh produce, a loaf of whole grain bread, and a couple of artisan cheeses—Diane looked forward to fixing herself a light dinner. Nearby to her cottage, she heard a man's voice raised in anger. She looked up to see two elderly men standing on opposite sides of the street. They appeared to be close in age, perhaps in their seventies or eighties—and they seemed quite distraught.

"Keep your cotton-picking fingers off my garbage can, Wheeland!" The slightly built man ahead of her shouted. He had on a plaid shirt and a brimmed cap.

"This is *my* can," the man in the knit vest standing on the other side of street yelled back.

"No, it is not!" the other one hollered, shaking his fist in the air. "And this is not the first time you've stolen my can, Wheeland!"

"Excuse me," Diane said gently to the red-faced man. "I'm Diane Spencer, your new neighbor." She smiled, pausing in the hopes that he'd introduce himself too, but he just stood there, fists planted on the hips of his baggy corduroy trousers, glaring across the street. "I'm not sure I can see any difference between the two trash cans." she said.

"You bet there's a difference." He nodded with stern blue eyes. "I clean my can out every week with bleach." He shook his finger at the befuddled looking man across the street. "Mr. Wheeland *does not!*"

"Oh." She made an uncomfortable smile at the other man. "Mr. Wheeland, I presume?"

He nodded with a sheepish expression. Diane's guess was that Mr. Wheeland was the friendlier of the two. "Do you think it's possible that you confused the cans, Mr. Wheeland?"

He threw his hands up and shook his head. "Maybe I did. But I could've sworn I put my can on the left side, as usual."

"You put your dad-burned can on the right side, you old fool!"

Diane hooked her loaded shopping bag over a shoulder, grabbed hold of the can still in its place by the curb, and wheeled it across the street. "Maybe we can resolve this peacefully," she said to Mr. Wheeland.

"Yes ... that would be nice." He looked down at the ground, reminding her of a little boy who'd been caught in the act. "Thank you," he muttered.

"Please, hold this for me." She handed him her shopping bag and then wheeled the second can to the other side of the street. "Is this better?"

But instead of answering or even thanking her, the old guy simply reached for the can and wheeled it away. She could hear him grumbling beneath his breath.

She returned to Mr. Wheeland and extended her hand. "Mr. Wheeland, I'm Diane Spencer, your new neighbor in that house right there."

Mr. Wheeland shook her hand. "Very nice to meet you, new neighbor. I'm so sorry you got caught up in our little squabble. Mr. Calder and I have never gotten along too well, but sometimes that man can be downright mean."

Diane smiled. "Well, at least I got to meet my neighbors."

"Not a very pleasant way to get acquainted," Mr. Wheeland said with a sigh. "But welcome to the neighborhood just the same."

CHAPTER TWELVE

B y the end of her second week in the cottage, Diane felt almost completely at home in Marble Cove. In fact, if the upcoming Sunday wasn't Mother's Day, Diane thought she'd be perfectly happy. But it *was* Mother's Day, and she wouldn't get to see either of her children this year. So she was feeling a little blue. With Justin deployed overseas, anything more than a phone call was unreasonably optimistic.

Jessica had called this morning, but instead of arranging when she'd be coming by, she said she would have to work the whole weekend. Being a first-year attorney in a prestigious firm would certainly look good on Jessica's résumé someday, but it came with a price.

Still, Diane was thankful that both her children had good jobs and fulfilling lives. If Justin ever figured out what he wanted to do, that was. As she folded towels later in the day, she decided to simply count her blessings and treat Mother's Day like any other Sunday. Perhaps she'd even visit one of the local churches. She might be given a carnation or something.

Warren, the tile man, was finishing grouting the new tiles in her kitchen today. The sand-colored soapstone looked clean and smooth, and she couldn't wait to try it out. She was so pleased with Warren's work that she asked him to come back and tile her bathroom as well.

"That's a bigger project," he told her. "Might take a whole week or more to finish up."

"That's fine with me," she said as she handed him a check.

"You pick out the tiles you want and leave 'em with Marge like you did with them others, and I'll see when I can fit you into my schedule."

Warren was putting on his coat when the appliance truck pulled into the driveway. "Just like clockwork," he said in his dispassionate Mainer's way. "What'd'ya know."

Diane kept Rocky with her as they watched the delivery men struggle to unload the first large box. It appeared to be the refrigerator, but it looked so big, Diane wondered if it would really fit. After a few minutes, they began wheeling the old refrigerator out of the house and toward the truck, when Shelley—holding Emma and pulling Aiden by the hand—hurried across the street with a curious expression.

"What's going on here?" she asked as the men set the old refrigerator on the lawn. "You're not moving out already, are you?"

Diane laughed. "Of course not. Just getting some new appliances."

"Can I pet your dog?" Aiden asked loudly.

"I think that'd be okay." Diane knelt next to Rocky, unsure how he'd be around small children. "Just remember that Rocky has a broken leg." She kept a firm hand on Rocky's leash and was prepared to jump if necessary, but the dog simply licked Aiden's hand, wagging his tail as if he'd just discovered his new best friend.

"How did Rocky break his leg?" Aiden asked tenderly.

Diane told a condensed version of Rocky's story, leaving out the possibility of abuse.

"Poor old doggy." Aiden made a sympathetic expression as he petted Rocky's head. "That must hurt." Rocky licked the little boy's face, making Aiden giggle and roll on the grass. "He likes me, Mommy! Rocky likes me!"

Satisfied that Rocky was good with kids, Diane let up on his leash and stood, tickling Emma's chubby chin. "How's my little angel?"

"Just about ready for a nap," Shelley said as the delivery guys hauled out the stove. "So what are you doing with your old appliances, Diane?"

"Oh, that's right," Diane said. "I was supposed to figure out where I want these guys to drop them. I don't really want to consign them. Is there a Salvation Army in town?"

"You know, our church has a big garage sale every Memorial Day weekend," Shelley told her. "If you wanted to donate them there, I'm sure no one would complain. Most of the proceeds go to a missionary family our church supports, although the church allows the garage sale workers to put in some of their own things as well. I plan to have a table this year. We can use the extra cash."

This reminded Diane of Dan's splurge on the big TV, and she felt sorry for Shelley. "Hey, how about if I just give my old appliances to you? You could sell them at your garage sale if you like."

"Really?" Shelley looked hopeful. "You'd do that?"

"Sure. Mostly I just want to get them out of here. Do you have someplace to keep them?"

"Dan's parents always let the church hold the garage sale in their barn. They're already stockpiling stuff there. I spent most of yesterday there, helping to clean and price things. Aiden and Emma came home filthy from head to toe. You should've seen the bathwater."

Diane laughed. "And I'll bet the ring around the tub was a good one too."

"That's for sure." Shelley looked at the avocado green dishwasher now coming out. "Do you think the delivery guys would be willing to take them out to the farm? It's only five miles."

"I'm sure they won't mind." Diane decided that if they did mind, she'd offer to subsidize their gas.

"Thanks." Shelley beamed. "I'm not sure what old appliances can bring in, but I won't complain." Then her smile faded slightly. "Of course, this will just give my mother-in-law a better excuse to insist I come out there to help them again."

"Well, that's it," one of the delivery guys told Diane as he tossed some pieces of cardboard into the truck. "You better go in and make sure we put 'em in the right spots."

Diane chuckled. "I don't think you had too many options on where to put them."

"Just the same, you gotta sign off that we delivered them in one piece." He held out a clipboard and pen.

"Okay, I'll go look." Diane headed into the house, looping the end of Rocky's leash around the handrail.

"And I'll come with you," Shelley called out eagerly. "I want to see what you got too."

Diane was surprised at what a difference the appliances made in the kitchen. So much lighter and brighter than the mismatched pieces from the sixties and seventies.

"Oh, Diane!" Shelley walked around the kitchen in wide-eyed wonder. "This is beautiful. You must be rich."

"Well, thanks." Diane tested the doors and lights, and Shelley gushed about how this kitchen could be featured in a magazine or home improvement show. Finally satisfied that all was well, Diane went out and signed the form; then she asked the guys to take the appliances to the address Shelley wrote down for them. When the truck left, Shelley and the kids went back to their home.

As Diane untied Rocky from the handrail, she watched Shelley tugging and pulling Aiden across the street. The lad was vehemently complaining. "I wanna play with the doggy," he yelled again and again, so loudly that the whole neighborhood could probably hear him. Then just as Shelley reached her own yard, Emma began howling full force. Poor Shelley—she had her hands full.

As Diane took Rocky inside, she briefly considered offering to babysit for Shelley again. However, the last time Diane had suggested this, Shelley had seemed more resistant than ever. For some unknown reason, Shelley seemed to think her children would fall totally apart if anyone besides herself cared for them. Diane chuckled to remember Shelley struggling to get her screaming children into the house. Perhaps there was more to Shelley's worries than Diane understood.

Diane walked to town in the afternoon. First she went to the stationery store and bought invitations for the open house she had decided to host. On her way past the Shearwater Gallery, she peeked in and saw some lights on in back. Not wanting to disturb Margaret, especially if she was painting, Diane lightly tapped on the glass door. She had promised to drop in sometime and look at the layout of the gallery. With her own house in order, this seemed as good a time as any. However, she probably should've called first.

Margaret came toward the door now, wearing a paint-smeared shirt and holding a brush in her hand. She waved to Diane. "Come in, come in," she said as she opened the door wide.

"I hope I'm not interrupting your—"

"Not at all. I was just ready to take a break."

Diane looked around the open room. "This is a lovely space." She took in the old wooden floors and brick walls. "Very charming."

"It has its challenges," Margaret said. "Getting the lighting right has been interesting."

Diane looked up to where the ceiling was painted black and tracks of various-sized spotlights were positioned. "That seems like a good idea," she said. "You can send the light where you need it."

"Precisely." Margaret walked over to where a number of framed works were leaning against a back wall. "I really should start positioning pieces, but I've been so obsessed with my own work." She frowned. "Also, I'm just not sure about the brick."

Diane studied the dark red surface. "Must make it tricky to hang paintings."

"Yes. Allan suggested we run strips of board up high and suspend wires down. I suppose that would work."

"How do the paintings look when they're up against the bricks?" Diane asked.

"I'll show you." Margaret set down her brush and carefully wiped her hands. She picked up a large seascape, holding it up. "What do you think?"

"It's hard to tell without the lights on, but my first impression is that paintings might be a bit dark on the dark brick wall."

Margaret set down the painting. "Exactly what I've been thinking. I've actually considered painting the walls white, but Allan says that's crazy."

Diane looked at the dark wood floors and the dark walls and frowned. "I'm not sure, but I think I agree with you, Margaret. How about if you turn on all the lights."

"Of course!" Margaret hurried back and now all the lights came on.

"That does help," Diane admitted, "but hold the painting up again so I can get the full effect."

Margaret complied. Diane studied it and slowly shook her head. "I still feel it's quite dark in here."

"So I guess I have no choice." Margaret set the painting down. "I'll have to paint the bricks."

"It does seem a shame to paint these lovely bricks." Diane ran her hand over a wall. "I wonder if there's any other way."

"Allan's gotten estimates for having walls built over the bricks, but it's so expensive. Painting is cheaper."

"What about fabric?" Diane asked. "I had my dining room upholstered with fabric. Mine was a printed pattern, but you could go with white."

"That's a thought." Margaret nodded. "Like a blank canvas."

They talked some more, kicking around ideas, and Margaret actually got paper and pen and made some notes. "This is so helpful," she told Diane. "You've given me some real inspiration. Thank you!"

"It was fun," Diane said. "I can't wait to see this gallery actually open. In fact, if you need any help, please feel free to call on me. I love things like this."

"Would you like to see what I'm working on?"

"I'd love to."

So Margaret led Diane to the back room and showed her a lovely seascape with a great blue heron in the foreground.

"Oh, Margaret, this is amazing."

Margaret looked pleased. "You really like it?"

"I love it. I would hang that in my house."

"Really?" Margaret was beaming now. "Why, thank you."

"See," Diane said, "you need to get this gallery open so people can see and purchase your work. Now I'm going to leave so you can get back to it. And, please remember my offer. If you need help, let me know."

Margaret thanked her again and Diane left. She'd had no idea Margaret was so talented. She suspected now that the pieces hanging in Margaret's home were from the early days of Margaret's art career. She'd obviously improved greatly since then. As Diane walked through her neighborhood, she not only felt fortunate to have a good friend in Margaret, but she also felt honored to know such a talented person.

She thought of her own novel. With proximity and a little luck, some of Margaret's creativity might rub off on her.

CHAPTER THIRTEEN

Whether it was from seeing Margaret's painting or perhaps something about the sunlight trying to break through the foggy air, Diane felt inspired as she walked down Newport Avenue. And the closer she got to her cottage, the more determined she was to go directly to her office, turn on her computer, and actually start that novel.

She was just passing by Mr. Wheeland's house when he came out and greeted her.

"How are you today?" she asked brightly.

"Very well. I'm expecting my daughter to arrive any minute." He glanced down the street.

"Oh, how lovely for you."

"Anna lives in Augusta. She works at the state office." She could hear the pride in his voice.

"Anna?"

"Did I say Anna? I meant Beverly." He cleared his throat. "She comes to visit me whenever she can. Unfortunately, it's not often enough." He looked a bit wistful now. "Oh, there's Beverly now," he said as a small car turned down their street and into his driveway.

A slender and stylishly dressed dark-haired woman stepped out of the car, looking curiously at Diane.

After giving his daughter a warm hug, Mr. Wheeland turned to Diane. "Beverly, I'd like you to meet Diane. She's just moved into the Bensons' old house. Diane, this is my daughter Beverly."

"We've just been getting acquainted," Diane said to Beverly.

She smiled nervously and shook Diane's hand. "That's nice. It's good for Dad to know his neighbors. I worry about him being alone so much."

"It's good for me, as well," Diane said cheerfully. "I love being in a neighborhood where everyone is friendly."

Mr. Wheeland rubbed his chin. "That gives me an idea. Beverly, are you still planning on making clam chowder tonight?"

"Are you hungry already?"

He chuckled. "No, that's not it. But I thought maybe our new neighbor would like to join us." He winked at Diane. "Beverly makes the best Boston clam chowder in these parts. Care to join us?"

"That's a lovely idea."

"I don't do much cooking these days," Beverly shot her dad a glance.

"Beverly uses her mother's chowder recipe," he told Diane. "It's my absolute favorite. And I'm sure you'd enjoy it too."

Diane didn't feel too sure as she watched Beverly biting her lip. "I, uh, wouldn't want to be any trouble. Maybe another—"

"Nonsense," he said. "One more person for chowder is no bother."

"Perhaps another night would be better," Diane said uncomfortably. As much as she wanted to get to know her neighbors, she could take a hint. And it was obvious that Beverly did not wish to entertain. Now she remembered something Mrs. Peabody had said about Beverly's standoffishness and realized it might be one thing Mrs. Peabody had gotten right.

"We'd love to have you." Mr. Wheeland looked so hopeful and pleased that Diane knew she couldn't disappoint him.

"Perhaps I could bring a green salad. I just bought some nice produce in town."

Beverly offered a stiff smile. "Let's say six-ish. Dad doesn't like to eat late."

He chuckled. "The older I get, the earlier I seem to go to bed ... and get up."

"Six-ish sounds perfect," Diane said, before going their separate ways.

After greeting Rocky, she set about making a pretty green salad. She tried not to feel guilty about her unorthodox dinner invitation.

As she set the salad in the fridge, she remembered how inspired she'd felt on her way home from town. For a nice change she felt ready to sit down at her computer and finally write with no distractions. She went into the study and sat down at the desk.

While she waited for the computer to be ready, she sat in her chair and stared at the beach treasures that used to adorn her kitchen window back in Boston. The shells and beach glass and miniature lighthouse were now arranged on her office windowsill. She focused on the lighthouse, willing it to inspire words that would breathe themselves into story. She looked at the magazine photos she'd collected from some catalogs, people who resembled the characters she was creating. She turned on her CD player and got the soundtrack to *Titanic* going.

She started her word-processing program and began a new file. Time to write down her notes. So far, all she knew was that this was going to be a mystery involving an unexplainable flash of light from her fictional lighthouse. So far, she had a heroine named Lucy and a villain who lived on the bluff, although she thought perhaps he might transform himself into a hero if she was patient enough. She had the seaside setting, of course, but beyond that, there wasn't much.

Nevertheless, she began.

After nearly two hours of growing desperation—and only a few new sentences to show for it—she turned off her computer. "I need a break, Rocky."

Rocky, who had taken up a position on the floor beside her desk, looked up at her happily. His tail *thunked* on the floor as he wagged it in anticipation of some change.

Diane pulled on her Bogs and polar fleece and picked up the dog leash. Her brain needed oxygen, and Rocky needed a walk. Diane had been increasing the length of their treks each day, but so far they'd made it only about halfway to the lighthouse.

Since that evening when she'd seen the mysterious flash of light, and after hearing Margaret's report about seeing it too, Diane had adopted the habit of carefully watching the lighthouse in the hopes she'd see it again. However, so far she'd seen nothing out of the ordinary. And as she walked down the beach today, the fog was so thick she couldn't see the lighthouse at all until it was time to turn back.

She stood there stroking Rocky's head and looking at the vague silhouette of the tall structure. "Someday you'll make it the whole way to the lighthouse. And maybe you'll even want to go swimming sometime ... when you're all well again." He looked up at her as if he understood, or maybe he just appreciated her. She couldn't believe what a big part of her life this dog had become in such a short time.

It was already close to six by the time they got back home, and Diane realized that her beach clothes probably wouldn't be a good dinner outfit. She didn't think this was a dress-up dinner, but Beverly had looked so stylish and, after all, Diane was their guest. So instead of going with her usual khaki pants and casual shirt, she put on a pair of nice trousers and a pale blue silk blouse. This was the best dressed she'd been since moving to Marble Cove.

As she walked down the street to the Wheeland house, carrying her green salad and wearing real jewelry, she felt slightly conspicuous. She wondered what Mrs. Peabody would think if she saw her, which she probably did. What would she have to say about Diane going into Mr. Wheeland's house at the dinner hour? Surely, Mrs. Peabody wouldn't assume that Diane had any romantic interests in the old man. Good grief, Mr. Wheeland had to be old enough to be Diane's dad. As she mounted the porch steps and rang the doorbell, Diane decided it was more likely that Mrs. Peabody knew all about Beverly's visitation schedule and would think nothing of this.

The door opened, revealing Beverly, who smiled. "Come in, come in." She had changed into more casual clothes but still looked pretty and stylish, although her face was slightly flushed and her dark hair a little messier than earlier. "I forgot that making clam chowder is so much work."

"Can I help?"

"No, I think I have it under control." Beverly led Diane inside and reached for the wooden salad bowl. "Thank you for this. I have some appetizers and goodies set up in the library." She nodded toward a partially closed door. "Why don't you join my father in there while I check on the chowder?" She lowered her voice. "Father isn't used to socializing much these days, so you might have to initiate the conversation. Do you mind?"

"No, of course not."

"Oh, thank you." Beverly looked relieved. "Now I better go make sure my chowder's not getting scorched."

Diane stood there for a moment, trying not to feel uncomfortable about being put in this position. Really, this was no big deal. Although she and Eric used to socialize regularly, in the past two years she'd gotten out of the habit. Still, she reminded herself as she reached for the doorknob, this was simply a low-key, casual dinner with two neighbors. She could handle this.

CHAPTER FOURTEEN

Diane smiled brightly as she entered Mr. Wheeland's dimly lit library. "Good evening," she told him. "Beverly said I should join you in here."

"Oh yes, hello there." Mr. Wheeland looked uneasy as he attempted to push himself from the leather chair.

"Please, don't get up for me," she said quickly. "You look so comfortable in here." She glanced around the cozy space. Tall bookcases stuffed full with books, a small fire in the fireplace, and a glass-topped coffee table with a pretty arrangement of appetizers and colorful napkins. "What a delightful setting!"

He smiled, waving to the chair opposite him. "Please, make yourself comfortable. Help yourself to Beverly's bounty. I think she was afraid I might starve before dinner."

"Thank you." She reached for a stuffed celery stick. "Very nice."

"Beverly tried to talk me into having our appetizers in the living room, but I dug in my heels. This is my favorite place in the house."

"I can understand why." She looked more closely at the bookshelves—a mixture of both nonfiction and fiction as well as a large selection of reference materials. "Surrounded by books. What could be better than this?"

He nodded slowly. "I couldn't agree more, but Beverly complains it's too dark in here during the daytime. I keep the curtains closed to protect both my eyes and my books. Some of these volumes are quite old."

"Are you a collector?"

"Not specifically. But I do have a few special tomes. Mostly I enjoy books for being books. Each one is like a good friend."

Diane smiled. "My late husband loved his books too. In fact, he taught literature at Boston College."

Mr. Wheeland's brows lifted. "Very impressive."

She waved her hand. "He didn't feel that way about his job. He simply did what he loved and loved what he did."

"I was a teacher too." Mr. Wheeland removed his glasses, wiping them with a white handkerchief. "However, I taught in high school. Social studies."

"Now that is *really* impressive. I suspect that educating teenagers is a lot more challenging than working with college students."

"You're probably right about that." He replaced his glasses. "I think I retired just in the nick of time."

"In time for what?"

"I got out just before computers and technology took over." He sighed. "I am a dinosaur when it comes to modern electronics. Beverly keeps pushing me to change my ways, but I have no intention of doing so. Computers will never be a part of my life."

"I can respect that. The truth is I have a bit of a love-hate relationship with my own computer."

"How so?"

"I love it when everything works as I expect it to work and when I accomplish what I set out to do, but I hate it when my computer does something I don't understand and I'm caught off-guard. It feels as if the computer wants to show off how it's so much smarter than I am."

He chuckled. "Similar to some high school students I've known."

She laughed. "I never thought of it like that, but that's a great metaphor."

"What sort of work do you do on your computer?"

"I used to write for a newspaper," she said. "But now I'm trying to write a novel."

"Really?" His eyes lit up. "What sort of novels do you fancy to write?"

"I'm thinking mysteries, perhaps with a dash of romance. And, of course, I want to use a seaside setting."

"Good for you." He nodded. "That sounds exciting."

"It might sound exciting, but with the progress I made today I am questioning myself."

"Writer's block?"

"I, uh, I don't know. I hope not. When you write for a newspaper, you don't even have the luxury of writer's block. I had a word count and a deadline, and there was no excuse not to get the story in."

"Perhaps you need those disciplines now. Can't you simply give yourself a word count goal and a deadline?"

She nodded as she considered this. "That's a good idea."

He sighed. "I once fancied myself to be a writer too."

"Really?" She leaned forward.

"Oh yes." He pointed to an old electric typewriter on a side table near his desk. "I've typed hundreds of pages. Unfortunately, the pages just never seem to make themselves into a book. That part of writing eludes me."

Diane frowned. "Goodness, I hope that's not going to happen to me."

"What's going to happen to you?" Beverly asked as she entered the room.

"Oh, I'm trying to write my first novel. Just started today, in fact. But I didn't get anywhere. Your father thinks it might be writer's block."

"Ah," Mr. Wheeland said. "It's nothing you can't get beyond."

Diane smiled. "Thank you, kind sir."

"All right," Beverly said, "dinner is ready. Shall we move to the dining room?"

"Excellent." Mr. Wheeland put Diane's hand on his arm as they walked. "You're fortunate to have begun writing while you are still young."

Diane laughed. "I guess *young* is all a matter of perspective."

"Father turns seventy-nine this summer," Beverly told her as they sat down to an elegantly set table.

"Well past my three score and ten," he said soberly.

Beverly laughed. "My father has been stuck on that old three score and ten saying for as long as I can recall."

He cleared his throat. "Well, remember your mother."

Beverly nodded. "Yes. Mother did pass on shortly after three score and ten. That was about four years ago."

As Mr. Wheeland bowed his head to say a short yet formal blessing, Diane realized that this little family—or what remained of their family—probably had quite a few untold stories. Suddenly she felt rather curious.

As they ate the tasty clam chowder, cornbread, and salad, Diane learned that Beverly was an only child and that she and her mother had been very close.

"Mother was a teacher too," Beverly told Diane. "That's how she and Father met."

"We would've celebrated our fiftieth anniversary last December," Mr. Wheeland said.

"At least we had a party for your forty-fifth," Beverly pointed out.

Now Diane felt it was her duty as their guest and social stimulator to direct this conversation along a more positive route. "I suppose you both know all about our neighbor Margaret and her art. She'll be opening her gallery soon."

"Margaret Hoskins is an artist?" Mr. Wheeland looked genuinely surprised. "I never would've guessed."

"Don't you talk to any of your neighbors?" Beverly asked.

He shook his head. "Apparently not. I suppose I left that to your mother."

"As it turns out," Diane said, "our quiet neighbor Margaret Hoskins isn't just an artist, she's a very talented artist. She does lovely seascapes and seabirds. Her gallery is going to be called Shearwater Gallery."

"For the seabird." Mr. Wheeland nodded.

"An art gallery in Marble Cove would be perfectly delightful." Beverly reached for the butter dish. "I've always felt this town was ready for more culture—something beyond the typical tourist shops."

"Margaret would like to open the gallery before Memorial Day," Diane said. "Although I know she's feeling a bit overwhelmed."

She told them about the challenges of the brick walls, and then the conversation turned to local architecture. It turned out Beverly knew quite a bit about it.

"Is that your line of work?" Diane asked as they were finishing up. "Architecture?"

"No ..." Beverly shook her head.

"Beverly's late husband was an architect," Mr. Wheeland said. "He even designed some important projects for the state."

For some reason this caught Diane off guard. She had assumed Beverly had always been single.

"I suppose I learned about architecture vicariously," Beverly said. "I met Will while he was working on a remodel for the State House."

"I think I mentioned that Beverly works for the Maine State House?"

"Oh yes." Diane remembered how professionally dressed Beverly had been earlier. "I'll bet you came here directly from work this afternoon."

"Yes. We had a half day today."

"Do you like living in Augusta?"

"Yes, most of the time. Fortunately, it's not quite two hours to get here. Well, depending on the time of year and the traffic."

"Beverly made that drive almost every weekend during her mother's illness." Mr. Wheeland set his empty water glass down with a sad expression. "She doesn't come nearly so much anymore."

"My job is rather demanding," Beverly told Diane. "It seems to get more demanding all the time."

"I know how that goes." Diane smiled sympathetically. "I sometimes felt that the more I was able to do, the more my boss loaded on to me."

Beverly nodded eagerly. "Yes, I feel just like that sometimes." After a beat of silence, she stood and began stacking the dishes. Diane stood to help.

"Please, let me get this."

"I can at least get these to the kitchen for you," Diane said as she gathered up a small stack.

"Then perhaps you ladies will excuse me for the evening." Mr. Wheeland made a partial bow. "Thank you for the delicious dinner, Beverly."

"Are you going to bed already, Dad?"

He nodded in a tired way. "It's been a long day, dear. And it seems the older I get, the earlier I go to bed." He turned to Diane. "It's been nice to get acquainted with you."

"And with you too," Diane smiled warmly.

"I hope you'll persist with your writing."

"I hope so too."

"If you ever need a set of eyes ..." He looked a bit uncertain. "I don't mean to overstep, but I am a good reader."

"You'd be willing to read some of my novel?"

"I'd be honored to read as much of it as you like."

"That would be wonderful. I know it's important to have other readers and to get honest, helpful feedback. As soon as I get something written, that is. Maybe when I have a couple of edited chapters together I'll take you up on that offer."

"And if Diane doesn't mind," Beverly said, "I'd like to put her phone number by your phone, Dad. Just in case you should need something. And I gave her your phone number as well."

"That sounds like a good plan," Diane said. "And I promise not to make a pest of myself. Just neighborly."

"Yes, I suppose that would be nice." He nodded to both of them. "Goodnight, ladies."

After he left, Diane insisted on helping Beverly in the kitchen. At first they made small talk, but by the time they got to the pots and pans, Diane decided to see if she could find out more. To prime the pump, she told Beverly a bit about her own life and how difficult it was for her to lose Eric when she did. "It was so unexpected—like someone had pulled the earth out from under me. I honestly felt I couldn't quite catch my breath for a while."

Beverly just nodded, scrubbing even harder on the stockpot. Her expression was hard to read, but Diane could tell she was losing her patience. Diane wondered if she'd pressed her too much. But at the same time, maybe she should push. Maybe Beverly needed a friend.

Something in Beverly's pretty dark eyes looked tired and worried and, unless it was Diane's imagination, slightly haunted. However, Diane wasn't sure it was her place to try to get to the bottom of it.

CHAPTER FIFTEEN

The week after Mother's Day brought sunshine and lilacs and the high hopes that Diane might actually be capable of writing a page or more of her first novel. The hopes turned into reality, and by midweek she was actually beginning her fourth chapter. They were short chapters, true, but she was so delighted at her progress that she was tempted not to answer her phone when it rang on Wednesday morning. However, just in case it was one of her children, she pushed her keyboard aside, slid back her chair and reached for her cell phone.

"Oh, Diane!" Shelley said, sounding unhinged. "I'm losing it."

"What is it?" Diane could hear someone crying in the background. "What's wrong?"

"I can't remember the last time I called to vent to someone, but I just needed some positive reassurance. You're always full of positive reassurance. My kids are driving me nuts. And then there's my mother-in-law."

Diane hit *Save* on her computer and leaned back in her chair. "What's going on?"

"My mother-in-law is insisting that I come over for the afternoon. She's complaining about how there's so much pricing to do, and the church garage sale is less than two weeks away. I reminded her that I had already tried to price some items with the wrong stickers. Then I told her I've got the kids and they're acting up, and she acts like that's nothing. Like I should be able to drag them out there, plop them down in the barn, keep tabs on them—and you should see some of the dangerous things out there. And then she actually expects me to have the clarity to price garage sale items—" She stopped suddenly. "Put that down, Aiden! Oh dear, I should go, Diane. Sorry to bother you."

"You're not a bother," Diane assured her. But, with the shrill sounds of Emma crying and Aiden yelling, Shelley cut the call short.

Diane's heart ached for Shelley. She looked out the window to see Shelley trying to get the kids out the front door. With a diaper bag slipping off her shoulder and a red-faced Emma flailing her limbs in her mother's arms, Shelley grabbed Aiden by the hand and attempted to drag him toward the car.

Diane suddenly experienced a strange urge, an almost physical pull to get out of her chair and help Shelley.

She turned off her computer and hurried outside just as the diaper bag fell to the ground and Aiden made his escape and ran toward the backyard.

Diane hurried across the street and picked up the diaper bag. "Let me stay with the kids," she insisted.

"No, no, I can't do that." Shelley turned to yell at Aiden who was halfway up a tree trunk. "They're both acting out today. It's like there's something in the air."

"I don't care," Diane told her. "I can handle it."

"But my house is a mess, Diane. I mean *really* a mess. Way, way worse than last time. There's no way I can let you in there—"

"Then let the kids come to my house."

She hesitated. "I can't do that."

"Why not, Shelley? It's a lovely day. We'll play in the backyard. Rocky will be happy to see Aiden." She called out to Aiden now. "Want to play with Rocky today?"

He slid down from where he was climbing and slowly sauntered over, looking suspicious. "Can I, Mommy?"

"And you can bring Emma's playpen over," Diane patted the diaper bag. "I assume there's formula in here."

"Yes, but—"

"Trust me," Diane said, locking eyes with Shelley. "We'll be fine."

Shelley looked torn.

Something compelled Diane to continue as she looked up to the clear blue sky. "In fact, I was about to take a break myself. I'll fix a little picnic for Aiden and me, and we'll play and have fun."

Shelley sighed. "Okay, you win. I hope you're not sorry."

"Here," Diane said as Emma began screaming even louder than before. "Let me take the baby while you get the playpen."

"I wanna come too," Aiden yelled from behind his mother. Shelley was trying to keep the front door closed, probably so Diane wouldn't see how messy it was in there.

"You *are* coming over, Aiden," Diane said. "But first you need to get some things. Do you have a dump truck or a pail and shovel?"

First he looked confused but then he nodded eagerly. "My sand toys!" He looked up at his mom. "Can I bring my sand toys to Diane's house?"

Shelley just shrugged. "I guess so."

"Okay." Diane slung the strap of the diaper bag over her shoulder. "I've got Emma and the bag. You guys get the rest and come over when you're ready."

Emma was still crying as Diane carried her across the street, but Diane kept chattering at her and bouncing her. By the time they got into the house, Emma seemed to be settling down. Now Diane took Emma on a little tour of her house, stopping to look at pictures on the wall or seashells on the mantle and even stopping to pet Rocky.

Then she took Emma into the kitchen and, using a damp paper towel, gently cleaned the tears from the baby's flushed cheeks and even smoothed her downy blond hair a bit. "See," Diane told her, "you're looking more like my little angel already."

It wasn't long until Shelley and Aiden arrived on the front porch, with the playpen and Aiden's sand toys in tow.

"Let's get those to the backyard," Diane said as she led them around the side of the house. "I started working on a garden bed, but right now it's mostly just a pile of sand and dirt, a perfect construction site."

"I hope you won't regret—"

"What a day!" Diane interrupted Shelley. "Can you smell those lilacs?"

Soon the playpen was set in the backyard and Aiden was playing with Rocky, running in circles and whooping wildly.

"I have something planned for our lunch," Diane assured Shelley. "And I put Emma's bottle in the fridge. So don't worry, we'll all be just fine."

Shelley frowned, looking from Diane to her kids, who seemed perfectly content. "I don't know."

"Trust me, everyone will have a good time. You have my phone number; I have yours. Go and take a break."

"I can't take a break." She let out a groan. "I have to help my mother-in-law."

"Then pretend it's a break. Maybe get yourself a latte on the way. At least you'll only have one thing to do."

"That's true. But I should probably just take the kids with me. My mother-in-law will want to know why I didn't."

"Tell her you needed a break," Diane said.

"I feel guilty—like she's right about me. Like I'm not a good mom."

"Even a good mom needs a break." Diane put a hand on her shoulder, gently nudging her toward the gate. "And the best moms make sure to take regular breaks."

Shelley pushed her hands through her long blond hair, pulling it back like a ponytail and twisting it. "Okay, okay, I'm going. Emma can have her bottle whenever you like. If she fusses again, it'll probably be because she's hungry. And you've got my number. If you need me, just call. I won't be gone more than two hours."

"Yes, yes. And my cell phone's right here in my pocket."

Shelley made an uneasy smile. "Thanks, Diane."

"You bet." Diane held up Emma's hand in a miniwave. "Bye, Mommy. And Shelley," she called as she closed the gate, "don't forget to breathe."

Shelley was barely out of sight when Emma started to fuss again, probably from seeing her mother leave. So Diane began another little tour, this one of the backyard. She showed her tulips that were sneaking through the overgrown flower beds and the bird feeder she'd hung recently. Then they went over to the garden patch where Aiden was busily digging a road with his shovel and dump truck.

Diane sat down on a lawn chair, and together they watched Aiden "working." Apparently he liked having an audience, because he seemed to enjoy explaining what he was doing and why. And Emma seemed to enjoy being outside. It was surprisingly easy to keep these two little ones entertained, although Diane realized if she did this regularly, she would need a whole new bag of tricks. Life with young children was demanding when a mommy was on call seven days a week, twenty-four hours a day.

Poor Shelley really did need a break. But maybe if all went well today, Diane could try to schedule a regular time, perhaps one morning a week, when she could go over to their house and let Shelley go off and do something besides the church's garage sale or marching to her mother-in-law's orders.

After a while, Diane enticed Aiden from the garden plot with the lure of a picnic. Atop a patchwork quilt on the grass she laid her makeshift meal on bright-colored paper plates. Something about the festivity worked to get Aiden to agree to hand-washing and joining her and Emma.

"Can we do this every day?" Aiden asked with a bite of apple in his mouth.

Diane laughed, bouncing Emma on her knee as she picked up a piece of Swiss cheese. "Not every day is as sunny and warm as today, Aiden."

"Picnics are fun."

Now Diane heard something jangling. Realizing it was her cell phone in her shirt pocket, she juggled Emma and awkwardly pulled the phone out and answered it.

"*Diane?*" said a guy's voice.

"Yes. Who is—"

"Do you have the kids?"

"Dan?"

"Yes! *Are the kids with you?*"

"Yes. They're right here. What's going on?"

"I'm on my way to the hospital. It's Shelley."

Diane felt an electric jolt of fear rush through her. But then she saw Aiden's face, watching her with a slight frown, so she took in a quick breath and kept her face neutral. "What do—"

"Car wreck. I'll call you back when I know more."

Diane hung up the phone and, inhaling deeply, turned around and forced a bright smile. "Who wants cookies?"

"Me!" Aiden exclaimed. Now he stood, doing a decent imitation of Sesame Street's Cookie Monster and making Emma laugh.

"Okay." Diane pointed at him. "You stay here and eat some more apples and cheese, and Emma and I will be back with cookies." He nodded with a sincere expression and she went back into the house. Her hands were trembling.

Perhaps sensing something, Emma began to fuss.

"No, it's okay," Diane said in a shaky voice. "It's okay."

First Diane got out Emma's bottle. She put it in a bowl of hot water to warm as she searched for cookies. She usually tried to keep a package of chocolate-orange mint cookies on hand for unexpected guests. Fortunately, she found them and just hoped Aiden would like them. She would give him only two. With milk.

Please, God, please, God, please, God, she silently prayed as she filled a small plastic cup with milk. *Please, God, please, God, please, God, let Shelley be okay, God, please!* She prayed over and over in her head as she dipped the bottle of formula up and down in the hot water.

"Diane!" yelled Aiden from the back door.

She jumped, nearly dropping the bottle.

"I ate my apples and cheese."

"Okay, I'm coming." She emerged with Emma and the bottle. "I need to get Emma settled with her bottle first," she told him. "So we can have cookies and milk while she has her milk too."

"Okay." He nodded and stood by watching as she settled Emma into the playpen, just as she'd seen Shelley do. She handed the baby her bottle, making sure she had it in her little hands, and then put the lightweight Winnie the Pooh blanket over her chubby bare legs. *Please, God, please, God,* Diane mentally cried out, *please let Emma's mommy be okay.*

As Diane returned to the house, she could hear Aiden doing his Cookie Monster imitation again. At least he didn't seem to suspect anything. Not yet, anyway. She returned with his cookies and milk. Then, as he celebrated with a happy dance, she checked to make sure her phone was still on and wondered what she could do ... besides pray and wait ... and play grandma to these two darlings. *Please, God!*

CHAPTER SIXTEEN

Just when Diane felt like crying out for help, Adelaide's head popped up on the other side of the fence.

"What are you doing?" she asked with childlike curiosity.

"We had a picnic," Diane said, shaking the remains of the cookies from the quilt. "Now we're just playing."

"Oh." Adelaide nodded with a sweet smile.

"Do you want to come over and join us?"

"Yeah." Adelaide's head disappeared from above the fence. But within seconds she was coming in through the side gate.

"Do you know Aiden?" Diane asked Adelaide.

"I saw him before." Adelaide smiled shyly. "You live in the blue house across the street."

"Uh-huh." Aiden peered up from where he was digging.

"I live next to Diane," Adelaide told him. "I have three cats."

Aiden's eyes got big. "Three cats?"

"Yeah." Now Adelaide told him her cats' names and why she'd named them the way she had.

"A cat named Oreo!" Aiden laughed. "Just like a cookie."

Adelaide laughed too. Then she kneeled down in the dirt and started playing with Aiden, helping him build his roads and complimenting him on his dump truck-driving skills.

Diane managed to keep herself from running over and hugging the dear girl. With Aiden occupied, Diane was free to keep Emma happy. But every few minutes she checked her cell phone, checked the time, and silently prayed that Dan would call soon and tell her that Shelley was going to be all right.

Finally it was nearly two o'clock, and Adelaide decided she'd had enough of Aiden. Diane couldn't blame the patient girl, especially since Aiden was starting to get cranky. Emma looked worn out too, and Diane knew it was their naptime, but she also knew it might be a challenge to get them to sleep at her house.

"I wonder if your front door is locked," she said absently to Aiden.

"That's a no-no," Aiden told her. "I get in trouble when I lock doors."

"Yes." Diane nodded. "I'll bet you do. But I wonder if your mommy locked the door."

Aiden looked uncertain, so Diane decided to find out for herself. "Come on." She hefted Emma in her arms and took Aiden by the hand. Then, hoping and praying the front door would be unlocked, she walked the kids across the street and over to their house. To her relief, the door wasn't locked. And why should it be in their sleepy little neighborhood?

Diane gently laid the nearly asleep baby into the crib; then she tiptoed to Aiden's room, where he was waiting for her to read him a story. He'd already picked one of her favorites, *The Cat in the Hat.* She read it to him.

But after she closed the picture book, he whined for another. "Please. Just one more."

So she resorted to bribery. "I will give you a very special treat if you take a good nap with no fussing or noise."

"What kind of treat?" he asked with sleepy skepticism.

"It will be a surprise. But you'll only get it if you close your eyes and don't make a sound." Then, prepared for him to let out a loud cry like she'd heard him do for Shelley, Diane quietly left the bedroom, waited in the hallway, and counted to twenty.

Fortunately, Aiden was either taking her bribe seriously or God was having mercy. More likely, the little guy was simply exhausted. And now the house was blissfully quiet.

On her way to the living room, Diane almost tripped on a stuffed doggy lying facedown in the hallway. Picking her way through what looked like a minefield of toys, Diane did a quick inventory of this house. As Shelley had warned, it was really, really messy.

Trying to decide if it was too soon to call Dan back, and not wanting to be a nuisance at a time like this, Diane decided to busy herself by putting the house back together. She remembered her promise not to clean house while Shelley was out, but the situation was different now. If Shelley was in the hospital, she wouldn't want to come home to a messy house. So Diane brought the toy basket from the family room and went about gathering up everything that was strewn from one end of the house to the other. She had just reached the kitchen with an overflowing basket when her cell phone rang.

"Hello?"

"She's alive," Dan told her breathlessly. "That's about all I know at the moment. The doctor is checking her out."

"What happened?" Diane asked.

"She was driving on the highway, nearly to Maple Road. She must've been on her way to Mom and Dad's, although I haven't called them yet. And I can't figure out why the kids weren't with her."

"Because they're with me."

"I know that now." He sounded frustrated.

"But how did you know that? Have you seen Shelley yet?"

"Not yet. But the paramedic who called me at work said Shelley had told her that. She said Shelley specifically wanted me to know that the kids were at Diane's."

"So Shelley was conscious? She could talk after the wreck?"

"Apparently. How are the kids, anyway?" He sounded worried. "I could call my mom and ask her to—"

"No, Dan, they're fine. They just went down for naps in their own beds. It's very quiet here."

"Good. I hate calling my parents until I know what's really going on. I heard there was a witness who came upon the scene. He said Shelley had her turn signal on and was about to turn left off the highway onto Maple Road when a big semi came barreling down the road behind her. Who knows what the truck driver was thinking. *He never even hit the brakes*—can you believe it? He just slammed right into Shelley's car. It's totaled."

"Oh no!"

"I gotta go. The doctor's calling me." And just like that Dan hung up.

Once again, Diane began to pray, only this time she whispered her prayer aloud. She set the toy basket down, and as she cleaned the kitchen, she prayed for God to intervene and for Shelley to make it through this nightmare.

Diane fought against feelings of guilt as she continued cleaning Shelley's house. She tried to distract herself by scrubbing countertops and sinks and toilets, but it was no use. Diane couldn't bear to think this might be partially her fault. If she hadn't urged Shelley to go, she'd be right here watching her children as they slept.

Finally, as she threw a load of dirty laundry into the washing machine, Diane faced the truth, asking herself, *What if she hadn't encouraged Shelley to go take a break?* She poured in the detergent and turned on the machine: *What if I hadn't offered to watch Shelley's kids?*

Why had Diane stepped in like that and interfered? And what was Diane going to do if Shelley was seriously hurt? What would Dan and Aiden and Emma do? Diane wished she'd never opened her mouth. Why hadn't she had the sense to mind her own business this morning? And now Shelley was lying in a hospital, possibly fighting for her life. And it was all Diane's fault.

No, Diane decided as she swept the floor, she was not going to give in to this kind of despair. She was going to keep praying. From that moment forward, each time a guilty thought or dark doubt crept in, Diane just prayed and cleaned all the harder. She knew from experience that worry is like an incessant wind that howls through the night—if she ignored the wind, it would eventually die down and go away; if she listened to it, obsessed over it, it could eventually drive her crazy.

It was nearly four when Diane realized her cell phone battery was dead. She considered dashing across the street for the charger, but what if Aiden woke up? It was about time and she just didn't want to risk it. Besides, didn't Dan know she was here at his own house? He could call the landline if he had news.

"Mommy, Mommy, Mommy!" Aiden cried from his room as if he'd awakened with a start.

It was probably a bad dream, but hearing him shrieking like that for his mother, so lost and desperate, sent a cold chill down Diane's spine. Then, before she could reach him, Emma began to cry as well. "I'm coming," she called. First she went to Aiden's room, reminding him that she was here and that everything was okay.

"Where's my treat?" he asked sleepily.

"Just a minute," she told him with a grudging smile. "We need to get Emma up first. And I need you to help me."

"Okay." He followed her as if he liked this idea.

Diane pretended she didn't know where things were. She asked him to find a diaper and powder and a pacifier. Finally they had Emma cleaned up, but she was still fussing. "Thank you, Aiden." Diane patted his head. "You're the best helper ever."

"Where's my treat?" he asked eagerly.

"Let's get Emma a bottle *first*, okay?"

"Okay, but this is taking a long time."

After a bit, Diane had Emma settled with another bottle of formula, and she began to search in the kitchen for Aiden's treat. She had no idea what to give him, but since she'd promised something "special" she couldn't very well offer him nothing better than a graham cracker.

Finally, Aiden stomped a little foot and pointed at the cabinet above the refrigerator. "Up there! That's where the treats are!"

Sure enough, in the cupboard above the fridge was a bag of leftover Easter candy. Diane pulled out a chocolate-covered marshmallow bunny wrapped in colorful foil and handed it to Aiden. She knew rewarding him with sugar probably wasn't the best thing, but under the circumstances, it seemed a small concern.

"But you need to have some milk with it," she told him. "And you need to eat it at the table."

Aiden was so enamored with the confectionary bunny that he went directly to his booster seat and began to peel it open. It was a messy ordeal, but Diane let him have at it. At least it was occupying him. She glanced at the clock and wondered about calling Dan's cell phone from the kitchen phone, except she only had his number on her cell phone, which was dead.

Then, just as Aiden was down to only the feet of the bunny, with chocolate smeared all over his hands and face, the kitchen phone rang.

Diane hurried to answer it, trying not to sound too worried. "Bauers' residence."

"Shelley's okay!" Dan said, clearly relieved. "They finished all the tests, and she's perfectly fine."

"Really?" Diane sat down on a kitchen chair, resisting the urge to break into joyful tears. "She's really all right?"

"Yes. They ran all kinds of tests and scans on her because the paramedics were certain that a wreck like that would've resulted in really serious injuries. But as far as they can tell, she's fine. Just a little bruised up and shaken. The doctor is releasing her now."

"Thank God!" Diane took in a deep breath.

"So, if you don't mind staying with the kids a while longer—or I could have Mom come over. She's here at the hospital now."

"No, no, the kids and I are fine." Diane looked to where Aiden was now smearing his chocolate-covered hands on the kitchen table—which she'd just cleaned—as if he were finger painting. "We're perfectly fine!" She laughed. "Take your time, Dan."

She hung up and turned to Aiden. "Hey, after you finish your milk, wash your hands and face, and brush your teeth, how about you watch a video?"

"Yippee!"

By the time Dan and Shelley came home, Diane, Aiden, and Emma had just settled comfortably in the family room and were watching *The Land before Time VII*.

The door opened and Dan led Shelley inside.

"Oh, Shelley," Diane jumped up and went over to hug her. "Are you really okay?"

"Besides being a little stiff and sore, I'm fine."

"I can't believe it!"

"Daddy!" Aiden called, running over.

"The car's totaled, though," Dan told Diane as he swooped Aiden up. "Hey, buddy. How's my little man?"

Diane bent down to pluck Emma off the quilt where she'd been playing with a teething toy. "Here's your mama, little girl. Say hello."

"Oh, sweetie." Shelley leaned over and kissed Emma on both cheeks. "It's so good to see you." Now she went over to Aiden and did the same. "My darlings, how I missed you!"

"Where were you?" Aiden demanded.

"It's a long story."

"I want to hear the story," he said.

"What about your movie?" Diane asked.

"I've seen it a million times."

Dan put Aiden down. "The doctor told Shelley to take it easy," he told Diane.

"That sounds wise." Diane put a hand on Shelley's shoulder. "Maybe you should go lie down."

"And that pain pill you just took will probably kick in any minute," Dan said. "Why don't you take a nap while I ride herd on these two?"

Shelley tossed Diane a sly but sleepy look. "I guess getting hit by a truck has a few perks."

"Oh my!" Diane shook her head as she led Shelley into the living room.

"I'm just kidding." Shelley sighed as she sat down on the couch. "Honestly, my head is still spinning—and not from the pain pills either. I just cannot believe I walked away from the wreck like I did. The car was totally demolished, obliterated, goners ... you know? The fact that I'm here and can even talk about it is nothing short of a miracle, Diane. A real honest-to-goodness miracle. Do you believe that?"

"I do." Diane put a lightweight throw over Shelley, tucking a pillow behind her. "Miracles might be rare, but they do happen. I believe it." Now she went to the kitchen to fix Shelley a cup of tea, still marveling at how Shelley was spared this afternoon. There was no denying that it truly was miraculous. Even so, Diane felt uneasy ... not to mention a bit responsible. What if she hadn't encouraged Shelley to go?

"I feel like a princess." Shelley made a drowsy smile as she sipped her tea. "Can you believe how this day turned out?"

Diane shook her head as she sat across from her.

"I feel so very, very lucky ... and blessed."

"And I feel guilty," Diane quietly confessed.

"*Guilty?*" Shelley looked confused. "Guilty about what?"

Diane tried to say it without breaking into tears. "I encouraged you to go today. I practically shoved you into your car. If I hadn't been so bossy, you wouldn't have gotten in a wreck, and you could've—"

Shelley looked up with big blue eyes. "You don't know what you're saying."

"But I urged you to go to your mother-in-law's, Shelley. It's my fault this happened!"

Now the tears came. She felt so awful she didn't care that Dan or anyone else might see her bawling. After some time, she felt a touch on her shoulder.

"Diane, stop." It was Shelley. "Diane, don't you see? You urged me to leave my kids with you. I was already determined that I was going out there no matter what, remember? If you hadn't stepped in, I would've eventually gotten Aiden and Emma into my car and taken them with me. Don't you see how today could've turned out so much differently?"

Like a jolt, realization set in. "Aiden and Emma would've been in the car with you ..."

"Sitting in the back seat. Diane, that truck hit me from behind." Shelley leaned back and closed her eyes, letting out a loud sigh. "You should've seen the back seat of my car—it was gone. Smashed into a space two feet wide. The paramedics couldn't believe I could walk away from that car—and I was in the *front* seat. They were certain I was seriously injured. They actually forced me onto the stretcher."

Diane took in a deep breath. "That's like a real miracle."

"It *is* a miracle. I know it is. God was watching over me today, and I'm not sure even why. But I'm so thankful. And I'm so thankful that you wouldn't let me take my kids with me. Honestly, Diane, that is the *real miracle*—that my kids weren't with me—they weren't hurt. *Thank you!* You saved my babies! I will never be able to thank you properly for that."

Diane wiped her face and accepted a gingerly hug from Shelley. "I'm so thankful you're okay, Shelley. I've been praying for you nonstop since I heard about it. I'm so glad you're all right."

"Thanks," she said in a drowsy voice. "Appreciate it ..."

"You get some rest, sweetie. I'll let myself out."

Shelley's eyes closed. The pain meds were taking effect. Diane just stood there staring for a moment as reality truly sunk in. This could've come out so differently. Instead of a miracle, it could have been a tragedy—two darling children could've been lost today.

Thank you, God, Diane whispered as she closed the front door. *Thank you, God!*

CHAPTER SEVENTEEN

"Can you believe that car?" Margaret held the newspaper out for Diane to see. "It really does look miraculous that anyone survived."

Diane was spending her Friday afternoon helping Margaret get her gallery set up. "Shelley's calling it a real miracle," she said as she slid one of Allan's beautifully crafted tables closer to a freshly painted white wall and then stepped back to see the effect.

It actually did look pretty good, though the cloth covering would've worked too. She would've liked to see the blank canvas effect.

"Hey," Margaret said, staring more intently at the newspaper, "you're mentioned in here. It says, 'Bauer's neighbor, Diane Spencer, was watching Shelley's children at the time. Or else both children would've been seriously injured or even killed upon impact.'" Margaret put down the paper and stared at Diane. "You never told me that part."

Diane smiled. "I guess you didn't ask."

Margaret took her glasses off. "Dear me, that's quite a story."

Diane looked over at the wall that was still its original brick color. "I like the juxtaposition of the white and brick walls," she told Margaret. "It's a nice contrast."

"You're sure you're not upset I wanted to go with the paint instead of your canvas idea?"

"*Pfft.* No worries. And you could always try that at some point in the future."

"Just so long as you're all right."

"Margaret, this is *your* gallery. And I do think the white and brick look great next to each other. In fact, it gives me an idea."

"Sounds like you're hinting that we should get back to work." Margaret set the newspaper down.

"I did think that was why I came here today."

Margaret laughed. "Yes, yes, I know. So, tell me your idea."

"What if we arranged Allan's pieces of furniture to look something like a room? Not a whole room, of course, but instead of setting all the tables in a row like they are now, why don't we put one of the larger tables against the natural brick wall and place one of the art glass lamps on it. And maybe put something in one of those ceramic bowls, like maybe shells or glass floats. Then we'll place a chair off to a side." As she talked, she picked up one of the lamps and set it on the table, adding a large blue ceramic bowl. "Do you get the picture?"

"Oh yes!" Margaret came over and helped Diane move the largest table into place. "Yes, that looks nice. And inviting."

"I thought if we focused the furniture and sculptures and three-dimensional pieces near the red bricks, we could reserve the white bricks for hanging the paintings." She pointed above the table. "However, a nice earthy landscape, like that one with the wildflowers and beach grass and pines, might look good here."

"That is one good thing about going with the lathe boards up high and the wires for hanging." Margaret moved her stepladder over and began to adjust a wire for the painting Diane was carrying over. "We can hang things wherever we want!"

"Exactly."

Margaret indicated a spot on the wall. "You think about here?"

"Yes, that's perfect." Diane held the landscape up to see. "This is a nice one, Margaret. I love the warmth of these orange lilies and black-eyed Susans."

"I did that one from a photo I took last August."

They continued working and chatting late into the day. Although Diane knew she'd sacrificed an afternoon of writing, she had no regrets. This was genuinely enjoyable work, and for all she knew, she might use it in a book someday.

"Oh, Diane!" Margaret clapped her hands to see the effect of lights illuminating the art they'd arranged. "I don't know what I'd have done without you."

"I don't know when I've had so much fun." Diane pointed to a spotlight that wasn't quite right. "I think that one needs to come to the right a little."

"Yes, I agree."

Together they moved the ladder, and Diane climbed up and tweaked the light. "That's better."

"It looks so good in here, I could almost imagine opening my doors this weekend. Do you think I dare?" Margaret was sweeping some of the packing materials into a pile.

"I don't know why not."

"Unless I want to stick with my original plan and do the big unveiling next Friday. That would coincide with the ad I plan to run in the newspaper."

"And it would give you a full week to work on your current painting."

"I might even get it finished in time for the opening." Margaret pointed to an area of wall that looked a little empty. "I'll hang it right there."

Diane strolled through the gallery, admiring how they'd arranged the pieces. "You know, Margaret, you could bring in some dried arrangements, like some sticks in that vase, or some pinecones here."

"Yes, good ideas!" Margaret ran over and grabbed her notebook. "Tell me more, and I'll make a list."

So, allowing her imagination to run freely, Diane walked around suggesting beach grass here and seashells there. "And you know what would be really nice in here," she said eagerly, "is some kind of water feature."

"Yes, you're right. And I know just who has one." Margaret made another note. "The ceramicist has one at her house. I'll see if she's interested in putting it in here."

"This is going to be a lovely gallery," Diane told Margaret. "I can't wait to see your grand opening. What a party it's going to be!"

"Speaking of parties. It was good of you to invite Adelaide to come to your open house next week. She's so excited about it."

"It's my pleasure. Such a dear girl. Oh, I almost forgot to tell you." Diane adjusted the angle of one of the side tables, placing a large red vase next to the handblown glass platter. "She was an incredible help to me the other day—you know, the day I had the kids and Shelley got in the wreck. I was about to fall apart, and Adelaide showed up like a ray of sunshine. She and Aiden got along especially well."

"Adelaide adores little kids."

"I could see that. And it gave me an idea, but I thought I should run it past you first."

Margaret leaned the broom against the wall. "What is it?"

"Before the wreck, Shelley was so overwhelmed she was practically in tears."

"Do you think that had anything to do with the wreck?"

"No, I really don't. According to the eyewitness report, Shelley was doing everything just right. She was just in the wrong place at the wrong time."

"Thankfully without her children."

Diane nodded. "Anyway, I'm happy to help Shelley with some relief care with Aiden and Emma. But I got to thinking about what a natural Adelaide is with kids and how Aiden liked playing with her, and I started wondering if Adelaide might make a good mother's helper."

Margaret frowned. "You mean like a nanny?"

"Sort of, but not exactly. I realize that might be too much responsibility for Adelaide. But what if Adelaide could visit at Shelley's house with the understanding that she's there to help with the kids so Shelley can, well, catch up with her housework, or maybe sit down and read a book? Allan mentioned she's looking for volunteer opportunities."

Now Margaret smiled. "Adelaide would probably enjoy that. *And* it would give her something to do."

"So do you want to talk to Adelaide about it?"

"Absolutely. And I think Allan will like this idea. Sometimes he gets overwhelmed too. Adelaide likes having someone to talk to, and she's delightful, but she can wear a person out."

"Kind of like Aiden." Diane chuckled. "You should've heard those two chattering like magpies while she was playing with him on Wednesday. Aiden loved the attention, and I think Adelaide enjoyed the admiration."

"Sounds like a winning combination."

"Worth a try?"

Margaret's expression turned thoughtful. "Yes, but how about if you run it past Shelley before I mention anything to Adelaide? I'd hate to see Adelaide get her hopes up and find out Shelley's not comfortable with the idea."

"I'll see what Shelley says and get back to you." As Diane walked home, she felt optimistic. As much as she loved Shelley and the kids, she realized they needed more than she was able to give. Shelley's euphoria over surviving that car wreck was beginning to wear off, and the daily grind of small children and housework was draining her again. As soon as she was inside her cottage, Diane called Shelley and explained the idea.

"Do you really think Adelaide is capable of watching my kids?" Shelley sounded skeptical.

"Not as a babysitter," Diane explained. "But more as a mother's helper. You would be in the house, but you'd also have Adelaide to actually play with the kids. I saw Adelaide interacting with Aiden, and they both had so much fun."

"So it would be kind of like a playdate?"

"Except that Adelaide wouldn't need as much supervision as a preschooler. Plus it would make Adelaide feel important, kind of like having a job."

"A job? Would I need to pay her?"

"No, I don't think so. Margaret just sounded like she and Allan would appreciate Adelaide having something to keep her busy. You know, something to make her feel needed."

"Okay...," Shelley said slowly. "I will try it out. And I have been trying to loosen up more with my kids. Maybe this would be a good step for me. I trust you, Diane."

Diane had mixed feelings as she hung up. She hoped she hadn't interfered too much. She'd have to watch out, lest her neighbors start calling *her* Mrs. Busybody.

CHAPTER EIGHTEEN

Diane thought that having an open house the weekend before Memorial Day would be the perfect way to meet and get better acquainted with her new friends in Marble Cove, including all her neighbors. To that end, last week she'd sent out invitations to everyone along Newport Avenue. And all but two households had responded. She wasn't terribly surprised that Mr. Calder hadn't gotten back to her yet. She was learning to accept that he wasn't exactly a friendly old man. However, she did wonder about the Littles.

"I don't want to seem pushy," she told Margaret as they sipped iced tea on the Hoskins' front porch on Thursday afternoon. "But I'd feel so bad if I found out they hadn't received their invitation and felt slighted."

"There's an easy solution to that." Margaret got up and, leaning over the porch railing, she waved vigorously to the blue Toyota pickup that was just pulling up to the house next door. "That's Detective Little right there."

A man with short-cropped gray hair emerged from the truck. With a worn briefcase and a bag of groceries, he started toward his house.

"Detective Little," Margaret called. "Do you have a moment?"

The man tipped up his sunglasses and peered at her. "Oh, hello, Margaret. I didn't see you there. How are you doing?" He walked over to the edge of his yard.

"I'm well," she told him. "I'd like to introduce you to our new neighbor."

Diane went over as Margaret introduced them, waiting for Detective Little to set down his briefcase and shake her hand.

"Welcome to the neighborhood," he said. "Call me Fred."

"Thank you." Diane smiled. "I sent you and your wife an invitation to an open house I'm having on Saturday afternoon, but since I didn't hear back, I wondered if perhaps it was lost in the mail."

"That doesn't seem likely." He made a slightly sheepish smile. "But my wife Cindy, well, she can be a little absentminded sometimes. Maybe she just forgot to RSVP."

"That's understandable. And it's not a big deal. Just a small gathering—a chance to get to know people. If you're able to come, I'd love to meet your wife."

He nodded. "We'd like to come."

"Wonderful! I'm glad to hear you can make it."

"Great." He nodded. "See you then." He picked up his briefcase and headed toward his house.

"That was easy." Diane grinned at Margaret. "Thanks for your help."

"And thank you for helping get Adelaide connected with Shelley. It's been the best thing for her. She calls herself a nanny and says she's going to work every morning. Those two hours have been wonderful for Allan. He'll probably be able to finish the console table he's working on in time for the gallery opening."

"That's wonderful. And how's your painting coming?"

"I finished the seascape I was working on and have already started a new one. I'm doing the Orlean Light."

"I can't wait to see it."

"It's something I've wanted to try for a long time, but I didn't want to attempt it until my skills improved. I don't want this piece to be just another lighthouse painting. So I'm working from some photos I took around dusk, trying to create a mysterious sort of look."

"I like the sound of that."

"I need to get out and take some more photos. I wish I could get a shot of one with the flash of light."

"Have you seen that again?"

Margaret shook her head. "Have you?"

"No. I've looked for it, but so far I haven't seen anything out of the ordinary."

"I suppose it could've been my imagination ... both our imaginations. Or maybe a reflection from one of the houses on the bluff." Margaret set her empty glass down. "But I haven't given up."

"If you do go out to take lighthouse photos—I mean, if it's late in the day and getting dusky—why don't you invite me to come along with you?"

"But I thought you said Rocky can't make it all the way out to the lighthouse."

"He can't yet. But he doesn't have to know I'm going to the beach without him." Diane patted Margaret's hand. "And I really don't like the idea of my good friend out there roaming the beach by herself after dark. She might decide to go for a swim with no one around."

Margaret laughed. "Okay, I'll make sure to call you first."

Diane pointed over to the moss green house on the corner—Mr. Calder's house. "I don't suppose you have any easy solutions for him."

"The truth is I've barely spoken to Mr. Calder myself. I think Allan has had a few conversations with him over the years. But Mr. Calder really is a bit of a hermit."

"So I should just give up?"

"I honestly don't know what to tell you, Diane. You've been incredibly successful at bringing the neighbors together already. But maybe you shouldn't set your hopes too high when it comes to Albert Calder."

"You're probably right." Diane looked at her watch. "I'd better let you get to your family."

"Yes, I suppose I should see if Allan wants help with dinner. It's his night to cook. You're sure you can't stay for dinner? He's making his specialty—meatloaf."

"That's tempting, but I'll pass. Thanks." Diane stood. "I think it's so sweet how you two share the household chores."

"Adelaide is getting to be a pretty good cook too," Margaret told her. "With supervision."

"Thanks for the tea, Margaret. And remember what I said about calling me before you go wandering the beach alone at night."

"You got it, neighbor."

★　　★　　★

Diane and Rocky took their daily before-dinner walk on the beach. They'd worked up to two-thirds of the way to the lighthouse. Diane suspected his leg was nearly healed, but she still didn't want to push him too hard.

By the time they returned home, Rocky was nicely worn out and happy to see his dinner and his bed. But Diane suddenly felt restless—and hungry. Now she wished she'd accepted Margaret's dinner invitation. Meatloaf sounded surprisingly good. Eric had always loved her meatloaf. Feeling blue, she opened her refrigerator and looked inside. Even if she did have the ingredients for it, which she didn't, she knew it would take more than an hour for it to be ready.

Maybe the hardest part of being single was dinnertime, Diane thought. Not just because cooking for one was a challenge, but because of the lonely feeling she sometimes got at the dinner hour. That had always been the time to gather. First with her family around her, and later when she and Eric would come together and share about their day, fixing food, laughing, making plans.

She closed the refrigerator and pulled on her fisherman knit sweater. "Rocky, I'll be back soon." She grabbed her purse and went out the door. No rules against a single woman going to a restaurant and eating by herself. At least that's what she told herself as she walked toward town.

She remembered times when she and Eric would be dining together and she'd see an older woman eating alone. For some reason it had always made Diane feel sorry for the woman. She would assume she was lonely and wonder what her story was. And now it was Diane whom people might feel sorry for. She hoped not.

Still, this idea of dining in public by oneself was new to her. And although she was hungry and happily devoured a lobster roll and cup of New England chowder, she was glad when she was finished and on her way back home.

Although it was nearly eight, it was still light out and a feeling of summer was in the air. The weather around here, especially in summer, was always unpredictable. One day could be chilly and foggy and the next sunny and warm. However, this was one of the many things she loved about Marble Cove—it kept her guessing.

As she walked down Newport Avenue, she noticed a silver Audi pulling into Mr. Calder's driveway. Curious as to who might be visiting the hermit, she slowed her pace. A youngish-looking man got out of the car—at least he looked youngish from a distance. As Diane got closer, she could see he was probably older, maybe forty or so. He was getting something out of the trunk of his car, and just as she was passing by the driveway, he turned to face her with a box in his hands.

"Good evening," she said cheerfully.

"Oh, hello." He smiled, balancing the box in his hands.

"Are you visiting Mr. Calder?"

"As a matter of fact, I am."

"Oh, that's nice."

He looked curious. "Do you know, uh, Mr. Calder?"

"No, I haven't had the pleasure." She pointed to her house down the street. "I recently moved into the neighborhood and I'm going to be having a little social gathering in my home—sort of an open house. I invited Mr. Calder, but he hasn't responded."

The man nodded with a knowing expression. "Yes, well, that's not surprising. You see, my grandfather isn't a very social sort of person."

"Your grandfather?"

"Yes." He set the box down on the stone wall that ran alongside the walk. "I'm Dennis Calder. Albert is my grandfather."

Diane shook his hand. "Diane Spencer. Nice to meet you. And it's so nice you're here to visit your grandfather. I'm sure he'll appreciate your company."

Dennis looked uncertain. "It's hard to tell. He usually does. I'm bringing him some food—some things my mother made for him. I'm sure he'll appreciate that, at least."

"Are you here into the weekend?"

"I actually live here in Marble Cove."

"Oh ... nearby?"

"I have a condo in Sunrise Shores. My parents live in Bangor, so my mom can't check on my grandfather as much as she'd like. She sends me these care packages to share with Grandpa, which forces me to come over here and invade his quiet little world."

"Your mother sounds like a thoughtful woman."

He grinned. "She is."

"If you're around this weekend and would like to accompany your grandfather over to my little soiree, you'd be more than welcome."

Dennis nodded as if considering this. "I'd love for my grandfather to get to know his neighbors better. My mom would appreciate it too. He really can be a sweet old guy, but he puts up these barriers." He picked up the box. "Kind of like these stone walls."

Diane chuckled. "It's been said good fences make good neighbors."

"Unless they keep you from engaging with your neighbors."

"That's true."

"Anyway, I'll mention your get-together to Grandpa and see if I can talk him into coming."

Diane nodded. "Thank you."

"Maybe if I agree to come with him, he'll consider it. I know he's lonely, so I'll do my best."

"How exciting!" Diane wasn't going to get her hopes up that Mr. Calder would actually come, but it was nice to meet his grandson. Dennis was a charming and strikingly attractive guy. He reminded her of a young Harrison Ford. Now if Diane were, say, twenty years younger ...

She chuckled. Other than Rocky, she was fine without a man in her life. Back when she and Eric had feared she'd be the first one to leave this world, he used to tell her that he was a one-woman man. Well, she felt fairly certain she could make the same claim. She was a one-man woman.

With a jolt, Diane realized Dennis was still standing there. "Something on your mind, Dennis?"

He looked nervous. "I was ... just wondering something."

She looked at him askance. "Yes?"

"You're having a party for the whole block. I just wondered if Mr. Wheeland has been invited."

"Why, of course. Oh, you think that will be a problem for your grandfather?"

"No," he said distractedly. "Well, yes. I mean, maybe. But it isn't what I ..."

She waited. "Spit it out, Dennis."

"I'm just ... I was ..." He took a deep breath. "Have you met Mr. Wheeland's daughter, Beverly?"

The shy look in his eyes suddenly made it all clear. "Ah, now I see." She smiled. "Yes, I've met Beverly. Lovely girl." She watched him closely. He seemed to agree with her assessment. "I have met her and, yes, she's in town and, yes, I've invited her to the party. So I'd say there's a good chance you could see her there." She tilted her head. "Another reason to try extra hard to get Gramps to come, eh?"

He didn't even try to hide his smile. "Excellent! We'll definitely be there."

She nodded maternally. "I can't wait."

Chapter Nineteen

Diane spent all of Saturday morning preparing for her open house. She had considered hiring caterers, but with fewer than twenty guests, she felt confident she could handle it herself. She used to put together parties like this all the time. And although she never considered herself to be much of a cook, she'd learned over time that a good party was mostly about organization. But as she looked around her crowded countertops, filled with platters and trays and all sorts of ingredients in various stages of preparation, she just shook her head and wondered what she'd been thinking.

She'd forgotten that, back when she'd thrown Christmas parties for Eric's staff, she'd had access to all kinds of stores and delis. She'd had a list of culinary experts who prepared delectable party trays and even delivered. All one had to do was transfer the goodies to nice platters, make flower arrangements, set out some pretty napkins and plates—and voilà, let the party begin.

Unfortunately, Marble Cove didn't have specialty food stores, and Diane was now up to her elbows in cheeses and cold cuts and veggies and crackers, hoping she wouldn't embarrass herself too badly today. But, really, she reminded herself, it was supposed to be about the people, not the food, right?

Finally satisfied that the food trays looked appealing, the beverages were ready, the flowers arranged, and her house spotless, she escorted Rocky to the makeshift doggy run she'd rigged up by the fence, just in case anyone had allergies. Diane estimated she had about fifteen minutes to get herself ready. Since the weather was acting like summer today, she decided to wear her white Capri pants and a blue-and-white-striped sleeveless blouse. Casual, yet fun.

She was just double-checking the guest towels in the bathroom when she heard a woman's voice calling through the screen door. "Hello to the house!"

"Shelley," Diane said as she went to open the screen door. "And Dan and Aiden and Emma! Come in, come in."

"Sorry to be so punctual," Shelley said, "but the kids' naptime is creeping up and I thought this way they could at least say hi."

"I'm so glad you came." Diane tickled Emma's chin and grinned at Aiden. "And don't you look nice in your red bow tie."

"He insisted," Shelley said. "He likes wearing it to church too."

"Wow, this place looks great," Dan said as they went into the kitchen.

"You had a lot to do with that," she reminded him.

"Yeah, but when I left, it didn't look anything like this. Wow, new appliances, new counters. *Swanky.*"

Diane heard someone else at the door. "Shelley, you give Dan the full tour if he wants and I'll get that. And the food is all set up in the backyard."

"Where's Rocky?" Aiden asked.

"He's in the backyard too," Diane called out as she went to get the door. "Penned up."

"Hello, hello?" Mrs. Peabody called.

"Welcome," Diane said, ushering her inside. "What a lovely dress."

Mrs. Peabody waved her hand dismissively. "This old thing? Why, I've had it for decades."

Diane didn't doubt that. But the purple and orange flowers were certainly colorful. "You look very festive."

"My, my." Mrs. Peabody looked around the small living room. "What a pretty place you have, Diane. So homey and inviting—and clean." She nodded with approval.

Shelley came over to introduce Emma to the elderly woman, and Mrs. Peabody was instantly beside herself making cooing noises to the pretty baby in pink ruffles.

Margaret and Allan and Adelaide were the next to arrive. Adelaide jumped right into her nanny role, taking Aiden aside to talk. Shelley looked greatly relieved. The guests visited among themselves, toured the small cottage, and slowly filtered out to the backyard where the food was set up and where Diane had arranged groups of borrowed lawn chairs here and there.

Detective Little and his wife Cindy arrived at the same time as Mr. Wheeland. But Diane was dismayed to learn that Beverly had decided not to come.

"She had some work to do," Mr. Wheeland said, but she could tell by his expression that he was disappointed too.

"I'm so sorry I forgot to RSVP," Cindy said to Diane. "Fred told me about my social faux pas." She patted her blond hair. "Never mind the blond jokes, though. I'm sure I've heard them all."

Diane laughed. "No worries. I'm just glad you could make it."

"Your home is lovely," Cindy said, gushing. "It looks like something from the pages of a magazine. Do you ever read *Coastal Living*? They have such gorgeous homes in there—as if everyone who lives on the coast has a beautiful home." She laughed. "I always dreamed of having a home like that. But after the kids moved out and we were left with all the worn-out furnishings, well, I decided I just didn't really care that much. We're hardly at home anyway."

"Come on," her husband urged her, "someone's here. Let Diane answer her door."

"I'll give Cindy the rest of the house tour," Shelley offered.

Diane thanked her as she went to the door. To her surprise, it was Dennis Calder, but he was alone. "Come in," she told the handsome young man.

"Thank you." His expression was somber.

"Is everything okay?" she asked.

He shook his head. "My grandfather."

"Is he unwell?"

"Just being stubborn." He nodded toward where an old man was lingering on the walk.

"Is he coming in?"

"He was." Dennis lowered his voice. "But then he saw Mr. Wheeland, and he dug his heels in."

"Oh dear."

"I suppose you heard about the garbage can war."

Diane couldn't help but laugh.

"When you're in your eighties, you take these things seriously."

"Is there anything I can do to help?"

Dennis shrugged. "Probably not. But I told Grandpa I was coming in here to say hello and ..." His eyes left her and scanned the room. When he looked back at her, he seemed doubly disappointed. "And I told him it was rude to get all the way over here and then turn around and go back. I think I might've made him feel bad."

Diane looked out to where the old man was shuffling his feet and looking at the ground. He reminded her of a boy who'd just been disciplined for breaking a playground rule. "How about if I go and have a word with him?"

Dennis' eyes lit up. "Would you?"

"Yes. And you go ahead and mingle with the guests. Get yourself a bite to eat. I'll see what I can do."

"Thanks!"

She turned to go but he touched her arm. "Um, Diane ..."

Then she remembered. She looked back over her guests as if someone new might've shown up without her noticing. "I'm afraid Beverly didn't come."

"Her father came, but she didn't?"

"I know; hard to believe. But that's what happened. I'm sorry." She looked outside at Mr. Calder. "You still want me to go out there? Maybe now both of you just want to go home."

He seemed to actually think about it. "Aw, no. It's all right. We're already here, and your spread looks nice. If nothing else, I'll get myself some finger food while you try."

She patted his arm. "All right, here I go."

Now, realizing she'd probably bitten off far more than she could chew, Diane pasted a smile on her face and went outside to meet her neighbor.

"Hello, Mr. Calder," she said brightly. "I'm Diane Spencer. We met the other day. I'm so happy you could come to my housewarming party. That's so kind of you." She looked toward her porch. "I had the pleasure of meeting your grandson. Dennis seems like such a nice young man. I'll bet he takes after you."

Mr. Calder seemed caught off-guard. "His mother, my daughter, thinks Dennis looks like my old photos, back when I was in the service."

"You were in the service?" she asked. "Let me guess. You're too young for World War II, right?"

He nodded.

"I'll bet you were in Korea."

He looked surprised, but nodded.

"My father served in Korea too," she said as she linked her arm in his. "Oh, my feet are tired. So much running around to get this party ready. Would you mind terribly if we went inside, so I could sit down while you tell me more about yourself?"

To her relief, he didn't resist. And soon she had him in her house and seated in one of the armchairs in the living room. It seemed a safer spot since Mr. Wheeland had migrated outside. As Mr. Calder talked about his time in Korea, Margaret, recognizing the situation, stepped in and fixed him a small plate of food, sending it back with Allan. And Before long, Allan and Dan joined him in the living room. Diane was able to excuse herself while the three men managed to have something of a conversation.

All in all, the party seemed to be a success. The only fly in the ointment Diane could see might be the history of enmity between some of the elders. But with Mr. Calder safely ensconced in the living room and Mr. Wheeland comfortably settled in the shade in the backyard with Mrs. Peabody by his side, Diane didn't think she'd need to worry about that today.

CHAPTER TWENTY

The next morning, Diane met Margaret and Shelley at the Cove on Main Street for coffee. To her surprise, Beverly was getting coffee too. Although Beverly returned Diane's warm smile with a small nod, she slipped a cardboard sleeve on her coffee cup and turned toward the tables in the back. But as she lifted the cup to her lips for her first sip, Margaret cornered her.

"Come, come," Margaret said. "We're all neighbors, Beverly. Let's sit down and enjoy some coffee together."

"Yes," Diane agreed. "Please, join us, Beverly."

Shelley smiled. "I've been dying to get to know you better."

Beverly held up a copy of the day's newspaper. "I'm just here to read the paper. Maybe some other time. Thank you, though." Beverly scooted past Margaret as Margaret shook her head at Diane.

Diane, Margaret, and Shelley found a table. For the first few minutes, Diane glanced several times at Beverly, and she was almost certain Beverly had one ear tuned in to their conversation. At the mention of Mr. Wheeland at Diane's party, Beverly looked up wide-eyed but then quickly looked back down at the paper when her eyes met Diane's. Diane talked a bit about her book, and Shelley told them about a new recipe she'd just tried. Then Margaret talked for a spell about her recent painting of the lighthouse.

"Speaking of the lighthouse," Diane said turning to Shelley, "Margaret and I have both seen it flash recently."

Shelley gasped and coughed as she cleared her throat of her muffin. "I thought my eyes had been playing tricks on me!" she said, coughing several more times.

"You've seen it too?" Diane said, as she scooted literally to the edge of her seat.

Shelley nodded and looked from Diane to Margaret. "What do you think it means?"

"Diane and I were trying to figure out what the source could be. So far, we've come up with nada."

"But we've all seen it?" Diane said.

"I've seen it too."

The three women looked up to see Beverly clutching her newspaper to her chest with one hand and holding her coffee with the other. After a beat of silence, Diane pulled out the empty chair next to her and motioned for Beverly to sit.

"When?" Diane asked.

"More recently when I was driving into town," Beverly said as she twisted the cardboard sleeve on her coffee cup. "But, like Shelley, I convinced myself it was nothing."

"Well, it definitely sounds like it's *something*," Margaret said with a resolute nod. "There's something so mysterious about that old lighthouse. That's what I try to capture in my paintings."

"I didn't know you were an artist," Beverly said to Margaret.

"I used to try to keep it a secret," Margaret said. "And I hope I'm not making a mistake by going public with it in the gallery."

"It's not a mistake," Diane said. "Your art is wonderful, Margaret."

Beverly turned to Shelley. "My father showed me the article in the newspaper about your car accident. That was incredible how you walked away with hardly a scratch."

Shelley filled Beverly in on some of the details. "But the most amazing thing is how different I feel now."

"What do you mean?"

"I used to be so much more uptight. It's hard to admit, but I obsessed over so many little things—small stuff that I can't really change one way or another, but I let it get to me. I let it steal my joy." She turned to Diane. "I think you tried to tell me that ... gently ... but I just didn't get it. And I'm not saying I'm a completely recovered worry-aholic, but maybe I'm moving in that direction."

"Nothing like a life-and-death experience to remind you of what really matters," Diane told her as she stirred her latte and looked meaningfully at Margaret.

"Have *you* had a life-and-death experience too?" Beverly studied Diane with a curious expression.

"It wasn't as dramatic as Shelley's narrow escape, but in its own way it was just as affecting." Without going into too much detail, Diane explained how she had gone through breast cancer treatments and how her doctors had all but given up on her. "There was no scientific or medical explanation for why the cancer disappeared," she said. "My daughter and I both attribute it to a lot of prayer. It was a real miracle from God. Although, if you'd asked me back then, I wouldn't have given God a second thought. Now I realize I was handed a new chance at life—and I'm thankful for it."

"Do you ever wonder ..." Beverly got a thoughtful look. "I mean do you ever ask yourself ... *Why was I spared?*"

"Absolutely." Diane nodded, surprised that Beverly was opening up like this. "Especially when I consider how some people aren't. I think there must be something I still need to do here on earth."

"So do I," Margaret said quietly.

Shelley looked at Margaret with wide eyes. "Have you had a brush with death too?"

Margaret recounted the time she'd nearly drowned. "I don't usually share this story, and I'd appreciate it if you didn't either. I don't want Adelaide to know about it because I know she'd worry. Her biggest fear is that something might happen to Allan or me."

"Wow, that's incredible." Shelley shook her head. "I had no idea. Although now that you mention it, I do remember hearing about a near-drowning and how someone rescued a woman. But I never knew it was you, Margaret."

Beverly shook her head. "And you never figured out who pulled you from the ocean?"

"It's still a mystery."

"Do you think it was an angel?" Shelley asked suddenly.

Margaret gave a half-smile and shrugged.

"I know that probably sounds childish," Shelley said. "But when I replay my car wreck in my mind, I sometimes wonder if an angel could've been protecting me. Because, really, I should've been killed."

"Wait," Beverly said, her brow creasing as she looked from one to the next. "*All* of you have had a near-death experience?"

One by one they nodded.

"That is so strange. I mean, what are the odds that four out of four women have survived death?"

"*Four out of four?*" the other three asked in unison.

Beverly pressed her lips together, as if she'd said too much.

"So you've had a brush with death too?" Margaret asked Beverly.

"Tell us!" Shelley said. "I want to hear your story too."

"Oh, it's not like yours. It's really nothing—"

"Come on," Shelley said. "You heard our stories. If you've escaped the jaws of death, we want to hear about it." She laughed. "Hey, maybe we'll start a club."

"Come on, Beverly," Margaret said. "I'd really like to hear your story."

"I would too," Diane said, scooting her chair closer to the table. "This is so interesting."

"Honestly, it's nothing." Beverly fiddled nervously with a napkin, glancing toward the door as if she wanted to make a fast break for it.

"Come on," Shelley urged her again. "You're the one who let the cat out of the bag. Tell us your story, Beverly."

"I've never really told anyone ..." Beverly pressed her lips tightly together.

"Then it's about time you did," Margaret insisted. "It's not healthy to keep secrets, you know."

"It's not a secret ... exactly." Beverly looked at Diane as if she might be able to help.

"I've learned that sharing stories is a great way to build friendships," Diane told her. "Even if it's hard at first. I'm sure you'll discover that when you take a chance and trust someone who cares about you, it's well worth the risk."

"That's right," Shelley assured her. "And you can trust us. You've heard our stories."

"My story isn't like anyone else's." Beverly still looked unsure. "In fact, I don't usually care to even think about it myself. I suppose the truth is that I feel a bit guilty."

"Tell us what happened," Shelley said.

"It was about three years ago, not long after losing my husband and my mother. That might be the main reason I have difficulty with the whole thing—so much was going on." She glanced at Diane. "Maybe you can relate since you lost your husband too ... I mean, it does make one wonder."

Diane wasn't sure what Beverly was implying, but she nodded anyway.

Beverly let out a long sigh. "I'd been in New York attending a three-day seminar related to my job. It was a Friday evening, and I was worn out and wanted to get home and just crash. So I hurried to the train station, fought my way through crowds, got my ticket, and had just stepped aside to check messages on my BlackBerry when the woman who'd been in line behind me started to melt down. She was crying and begging the ticket agent to help her get to Boston."

Beverly held up her hands. "It turned out that I'd been given the last seat on the train. And this woman was sobbing and saying how it was her tenth anniversary and she had to get home to be with her husband. My first reaction was a bit jaded. I was thinking, 'Lucky you, you still have a husband. Get over yourself.' Then I felt guilty for being so selfish. So I . . . gave her my ticket." Beverly's eyes filled with tears.

"*And?*" Shelley leaned forward. "That's it?"

"*And* that train derailed just past New Haven."

Shelley's hand flew over her mouth, and Diane let out a little gasp.

"The woman sitting in my seat never made it home in time for her anniversary—she never made it home at all. She died that night."

Margaret seemed strangely calm. "You said you felt guilty. Do you blame yourself for that woman's death, Beverly?"

"Sometimes I do." Beverly used a napkin to wipe her eyes.

"But you know that's ridiculous, don't you?" Diane asked her. "You had no more control over the derailment of the train than I had over my breast cancer."

Beverly sniffed and nodded. "I know."

"And you were just trying to be nice," Shelley told her. "That was generous of you to give up your seat. You had no idea what would happen."

"The ways of the universe are mysterious," Margaret said slowly. "But I do believe there is a plan of some kind. I believe we're put here for a purpose, and we can't leave here until we accomplish that purpose."

"I believe God spared me for my kids," Shelley said with conviction. "They need me."

"I believe God spared me for a reason too," Diane added. "I'm just not sure what it is. Perhaps for my kids, although they're grown and independent, and a lot of the time I feel like they don't really need me anymore."

"I need you!" Shelley said.

Margaret nodded. "So do I."

"I think maybe I do too," Beverly quietly admitted.

Diane smiled at them. "Maybe we all need each other."

"It's like I said earlier," Shelley said with youthful enthusiasm. "I think we need to form a club. A survivors' club." She laughed. "But not like that TV show. There will be no voting anyone off this island." Shelley's brows arched when she looked at her watch. "And speaking of getting off the island, I better get home. I'm surprised Dan's mom hasn't called by now. She's watching my kids."

"I should be on my way too," Margaret said.

Diane stood and gathered her things. "But I do think Shelley's on to something. We should form an alliance, a club for miraculous survivors."

"I agree." Margaret set down her empty coffee cup.

"Yes," Shelley stood. "And Rocky should be our miracle mascot."

"I think the miracle mascot is probably wishing I'd come home and take him for a walk," Diane said as they went to the door. "Anyone care to join us?"

"I'd love to, but it's my turn to cook tonight," Margaret said, "and I still need to get groceries. Next time."

"I'll go with you," Beverly said. "I could use some exercise after overindulging on that cinnamon roll."

"What a lovely surprise," Diane said. "This will be so much fun."

⋆   ⋆   ⋆

Before long, Diane, Rocky, and Beverly set out for a midday stroll down the promenade. The sea air was surprisingly warm, almost balmy. Rocky seemed to respond happily to it, running down to the edge of the water and back.

"What a gorgeous day this is," Diane said. "This is the kind of weather I used to long for as a child, back when my family visited Marble Cove for summer vacation."

"Well," Beverly said, "like my father says, when you grow up here, you learn to make the most of the good days when you get them and to make do when it's windy or cold. However, as I've gotten older, I find I get more impatient with bad weather."

"That's funny. I think I'm learning to appreciate it." Diane chuckled. "Maybe it comes with old age."

They walked quietly for a while, listening to the sound of the waves rolling in and splashing onto the sand, the occasional shriek of a seagull, and the laughter of children as they chased each other down the beach.

"You said something earlier," Diane said carefully, "about how I might understand something in regard to your husband's death."

"Did I?" Beverly stooped to pick up a shell. She made a show of examining it closely in the long rays of late-day sunlight.

"I'm curious about your husband. You don't seem to speak of him much."

"I suppose there's not really much to say." They began walking again. "Will and I were only married a few years before he, uh, passed."

Diane knew that Beverly was politely telling her to back off and respect her boundaries.

"Sometimes it helps to talk about these things, Beverly. I don't want to force my friendship on you, but if you ever need to talk ... I'm here."

"Thank you. I will keep that in mind." Beverly's voice had a tone of finality in it—like the sound of a closing door.

However, Diane would be watchful, and if she saw that door crack open, she would give it another firm nudge. Because, for reasons she couldn't fully understand, Diane knew that Beverly needed to talk to someone.

CHAPTER TWENTY-ONE

Diane was barely through the door of Marble Cove Community Church when she realized she felt right at home.

Maybe it was the music she liked so much. Maybe it was the charming old building, which used to be a barn and still had a faint aroma of old hay. Maybe it was seeing a couple of faces she recognized from town—Lee Waters from the Pet Place and Marge, the appliance salesperson. Whatever it was, Diane felt she'd landed in the right place.

The congregation was not too big, not too small. The music was not too boisterous, not too sleepy. The sermon was not too long, not too short. She felt like Goldilocks, because *this church was just right*. After the service she shook hands with Pastor Carl, promising she'd be back next week.

"I'm so glad you came." His blue eyes sparkled merrily through his wired-rimmed glasses. With his snowy white hair and rosy cheeks, she could imagine him playing Santa Claus at Christmastime.

"I felt right at home," she told him. "And your sermon was *just right.*" She refrained from mentioning Goldilocks.

"Thank you." He rubbed his chin. "But if you ever don't care for a particular sermon, I hope you'll feel free to express your opinions. There's always room for improvement."

Of course, that simply made her like him even more. A pastor who invited critiques ... that was a rare quality indeed. Diane caught herself humming a worship song as she drove home. She felt so close to perfectly happy that she wondered if she should be looking over her shoulder. Not that she expected some calamity to befall her, exactly. But the last decade had conditioned her to expect the unexpected—both good and bad.

She had just pulled into her driveway when she saw someone hurrying down the sidewalk toward her. It was Beverly, dressed in jeans and a T-shirt and waving as if something was wrong.

Diane hurried out of her car and went to meet Beverly. "What's wrong?"

Beverly looked as if she'd been crying. "Oh, Diane."

"Is it your father?" Suddenly Diane imagined Mr. Wheeland unconscious.

"No, not really. I think maybe it's me." Beverly pulled a tissue out and blew her nose. "Do you have time to talk?"

"Sure." Diane reached in the car for her purse. "Come on into the house."

Curious as to what had brought this on, Diane led Beverly into the house, greeted Rocky and sent him out into the backyard. "Sit down." Diane pointed to the living room. "Can I get you something? Tea? Water?"

"Water. *Please.*" Beverly slumped onto the sofa like a rag doll. "Oh, your house is lovely. I'm sorry I didn't come to your party."

Diane poured her a glass of water. "Don't worry about that now, dear. Just tell me what's wrong."

"I feel like I'm falling apart."

Diane brought two glasses of water and a box of tissues. "Everyone falls apart sometimes," she said, handing Beverly a glass.

"I probably look like a crazy woman." Beverly took a long sip of water. "I was trying to talk to my father about it just now. But I could tell he was feeling stressed, and I realized I couldn't say too much without upsetting him."

"Upsetting him?"

"It's just that I'm worried about him. He's getting so old and forgetful. Just this morning, I found him in the backyard with no shoes on."

Diane suppressed the urge to laugh. "And there's a problem with that?"

"I know it sounds silly, but with his diabetes, he's prone to very cold feet. His circulation isn't good."

Diane nodded. "Oh, I didn't know he was a diabetic. Yes, I see what you mean now."

"Sometimes he doesn't even feel how cold his feet have become. And to stand out there in the dewy grass on such a cool morning, well, it was just plain foolish. And it won't always be this warm here."

"Why was he doing it?"

"He told me he'd gone out to fill the birdfeeder but then he'd stayed out longer than he'd planned."

"That seems understandable."

"Maybe, but it's still dangerous. Can you imagine what would happen if he did that in the winter?"

Diane didn't know what to say.

"I'm not suggesting Dad is losing it mentally. But the problem is, I'm just not sure. He's alone so much of the time and, well, I feel like I'm responsible, but I don't know what to do. I can't be here all the time."

"It doesn't seem there's much more you can do than what you're already doing, Beverly."

Beverly stood now, pacing back and forth as if this problem was really much larger than it seemed to Diane. "I feel so trapped. I have to work. I need my job. Most of the time I actually like my job. But then there's Dad. I feel I owe him more."

Diane nodded thoughtfully. "I once heard someone say that children do not owe their parents anything."

Beverly looked surprised.

"I know I don't expect my children to drop everything to come and care for me if I should need it."

"You don't?"

"Not a bit. In fact, I would be quite concerned if they did. After all, they have their own lives and livelihoods to look after."

"But my mother always told me that family comes first."

"I don't disagree with that. In fact, I'm sure I'd do anything for my children."

"But not for your parents?"

Diane made a sheepish smile. "I can't really answer that since my parents have passed on. I suppose if it came down to it, I'd feel pretty much the way you feel, Beverly."

"Right. Exactly. So what am I supposed to do?"

Diane shrugged. "Tell him to put his shoes on before he goes outside to feed the birds?"

Beverly almost smiled. "Does it sound like I'm making a mountain out of a molehill?"

"Not exactly. It sounds like you love your father."

"I do. And I don't want to let him down."

"Oh, Beverly, I doubt you've ever let him down."

"Don't be so sure." Beverly turned away and looked out the window.

Diane wanted to ask what that meant, but she held her tongue. If Beverly had something she needed to talk about, something more than her concerns for her barefoot father, she knew Diane was here.

"I suppose I just needed to vent," Beverly said with a sigh. "Thank you for listening."

"Anytime," Diane said. "That's what friends are for."

Beverly looked slightly taken aback. "Friends ..." She shook her head in a doubtful sort of way. "I like the sound of the word, but sometimes I find it hard to understand."

"How so?"

"It's just difficult to believe that friends, I mean *real* friends, exist."

Diane tried not to look surprised. "Surely you have friends at home ... in your neighborhood ... at work?"

Now Beverly made that businesslike smile again. "Of course I do. But I suppose I've learned to be cautious in my friendships."

Diane was unsure of her meaning. "I've learned that my best friendships are the ones where we trust each other. But that takes a measure of faith, doesn't it? It's not always easy to do that in a new relationship."

"Yes, I suppose it takes time."

"I'll bet you were close to your mother," Diane said absently.

"Yes, she was truly my best friend." Beverly looked ready to tear up again. She reached for a tissue. "I miss her."

"That probably makes it even more difficult with your dad." Diane regretted how lightly she'd swept over this now. Really, what did she know about aging parents?

Beverly nodded. "Speaking of my dad, I should probably go and reassure him I'm all right. He could tell that I was having a meltdown of sorts. Although he probably attributes it to hormones since that's what my mother always told him when she was upset." She let out a stiff-sounding laugh. "Who knows, maybe that's what it was. Suddenly everything seemed so overwhelming and difficult." She made what looked like a genuine smile. "I'm sorry for dumping on you like this, Diane."

"Please, don't apologize, Beverly. Anytime you need to talk, I'm happy to listen. I mean it."

"Thank you."

"And be assured, when you're back in Augusta, I'll try to keep an eye on your dad. And I'll call you if I think anything is amiss. You can trust me."

"I know I can. And I truly appreciate it." Beverly excused herself and left.

Diane watched her go down the sidewalk. She could tell that something was still troubling that woman, and she suspected it was more than anxiety about her father. She hoped the time would come when Beverly would be ready to talk openly. Until then, Diane would try to show herself to be a trustworthy friend.

CHAPTER TWENTY-TWO

Later in the day, Diane decided to invite Beverly for a beach walk. "I thought you might like to stretch your legs."

Beverly stood at the front door, looking uncertain.

"Come on," Diane said. "It would do you good to get some fresh air before your drive back to Augusta."

"Maybe you're right." Beverly shut the door and joined Diane and Rocky on the sidewalk. "A walk might regenerate me."

"Rocky has been begging to go out," Diane said. As if to prove her point, the dog pulled at his leash.

"It looks like he's recovering nicely," Beverly said as they started down the boardwalk.

"He seems to be getting more and more rambunctious." Again, as if listening to them, Rocky took off toward the water's edge. "Come back, Rocky," Diane called out. But the silly dog plowed directly into the surf, cast and all. Diane called again, but he continued splashing in the water. She shook her head. "He's like a disobedient child."

"Or like my dad going barefoot this morning." Beverly actually laughed. "Anyway, it looks like Rocky's enjoying himself."

"Yes, but I don't think he's supposed to get his cast wet." Diane whistled for him.

"Too late for that now," Beverly said. "And maybe it's a good sign. Maybe his leg is healing."

Now Rocky came back and gave himself a good shaking, splattering Diane and Beverly with seawater.

"Silly boy." Diane leashed him up, and they continued along.

"I want to thank you again for listening to me today," Beverly said as they walked. "I don't know why I fell apart like I did. I guess I'll chalk it up to hormones like my mother used to do."

"Hormones or whatever, I'm just glad I could be there for you." Diane peered out to the horizon where a thick layer of afternoon fog was starting to roll in. She suspected the afternoon sunshine would soon be obliterated.

"I tend to stress out over things," Beverly said, "but I think our little talk helped to let some of the pressure off."

Diane smiled at her. "Keeping things bottled up inside us usually just makes matters worse. At the very least, it can make things *seem* worse. Whether our problems are big or small, I believe it's better to bring them out into the light of day."

"Maybe so ..." Beverly frowned. Once again, Diane decided not to push.

They were going farther than Diane usually went with Rocky, but Beverly seemed to need the walk, and despite his "swim,"—or perhaps because of it—Rocky was more energetic than usual. Up ahead, the Orlean Light came into view.

"I just love that old lighthouse," Diane said.

Even slightly draped in the pale fog, the structure looked dependable and solid, like a promise of safety and refuge.

"So do I." Beverly nodded. "As a child I used to imagine living in there."

"Wouldn't that be fun? I'll bet the view from it is amazing."

"Hey, do you see that?" Beverly pointed up to where a lone figure was running across the beach and directly to the lighthouse.

Diane watched as the person now darted behind the lighthouse, almost as if trying to conceal himself. "Maybe someone's playing hide-and-seek?"

"Seems a little old for that."

Diane glanced around to see if anyone else was on the beach, someone who might be with the person acting strangely. "I'm sure it's nothing. But I have to admit the fog makes it feel a little mysterious." She chuckled nervously. "I always did love a good mystery."

"Unless it's something sinister." Beverly stopped walking. "I didn't notice anyone else on the beach, Diane. In fact, I haven't seen anyone else for a long time."

"Maybe we should turn back," Diane said. "It does seem a little deserted down here. Well, except for whoever that is hiding up there."

"I think that's a good idea," Beverly said. "Something about that scene doesn't feel right to me."

Diane watched a bit longer, curious to see if the person would make another appearance. Then they turned around and began walking back. "Over the years, I've learned it's good to listen to your instincts. Sometimes you get a feeling like *don't do this* or *slow down* ... and it's your inner voice trying to protect you from something."

"Like the day I gave the woman my seat on the train?"

"Maybe so." Diane patted Beverly on the shoulder. "Or maybe you were just being kind that day ... and God had other plans for your life."

Beverly sighed. "I wish I could believe that."

"I have a feeling life is going to get better for you."

"I hope you're right."

"Now, excuse me for being nosy ..." Diane hoped she wasn't overstepping her boundaries. "Maybe it's because I feel slightly maternal toward you—"

"*Maternal?*" Beverly laughed. "You're not old enough to be my mother, Diane. Don't forget you're only twelve years my senior."

"Okay, then think of me as your big sister." Diane chuckled. "Your older and wiser big sister."

Beverly nodded. "Yes, I like the sound of that."

"So, anyway ... I met someone who knows you."

"*Hmph*, everybody knows me here."

"Yes, but this person seemed interested in knowing you better."

Beverly looked at her sidelong.

"I'm talking about Dennis Calder."

Beverly stopped. "You met Dennis?"

"*Mm-hmm.*" Diane pulled Rocky up to where Beverly was standing. "And I couldn't help but notice that he seemed rather interested in you yesterday."

Beverly actually giggled. "Where did you even meet him?"

Diane shrugged with nonchalance. "That'll teach you to skip one of my parties ..."

They started walking again.

"He's in town then?"

"*Mm-hmm,*" Diane said. "And when he spoke of you, he had more than just neighborly interest in his eyes."

She giggled again. "Really?"

Diane noticed Beverly was getting a little spring back in her step as they turned onto Newport Avenue. "Now you drive safely back to Augusta," she told her. "And don't worry about your father, okay?"

Beverly nodded and thanked her again. Then they hugged one more time, and Diane and Rocky went into the house.

Diane felt good about the time she'd spent with Beverly, and she wished Beverly didn't live so far away. She could tell the younger woman was carrying some heavy burdens and seemed to desperately need a good friend. But Beverly kept up some obstacle, like an invisible wall. Still, Diane felt she'd made a little progress with her today, perhaps chipping away a couple of bricks.

*   *   *

On Thursday morning, Diane realized Rocky had been chewing on his cast. "Oh, you silly boy. How are you going to get well if you do that?"

Fortunately, Dr. Spangler had time to see him. After removing what was left of the raggedy cast and taking new X-rays, the vet proclaimed Rocky to be well. "You've taken good care of him," he told Diane. "He looks healthy and happy."

"Thank you." Diane clipped Rocky's leash to his collar, giving his ear a gentle twist. "Now you can jump into the ocean without being yelled at."

Rocky wagged his tail like he understood.

Dr. Spangler walked her out to the reception area. "I was sorry to miss your open house last Saturday. But my niece never would've forgiven me if I'd missed her wedding."

"Oh, of course," Diane said. "It was just a little gathering of neighbors and friends," she said in an offhanded way. "Not a big deal. Although we did enjoy ourselves."

Dr. Spangler bent down to stroke Rocky's head. "I suppose you don't give rain checks."

Diane wasn't sure how to respond, but when Dr. Spangler stood and looked at her, he had such a hopeful expression that she simply said, "Why not? Come by any time you like."

He nodded with a twinkle in his blue eyes. "Who says doctors don't make house calls anymore?"

She laughed and thanked him, feeling a little uneasy as she went out to the parking lot. Was Dr. Spangler flirting with her? It wouldn't have been the first time someone had flirted with her since Eric's passing, but it always caught her off guard.

To celebrate Rocky's new freedom from the cast, Diane decided a beach walk was in order. She had just started out when she remembered the person she and Beverly had spotted lurking around the lighthouse yesterday. She knew it was probably nothing, and she felt relatively safe with a big—and healthy—dog by her side, but she knew she'd exercise caution. Although the beach was still socked in by the fog that had rolled in yesterday afternoon, the air temperature, warmed by the afternoon sun, was comfortable.

They were nearly to the lighthouse when Diane began to question herself. Was it really wise to be out here walking on the beach when it seemed no one else was around? Especially after what she and Beverly had seen yesterday? Or was she just being silly and making a mountain out of a molehill? Really, what could happen?

Even so, she realized she was looking forward to the beginning of tourist season, which was nearly here. With Memorial Day weekend ahead, the beach would soon be teeming with people, no matter the weather. Today, however, it felt lonely and slightly spooky.

"Want to head back?" she asked Rocky as she peered at the lighthouse. Her voice sounded flat in the thick fog. Then, through the misty air, she noticed a flash of light.

She blinked and looked again, peering directly at the lighthouse, but she saw nothing. She stood there for a couple of minutes, just staring. Still nothing. Just the fog-draped lighthouse, mysterious and compelling.

The last time she'd seen a flash like that, she'd nearly convinced herself it was her overactive imagination. This time she felt sure it was not. Still, she had no idea what had caused it or how a decommissioned lighthouse could possibly transmit a light. Perhaps it had something to do with the mysterious character she and Beverly had spied. In that case, she wasn't sure she wanted to be out here by herself, dog or no dog.

"Come on, boy," she tugged at his leash and began walking back. It was possible she'd imagined that light—again—but she really didn't think so. Whatever it was, it was intriguing and somewhat exciting. And, if nothing else, it motivated her to go home and continue writing her mystery, where the lighthouse was acting more like a character than an inanimate object.

Chapter Twenty-Three

The knock on the door startled Diane. She looked up from her writing and saw that it was already four o'clock. She'd been so caught up in her writing she hadn't even eaten lunch. "Coming."

It was Margaret at the door.

"Oh, Margaret. Come in!"

"Sorry to crash in on you." Margaret had a somewhat sly expression. "The day has turned out to be so lovely I decided to sneak out for a swim, and I thought you might like to join me. Besides, you made me promise to tell you before I went out again. So here I am. You want to come?"

Diane ran a hand through her hair and wondered if she was really up for that much adventure. "I, uh, I guess so. But let me grab a bite to eat, or I might pass out on you."

"Sure." Margaret went over to see Rocky and bent down to pet him. "Hey, your cast is gone."

As Diane fixed herself a quick peanut-butter-and-jelly sandwich, she explained about their vet visit earlier this morning. "I already took him for a long walk to celebrate. And Margaret, you'll never guess! I saw the mysterious flash of light again! It actually inspired me to come back here and write and write. That's what I've been doing for the past five hours."

"So you think it was really a light?" Margaret asked. "Or just a reflection?"

"It was too foggy to be a reflection," Diane said between bites. "What could it reflect?"

"Interesting." Margaret nodded toward the window. "Well, the fog's burned off now."

Diane swigged down some milk, wiped her mouth, and then frowned. "Oh dear, what about what they say about not swimming right after you eat?"

Margaret chuckled. "It's only an old wives' tale. But, since I'm an old wife, I'm inclined to respect it. Still, it'll be about thirty minutes before we get to my favorite swimming spot. You should be okay."

"Let me get my suit on," Diane said. "Don't you bring a towel?"

Margaret pointed to a cotton scarf tied around her neck. "I use this so Adelaide doesn't ask questions."

"I intend to use a real towel," Diane called as she went to her room to change. When she came back out, Diane had two towels with her. "Here, use one of my towels, and Adelaide will never know."

"Thanks."

Because Rocky had already had one walk today, and because she wasn't completely sure about his swimming skills, Diane decided to leave him behind this time. Besides, it was good being able to focus her attention on Margaret, listening as her friend updated her: preparing the gallery opening tomorrow, finishing her last painting, and Adelaide still enjoying her "job" as a mother's helper.

"And Shelley is like a new woman," Margaret said as they walked down the beach. "As though she's finally caught her breath."

Diane shared a bit about Beverly. Not too much, since she knew Beverly was a very private person, but enough to assure Margaret that Beverly's friendship was important to Diane. She wanted Margaret to understand that the younger woman was more than just a pretty face.

"Here's my spot," Margaret said and immediately began peeling off her outer clothes. "Isn't it amazing how we've all experienced a near-death experience?"

"I think it's fascinating." Diane peered down at the lighthouse, which was shimmering in the afternoon light. Tall and white and stately, it was such a comforting symbol—constant and reassuring. "As I was writing today, I kept thinking about the lighthouse and how it's like a metaphor for hope. Do you know what I mean?"

Margaret nodded as she adjusted a strap on her bathing suit. "That's how I feel when I'm painting it too."

"And all four of us love lighthouses," Diane said as they walked toward the water's edge. "Shelley's house is full of lighthouse stuff. She even has a cookie jar that looks like a stout little lighthouse."

Margaret laughed.

"And you paint lighthouses, and I write about them, and even Beverly mentioned how much she's loved the

Orlean Lighthouse since childhood. It makes us connected somehow, don't you think?"

Margaret nodded as she peered down at the lighthouse. "It's a good symbol for miracles ... and we've all experienced miracles." Now she turned and ran toward the ocean, plowing through the ankle-height waves and then plunging into the waist-high surf and eventually diving directly into an oncoming wave.

Following suit and trying not to be too jolted by the shocking chill of the water, Diane did likewise. Soon she was fully in and swimming out to where Margaret was wearing a big grin and bobbing like a cork in the gentle waves. Diane laughed and waved and continued to swim. Margaret was right—*this was invigorating!*

They both swam for a while, pausing occasionally to chat or point out a seabird. Finally, they turned back and swam side by side toward the shore.

When Diane got out she couldn't help but laugh. "That was so amazing, Margaret. Now I understand why you love it so much."

With a broad smile, Margaret shook her short-cropped gray hair, running her fingers through it. "Nothing like it."

"Feel free to invite me anytime you like." Diane reached for her towel and began to rub her slightly numb limbs.

"As long as the tide is right and there's no undertow."

They toweled dry and wrapped up in their towels. Then they perched on a log and soaked in the late afternoon sun.

"In a few days this place will be crawling with tourists," Margaret said a bit sadly.

"I know." Diane looked out over the gorgeous span of blue upon blue, not a cloud in sight. "It's funny being on the other side of that phenomenon. You know, I used to be a tourist and now I'm a local. I need to adjust my thinking."

"To be a real local you have to complain about the tourists," Margaret said wryly.

"So will you complain?" Diane asked her. "When they come to your gallery and purchase your art?"

Margaret laughed. "Good point. I suppose not."

Diane stretched her arms up into the air. "I can't think of anywhere I'd rather be, Margaret. Nowhere else on the planet is quite like this."

"*Look!*" Margaret pointed down the beach.

Diane jerked her head in time to barely see the edge of a flash of light.

"Did you see it?" Margaret stood, hands on hips, staring down at the lighthouse.

Diane nodded with wide eyes. "I did."

"Was it your imagination?"

"No." Diane felt a rush of excitement that reminded her of childhood.

Margaret looked up toward the bluff, then back out over the ocean. "Was it a reflection?"

"I don't know ... for sure."

Margaret turned to Diane and frowned. "I don't know for sure, either, but I don't think it was. I honestly think something is going on up there."

Diane bit her lip. As curious as she was to get to the bottom of this, she just wasn't sure. Maybe if Rocky were with them. Or if she'd brought a cell phone.

"I need to get home and start dinner," Margaret said as she pulled on her plaid flannel shirt. "Otherwise, I'd say let's go find out what's up there."

"Maybe next time ..." Diane looked wistfully toward the lighthouse. Part of her wanted to know exactly what was going on. Another part of her wanted to simply enjoy the romance of the mystery. She turned and followed Margaret back up the beach.

As they got closer to town, they noticed more people out walking on the promenade and playing on the beach.

"The annual migration has begun," Margaret declared as they turned off the promenade toward their neighborhood.

"It is kind of fun," Diane said. "Like waking something up."

"Looks like the Simpsons' vacation cabin is going to be occupied." Margaret pointed down Newport Avenue to where an SUV was pulling into the house across the street from her own house.

"Is it usually filled throughout the summer?"

"Pretty much. Sometimes it'll sit vacant, but not usually for long. One summer it was rented to the same family the whole time."

"Was that nicer?"

Margaret frowned. "Not in the case of that particular family. They had five very noisy children who ran unsupervised most of the time."

"Too bad Adelaide didn't know about her mother's helper skills back then."

"Unfortunately, Adelaide was only a child herself at the time." Margaret grimly shook her head. "And some of their kids were very unkind to poor Adelaide. I wasn't a bit sad to see that family go home."

As they neared their homes, Diane took her towel from Margaret lest Adelaide pop out and see it. "Thanks for inviting me to swim."

"Sure," Margaret said. "You're coming to the gallery opening tomorrow night?"

"Of course."

"It's not going to be the grand opening," Margaret clarified. "I'm trying to get another artist from the city out to display her work with me for that—and then I'll have a big shindig with live music and the works."

"Sounds like a great plan."

"But tomorrow should be fun with locals and friends. A bit like priming the pump."

Diane waved to Margaret, and they went their separate ways.

Before going into her cottage, Diane looked around. Whether it was the sunshine or the couple across the street chatting eagerly as they unloaded their car, it really did feel like something was in the air. Diane remembered how excited she felt as a child upon arriving in Marble Cove. She always felt like an adventure was around the corner: she couldn't wait to go to the candy store, and going to sleep with the feeling of gritty sand on sun-dried sheets felt good.

She chuckled as she stepped onto her front porch. She could experience that sand-on-sheets sensation tonight if she wanted. In fact, she'd just put line-dried sheets on her bed this morning. She opted for a nice hot shower instead.

Still feeling energized, she put on fresh clothes, leashed up Rocky and walked to town. Her plan was to get some fresh produce and seafood at the grocer's and come home and make a salad. Rocky was still learning to heel, but for the most part it seemed he wanted to please her, and going to town was a good opportunity to practice his best canine manners.

Fortunately, Marble Cove was a very dog-friendly town. Most business owners didn't mind if a patron tied a well-mannered dog outside of their shop. Some even let the dogs come inside. And some were kind enough to set out bowls of water on hot days to accommodate their furry friends. Also, Diane had discovered that going to town with Rocky by her side, especially when he had his cast on, was always a good conversation starter with others. All in all, it worked out nicely for both of them.

But just as Diane was passing by Mr. Calder's house on her way toward town, a fat gray cat emerged from the flower bed, arched its back and hissed. Naturally, Rocky barked and lunged, which frightened the cat away.

"No, Rocky!" Diane said, trying to pull him with her down the sidewalk. But not in time, because Mr. Calder was just emerging from where he'd been sitting in the shadows of his porch, probably watching the whole embarrassing ordeal.

"I'm so sorry," Diane called to him. "I hope Rocky didn't frighten your cat too badly."

The old man was making his way steadily toward her, and although he didn't look malicious, Diane had seem him blast his neighbors for any infractions or offenses.

"I'm terribly sorry, Mr. Calder." She tugged on Rocky's leash again. "I hope your cat's not—"

"That wasn't my cat," he told her gruffly.

"Oh well, then." Diane shifted her weight, still holding tightly to Rocky's leash.

"Your dog could eat that durn cat for supper, for all I care."

Diane couldn't help but chuckle. "Sounds like you don't like cats much."

"Not that one, for sure." He pointed to his flowerbeds. "That cat is ruining my begonias."

"Cats never seem to understand boundaries."

To her surprise, Mr. Calder bent down and patted Rocky on the head. "Good boy," he said. "You can chase that cat any ol' time you want."

"I didn't get a chance to talk to you much last Saturday after you came in," she said. "But I was so glad you and Dennis came over for my open house."

He made what looked like an uncomfortable smile. "It was a nice little get-together. Thank you for having us."

Diane remembered something Mrs. Peabody had told her about Mr. Calder, or maybe it was his father, but Mrs. Peabody had mentioned that someone in the family used to have a connection to the lighthouse. Maybe they'd helped to build it or worked in it or something. How to bring it up? "I really love living in this neighborhood," Diane told him, "and being so close to the beach and the lighthouse."

He nodded, but there was a flicker of something in his expression. Was it interest—or impatience?

"Did I hear that your family has a connection to the Orlean Lighthouse?" she asked hopefully.

Whatever friendliness she'd thought she'd seen in his eyes suddenly went out—as though someone flipped a switch from on to off. It was gone.

"Anyway," she continued nervously, "I'm writing a book. A novel actually. I might've mentioned it to you already. I've decided to include the lighthouse in my storyline, and I thought if I have questions about this particular lighthouse, well, perhaps you'd have some answers for me."

"I don't know nothing about that lighthouse." He briskly stepped away from her, barely tipping his head. "Good evening." He turned and hurried back up the steps to his house.

"Good evening," she called meekly after him as his front door closed with a loud *clunk*. She tugged Rocky's leash. "Come on, boy." She walked him away from the house, trying to figure out what had just transpired. For a moment she'd felt a sense of kinship with Mr. Calder, and it seemed the old man had liked her dog. But the instant she brought up the subject of the lighthouse ...

Another mystery.

CHAPTER TWENTY-FOUR

Diane waited anxiously as Mr. Wheeland went over his notes. He'd invited her over for coffee this morning—and to offer her a critique on her first chapter, which she'd let him read. Naturally, she was apprehensive.

He cleared his throat and adjusted his glasses. "I think you've made a very good first effort on this chapter, Diane." He paused.

"But ... ?"

He smiled. "Well, as I said, 'a first effort.' In my opinion, it is still rather rough."

"Can you give me some specifics?"

"Yes." He held up several pages. She could see red marks and handwritten notes filling the margins. "I've made lots of notes."

She nodded with wide eyes. "Yes. That is a lot of notes."

"I didn't feel that I understood your character," he said. "What is her motive? And what really drives her?"

"You mean besides the mystery?" she asked a bit timidly.

"Yes. I want to know more about her, Diane."

Diane nodded. "Yes. That makes sense."

He went over a few more details. The more he talked, the more she realized he was genuinely interested in helping her improve and wasn't just trashing her work. They were wrapping it up when someone came into the house.

"Oh, that must be Beverly." He stood happily. "I nearly forgot she was coming today."

He went to the door, and Beverly came in.

"Hello, Dad." Beverly hugged him and then looked surprised to see Diane.

"Welcome back!" Diane reached out to give Beverly a hug too, but Beverly looked slightly taken aback. Diane wondered if she'd overstepped her bounds. Like the first time they'd met, Beverly was impeccably dressed in a business suit, with her dark brown hair perfectly in place.

"It's good to see you," Beverly said formally.

"I'm surprised you're back in town so soon."

Beverly made a sheepish smile. "I had such a great time last weekend, I couldn't wait to get back. And because this is a holiday weekend, everyone in our office gets Friday off as well as Monday. So I wasted no time."

Diane couldn't help wonder if she might be hoping to accidentally run into Dennis. "Well, I won't keep you." She picked up Mr. Wheeland's notes.

Beverly looked at the papers on her father's desk. "Dad said you let him read your opening chapter."

Diane felt embarrassed now. "Yes, well, I uh ..." She held up the pages of notes. "We were just going over that. I think I still have a lot of work to do."

"He said it was delightful, Diane."

Diane felt her hopes soar. "Really?" She turned to Mr. Wheeland. "You mean you really liked it?"

"He didn't tell you that?"

Mr. Wheeland chuckled. "Well, I never quite got to that part."

Beverly nodded with a knowing expression. "He was probably playing schoolteacher first."

"Of course." He grinned.

"That's okay," Diane said.

"When you get to the last half of my notes, you'll see how much I did like it," he said.

"Thank you." She smiled happily. "I should get home now." She turned to Beverly. "But I'm glad you're back."

"So am I!" Beverly looked happier now. Surprisingly so. She seemed happier than Diane ever remembered seeing her.

"You're coming to Margaret's opening tomorrow, aren't you? You and your father?"

"Wouldn't miss it."

Diane waved. "See you then!"

★   ★   ★

The opening of Shearwater Gallery was relatively quiet, but nice. Over the course of the two-hour event, nearly thirty people stopped by. But there were never more than twelve in the place at any one time, which felt just about right.

Margaret had chosen some delightful piano music to play quietly in the background, and Diane appointed herself mistress of refreshments. Shelley became the chairwoman of the welcoming committee, and Beverly very rapidly mastered the story behind each of Margaret's pieces and was quick to share with anyone who looked even halfway interested. Allan did whatever lifting or running around needed to be done.

The little sitting area Diane had suggested was a big hit. The chairs were never empty, and it seemed the gravitational center for anyone wanting to chat while they enjoyed hors d'oeuvres. Everyone Margaret had expected to see at the opening did show up. And a few unexpected arrivals came, too, including a man who said he'd stumbled in just looking for directions in town but ended up buying one of Margaret's small pieces.

The last guests stayed twenty minutes beyond the announced closing time. But eventually it was just Margaret, Diane, Shelley, and Beverly.

"We'll really do it up right in about three weeks," Margaret said as they were closing it up for the evening. "I just contracted Dorothy Granger to show her oils, starting in late June and clear through until Labor Day. I plan to have a Shearwater summer solstice party on the first day of summer. I've got a jazz quartet from the high school lined up to perform, and I'll put ads in several of the newspapers in this area."

"That sounds like fun," Shelley said. "Maybe I can talk Dan into watching the kids for me again." She sighed. "It's so much fun being out like this on a Friday night. I feel almost like a grown-up."

Diane laughed. "I remember those days."

"Will you run an ad in an Augusta paper?" Beverly asked. "I'm sure lots of people there would be interested, even if they just drove out for a day."

Margaret nodded. "That's a good idea. I'll let Allan know as soon as I get home."

They worked quietly for a while, all helping to clean up the remnants of the cheese and cracker plates and dispose of paper napkins and plastic cups.

"That's the last of it," Margaret told them. "Thanks for all you three did." She held her hands up in the air and did a little turn. "I feel so happy—I don't want to call it a night."

"It's a beautiful evening out there," Beverly said. "I noticed a full moon coming up when I drove my father home earlier, and it's not even very cool out. Anyone care to take a moonlit stroll on the beach?"

"I'd love to," Diane told her. "I mean, um, 'so didn't I.' Did I say that right?"

Margaret laughed. "Not really, dear, but points for trying."

"I want to come too!" Shelley clapped her hands. "I haven't done anything like that in years—not since Dan and I were dating."

"Count me in." Margaret jingled her keys. "Let me lock up, and we can go."

Within minutes the four of them were walking along the beach with their shoes off. Others were on the promenade, and a few brave souls were even splashing in the ocean. The moon was so bright you could easily see.

"This is enchanting," Diane said as they strolled down the beach. "I wonder if you could paint this, Margaret."

"Might be fun to try." Margaret said. "Although I don't know that my camera could capture anything in this light."

Shelley was actually dancing now, doing some kind of beach ballet. To Diane's surprise, Beverly joined her.

"It does make one feel younger, doesn't it?" Diane said to Margaret. "Being out here in the moonlight like this."

Margaret nodded. "I'm tempted to take a moonlight swim."

"Really?"

"Well, not really. After all, I have on my good clothes, and I haven't checked the tide tables."

Diane looked out over the ocean, watching how the dark shiny waves reflected the pure white light. "Truly magnificent."

After a while, their foursome was farther down the beach than most of the tourists, and Margaret began crooning the old "Buffalo Gals" folk song. Soon the others were singing along with her.

> Buffalo gals, won't you come out tonight?
> Come out tonight, come out tonight?
> Buffalo girls, won't you come out tonight,
> And dance by the light of the moon.

With Margaret's help they made it to the girl with the hole in her stocking and her heel kept a-rocking before they all burst into loud laughter.

"I'm glad the tourists aren't down the beach this far to hear us," Margaret said between giggles. "We might scare them away—and I can use their business."

"Hey," Shelley yelled. "What was that?"

"What?" Diane asked.

"Down the beach. The lighthouse. Look!"

They all turned and looked down toward the lighthouse, but nothing out of the ordinary seemed to be happening.

"It was a light," Shelley told them. "I'm positive I saw it."

"Could it have been the reflection of the moon?" Beverly asked.

"No," Shelley said. "It wasn't like that."

"You know," Diane said, "Margaret and I have—"

"Look! There it is!"

This time there was no denying it. All four of them saw a flash of light—coming directly from the lighthouse.

"See!" Shelley yelled.

But as quickly as it came, the flash of light was gone.

Shelley looked at them, a little worried. "You guys saw that, right?"

"That was definitely a flash of light," Margaret said.

"Okay, good. I thought I was nuts."

Now they all began to talk at once, trying to decide what it was. Was it a reflection? A flashlight? Something reflected from one of the houses on the bluff? Maybe fireworks? The moon? They couldn't agree. But the one thing they could all agree on was that it was *not* their imagination. They stood there for about ten minutes, just waiting and speculating and waiting some more.

Shelley let out a loud sigh. "I wish I could stick around and figure this thing out, but I promised Dan I'd get home in time to put the kids to bed." She giggled. "Although it may be too late now."

"It's good for Dan to help out," Margaret told her as they all turned around and began heading back home. "Those are his kids, too, you know."

"Believe me, I know. And from what I'm hearing, Dan may have more time to help out soon," Shelley said a bit sadly.

"Why's that?" Diane asked.

"The shipping company ... it's not sounding too good."

"That's nothing new," Margaret said. "For as long as I can remember that company has been up and down. And yet it's still here, isn't it?"

"It is for now." Shelley's voice was laced with uncertainty.

As bad as Diane felt for Shelley and Dan's situation, she was distracted by the strange phenomenon of the flashing light at the lighthouse. She enjoyed the mystery and intrigue of not knowing what was causing these unusual occurrences, yet she was growing more and more curious. As a reporter, she wanted to get to the bottom of it. As a novelist, she wanted to tell the story.

Just how was it possible that a decommissioned lighthouse was capable of randomly flashing a light? Didn't that suggest that someone might actually be inside the lighthouse? And if so, why were they flashing a light? Were they trying to signal someone? And if so, who? And why? Was someone smuggling stolen goods? Could it be secret military messages? And whoever this person or people were, were they supposed to be there? Were they there legally? And if not, why wasn't anyone doing anything about it?

Diane knew from years of newspaper reporting that the most common criminal element was usually related to trafficking of some sort. But the idea that someone in their quaint old town might be using their beloved lighthouse as a haven for smuggling sickened her. Not only was it an insult to the lighthouse, but it could be hazardous to the community as well. As they turned onto their street, Diane remembered what Dr. Spangler had said about Rocky's injury—that it could well have been intentionally inflicted on the dog. What if that had something to do with a criminal element?

By the time the four friends said good night and parted ways, Diane knew she wanted to bring her concerns to the attention of the law. She was tempted to just go knocking on Detective Little's door on her way home, but she knew it was a bit late for that and would probably be an unwelcome intrusion into his personal world. As eager as she was to hear Detective Little's reaction to her crime theories, she knew it would have to wait until morning. So she went on home and flopped on the couch beside Rocky in his bed.

Unfortunately, the wheels in her mind were now turning. She hadn't given a thought to security since moving to Marble Cove. But being a single woman, all alone, living in a small cottage that was at the end of the street, closest to the beach, did bring its own set of concerns.

She looked over at Rocky, sleeping serenely in his doggy bed, and wondered ... *What had happened to him? Who was to blame for his injury?* Too bad Rocky couldn't talk. She wondered if he would have a negative reaction if he were to see his abuser, if there really was an abuser. Or would he, in the same way that some abused wives and children might do, rush straight into the arms of his enemy?

For peace of mind's sake, Diane went around her house checking the locks on windows and ensuring the deadbolts on the doors were secure and even leaving the exterior lights on. Then, reminding herself that she was safe in God's care, she went to bed ... and attempted to sleep.

But for the first time since relocating, she couldn't drift off to sleep, and she was forced to read until nearly two in the morning.

★　　★　　★

Even so, she was up fairly early Saturday morning. Diane knew that neither of the Littles worked on the weekend. And remembering the old days when she and Eric put in a long work week and how they relished sleeping in on Saturdays, she decided it would be imprudent to show up on their doorstep earlier than ten.

So she decided to make sugar cookies and even put a flag up by her front door in honor of Memorial Day weekend.

Finally, after tidying her house, weeding the flower bed and taking a shower, it was finally nearly ten. Even so, she made herself wait just a bit longer.

Finally, and feeling as if she might burst, at a little past ten she carried a paper plate of sugar cookies over to the Littles' and quietly knocked on their door.

"Oh, hello!" Cindy Little said. She was wearing a combination of pajama bottoms and a sweatshirt, and she looked surprised.

"I'm sorry. Is it too early?" Diane was embarrassed now. "I wanted to discuss a ... well, a legal matter with Detective Little." Diane pushed the plate of cookies toward Cindy now. "But I can come back—"

"No, no, it's fine," Cindy said. "Fred, there's someone here for you."

"Coming," Detective Little called from somewhere in the house. "Come on in."

"Yes." Cindy nodded with an uncertain look. "Do come in. And excuse the mess. As I said, housekeeping—especially after the children moved out—is not my strong suit."

"I'm afraid I should've called first," Diane said apologetically. "I didn't have your number, and I just thought—"

"It's okay," Cindy said as she moved a pile of newspapers from a chair. She sniffed the cookies. "*Mmm* ... these smell good. Would you like some coffee, Diane? I do make good coffee."

"That would be lovely, Cindy. Just black is fine." Diane felt like such a fool now. What had she been thinking to come barging in on their Saturday morning like this? Really, was she losing her mind?

Detective Little came into the room, hair a little messy, unshaved, and wearing sweats and a T-shirt. He sat down in an easy chair near Diane. "So what brings you over?"

"A concern," she said evenly. "I don't usually think of myself as an alarmist. And I lived in Boston for years, worked on the newspaper, so I'm not easily rattled."

"Oh," he said, rubbing his face. "So it's business, not pleasure, eh?"

Diane felt like saying, *But I brought cookies!* "Um, yes. Is that all right? I could come to your office on M—"

"No," he said. "I just needed a second to get my work brain on. Okay ... so what has you rattled?"

Diane sighed. "Well, last night I saw something and ... I got a bit worried."

He leaned forward. "What did you see?"

"Here you go." Cindy handed Diane a mug of coffee. Now she looked uncertainly at her husband and Diane. "Should I go somewhere else?"

"I don't mind if you hear this," Diane said quickly. "Like I was saying, I don't want to be an alarmist, but I just felt I needed to voice a concern." She replayed for them the recent events related to the lighthouse. "If I was the only one who'd seen these things, or if it was an isolated case, I would probably just brush the whole thing off."

"So, let me get this straight. You and your friends have seen a light coming from the lighthouse? Or a light flashing on to the lighthouse?"

"I'm not exactly sure. Maybe both."

He nodded, rubbing the stubble on his chin. "It's probably some old faulty wiring. Seems to me the electric company never got around to shutting the power off." He reached for a cookie.

"I realize this. But last weekend, Margaret and I saw a suspicious person at the lighthouse."

"Suspicious in what way?"

"Running away! And seeming to hide."

He didn't look very concerned. "Hmm. Well, Diane, kids and teenagers like playing games down there. Especially around Halloween. I've learned to look the other way. Kids need to have fun—as long as they're not breaking the law, that is."

"But that wasn't the only time someone had been seen lurking about down there. Remember Margaret's mysterious rescue and the footprints that led to the lighthouse?"

"Wait—is this another rescue?"

Diane felt the moment slipping away. "No, it happened a while back. I don't know exactly."

He checked his watch. "I see."

"And then, of course, there's Rocky."

He frowned. "Rocky?"

So she told him about her dog, his broken leg, and how she'd seen someone that day. "The vet says the break appeared to be the result of high impact, like someone beat him."

"Oh my!" Cindy looked horrified.

"But he's doing great." Diane knew she was overstating things, that the vet had said it *might* have been abuse, but she needed to get this detective on the hook somehow. "Still, I got to thinking about all these things last night," she said eagerly, "and I began to feel seriously concerned. You know as well as I do, Detective, that most crimes are drug-related. And I started thinking—what if some kind of drug-trafficking ring is using our lovely little lighthouse to smuggle drugs?"

"Oh, my word!" Cindy turned to her husband. "You have to look into this, Fred!"

He nodded, taking another cookie. "Yes. I will look into it. Be assured."

"Thank you. I'm so relieved." Diane stood now. "I'm sorry to have come unannounced like this. But maybe now you can understand how concerned I was. Last night I actually went around double-checking all my locks, and I left the exterior lights on too. My house is so close to the beach ... and I am alone."

"I don't blame you one bit," Cindy told her. "I would do the same thing."

"Will you let me know if you find anything?" Diane asked the detective.

"If he doesn't, I will," Cindy said.

"Don't worry," he assured them both as they walked to the door. "I'll tell you how it turns out."

"Thanks so much."

"Most likely, it's nothing more than light reflecting from a boat or a house or a car, combined with an overactive imagination." He chuckled. "You did say you're a novelist, right?"

Diane's hopes dimmed a bit. "I am working on a novel, yes."

"Does it by any chance involve a lighthouse? Or some kind of criminal element?"

She felt her cheeks blush. "As a matter of fact, yes ..." She tipped her head to one side. "How did you know that?"

He laughed loudly. "I'm a detective, Diane. It's my business to figure these things out."

"Good," she told him. "Now, please, go figure out what's going on up there and let me know if you solve this mystery. Cindy, thank you for the coffee. Maybe tonight we'll all get a good night's sleep."

Diane felt better as she went home. She hoped Detective Little would get to the bottom of it. It wasn't easy passing off a good mystery to someone else, because as an investigative reporter and novelist, she wanted to figure it out herself. However, there was a time for sleuthing and there was a time to leave it to the law. The idea of going out to the lighthouse on her own to snoop around, possibly at night, just didn't sit well with her.

CHAPTER TWENTY-FIVE

It was Sunday afternoon before Detective Little got back to Diane—and it happened mostly because she caught him in passing. She'd already exercised a great deal of self-control in not calling him on Saturday night. She'd kept reminding herself that no news was probably good news. But by Sunday morning, she felt she deserved some kind of response or explanation. If criminals were wandering around at large, she wanted to know. How long would it take to check this out, anyway? Even so, she didn't disturb the Littles on Sunday morning. Instead, deciding this was her opportunity to practice patience, she went to church.

Then, just a little past one she was out in the front yard pulling some last weeds from the flower beds and watering the window boxes. She'd recently planted the boxes with pansies, alyssum, and lobelia, and already they were looking very festive. She was just finishing the last one when she spied the detective opening the door to his pickup.

"Hey, Detective." She dropped the watering can and hurried past the Hoskins' yard and on to the Littles'. "Got a minute?"

"Sure." He gave her a polite smile. "How're you doing, Diane?"

"I'm okay." She wondered if he even remembered their conversation yesterday. "Did you have a chance to check out the lighthouse situation yet?"

He leaned against his pickup, pulling his aviator sunglasses out of his shirt pocket. "Oh, didn't Cindy tell you?"

"Tell me what?"

"That it was nothing."

"*Nothing?*"

"Well, not nothing *exactly*. But Officer Crawley figured it all out."

"Officer Crawley?"

"Sure. Crawley lives over on Hobnail, and he explained the whole thing to me. You familiar with raised trucks?"

She frowned. "Raised?"

"A pickup with an elevated chassis. You ever seen one?"

Diane shook her head. "I'm not sure what you mean."

"Some of the kids jack up their rigs, and they ride high." He held his hand up to his shoulders to show her. "Practically need a ladder just to get into the cab."

"Oh yes. I suppose I've seen those before. Not so much in Boston, though."

"It seems that every time one of those tall bad boys goes 'round Hobnail Turn, the headlights hit the glass on the lighthouse, especially if they're on high beam. And if you're in the right place at the right time, it bounces off the glass and looks like the lighthouse is actually running." He chuckled. "I guess lots of folks have been tricked by it over the years."

"Really?" Diane frowned, trying to take this in. Was it really possible that raised pickups were responsible for the unexplained flashes of light? Or was this detective just taking the easy way out?

"So, anyway, you can sleep well tonight, Diane." He opened the front door of his truck. "And don't let your imagination run away with you—well, unless you're writing your novel." He shook his head. "I sometimes wonder how Stephen King sleeps at night."

Diane was trying not to feel offended. "Then, if I understand you correctly, you never actually went down to the lighthouse to see if anyone was inside it?"

He laughed. "No, no ... I don't think that's necessary. Really, Diane, what do you think the chances are that someone would pick little ol' Marble Cove for his drug-smuggling headquarters?"

She shrugged, picking at the cuffs of her pink polka-dot gardening gloves, fully aware he was making fun of her.

He put his sunglasses on now, giving him a slightly hardened appearance, probably another hint he was ready to move on. "But you be sure and let me know if you see any more mysterious strangers running around and hiding out down there at Orlean Point now, won't you?"

She knew he was teasing but simply nodded. "Sure, you bet."

"See you around." He tipped his head to her and climbed into his pickup.

She just waved and turned back to her house as he drove away. "Well," she muttered, "*that* was a waste of perfectly good sugar cookies."

Detective Little had probably written her off as overimaginative. Or maybe he suspected she was a younger version of Mrs. Peabody. Whatever he thought, she'd felt dismissed by him, as though he had better things to do than placate an eccentric neighbor.

Oh, the raised pickup explanation was somewhat believable. Except they'd never been in the same place when they'd observed the flash of lights—sometimes they were near the lighthouse, sometimes not, and sometimes right under it. One time Margaret saw the light in broad daylight, and another time Diane had witnessed it in the fog. *Hmph,* she thought as she walked up to her house.

She was not buying Officer Crawley's half-baked theory or Detective Little's dismissal. In her opinion this was a case of plain old laziness on the part of the local police. Really, how hard would it have been to simply go down there, poke around, try locks on doors, and look for footprints in the sand? It wasn't as though there was a whole lot else going on in Marble Cove. At least she didn't think so.

"You look like someone just rained on your picnic." Margaret grinned at Diane from her front porch. "You okay?"

"Oh, sure." With a reluctant smile she walked over, meeting Margaret at the short picket fence that separated their properties. "I'm just trying not to be too miffed at Detective Little."

Margaret's brows lifted. "Miffed about what?"

Diane filled her in, explaining her theory and the clues she'd strung together herself.

At the end, Margaret seemed as upset as Diane was. "Raised trucks? Fiddlesticks!"

Diane laughed. "I realize I could be all wet. But everyone knows that drug smuggling *does* happen in small coastal towns just like Marble Cove. I hope that's not the case this time. But if the local police aren't willing to at least check it out ... well, what's a concerned citizen supposed to do?"

"Go check it out for herself?"

Diane planted her hands on her hips. "You know, that's very tempting."

"Don't forget you're in Maine now, Diane."

"What's that supposed to mean?"

"Folks are independent out here. Some Mainers consider Maine to be a country unto itself."

Diane laughed. "Meaning we can take the law into our own hands?"

"Not exactly. But a can-do attitude is almost expected in Maine."

Diane nodded. "Fine. I *can do* too. I'll go check out that lighthouse by myself then. Well, Rocky and I will, anyway."

"Not by yourself." Margaret waved to where Beverly was just coming over from her father's house. She had a cup of coffee in hand and looked as if she wanted to join them. "I'll go with you," Margaret declared as Beverly came into the Hoskins' yard.

"Oh, are you two off to somewhere?" Beverly asked hesitantly, as if she were about to scurry back home. "I don't want to interrupt."

Diane quickly explained her encounter with Detective Little. This time she tried to be a little more gracious. "I'm sure he's got his hands full ... but ..."

"Hands full with what?" Margaret asked.

"It is a holiday weekend," Diane pointed out. "The police are probably busier than usual."

"Yes, busy ticketing the tourists," Beverly said.

They all laughed loudly.

"Hey, girls!" Shelley called from across the street. Dan was outside playing chase with Aiden in their front yard. Shelley hurried over to join them. "Looks like this is where the party is today. What's up?"

Diane filled her in, careful to put an even better spin on the story this time. She didn't mean to malign the local police force—and him a neighbor, to boot.

But Shelley just nodded. "That's actually true about the traffic patrol. I saw two cars getting speeding tickets just outside of town. Tourists too." She giggled. "Sometimes I wonder how the cops are so good at picking out the tourists. I used to speed on that same strip of road, back before I had kids, anyway, and I was never ticketed once."

"And don't forget that cops have to get their quotas," Margaret told Diane. "Can't really blame them for trying to pay their own salaries."

"And the tourists *do* drive too fast," Beverly said.

Diane nodded. "That's true."

"So, anyway, Diane and I are taking matters into our own hands." Margaret had a mischievous twinkle in her eye. "We're going rogue."

"*Ooh,*" Shelley said.

"Yes," Beverly said, taking a sip of her coffee. "You're real rebels."

"Well," Diane said, lifting her nose imperiously, "perhaps not. But we're going to go check out the lighthouse ourselves."

"When?" Shelley asked with interest.

"Right now," Diane said with a resolute nod.

"Oh no, I can't right now!" Margaret said. "Allan's keeping shop at the gallery for me this afternoon. And I promised Adelaide we'd go get an ice cream."

"How about if we go this evening?" Beverly suggested.

"We?" Diane pointed to her. "You're coming too?"

"Do you mind?"

"Of course not. If you can handle being a rebel with us."

"Maybe just this once."

"I want to come too," Shelley said eagerly. "If you wait until after bedtime, like around seven, I could get Dan to sit with the kids."

"And the later we go, the better our chance of seeing the light," Diane said.

"And the less chance that we'll be seen," Beverly said.

"So," Diane said, looking curiously at her three friends, "we're all going?"

"I know! Let's make it a picnic," Margaret said. "A moonlight picnic."

"Yes!" Shelley clapped her hands. "It can be potluck. I'll bring spaghetti—I'm making it anyway. I'll just make a big batch."

"And I'll bring a salad," Diane said.

"I'll make dessert," Margaret said.

"I'll pick up a good loaf of bread and drinks," Beverly said. "Does that about cover it?"

"Yes," Diane said. "And I'll bring a picnic basket with plates and things in it."

"That way we won't look suspicious," Margaret said. "Just four friends out for a moonlit dinner picnic on the beach."

"I *love* this idea!" Shelley was actually dancing in the driveway now. Diane couldn't help but chuckle.

"So we'll meet around seven?" Margaret said.

"We'll need flashlights," Diane said. "And I'll bring my cell phone. And Rocky."

"I need to go," Shelley said suddenly. "I want to wake Emma from her nap early, and if I let Aiden skip his nap, both kids will be falling asleep by dinnertime."

So it was settled, they'd meet at Diane's and then, before the sun set, they'd venture over to the lighthouse to see what was really going on.

⋆   ⋆   ⋆

With their portable potluck, blankets, flashlights, and mascot—Rocky—the four women set out for their evening picnic.

"This is so much fun," Shelley said. "I wish Dan liked to do things like this. But at least he didn't mind my going."

Diane knew that for their marriage to get better, it would probably require more hard work from both of them. Good marriages don't just happen. She was glad to have seen Dan playing with Aiden and now watching the kids and encouraging Shelley to have a night out with the girls. Maybe he was learning.

They found a good spot to arrange their picnic—not too far from the lighthouse so they could easily see it, but not too close either. The plan was to be inconspicuous. Diane had hoped to go poking around the lighthouse before dark, but the other women seemed hungry, and Shelley warned them that the spaghetti would get cold.

So they arranged the blankets and dished out the food and were soon having such a good time that Diane nearly forgot they were on a mission. Rocky was happy to be included. He was the life of the party, and he worked his charms on all of the women.

"This spaghetti is delicious," Margaret said as she took a second serving.

"It really is," Diane told Shelley. "I didn't know you were such a good cook."

Shelley laughed. "Because I don't usually have much time to cook." She nodded to Margaret. "That is, until Adelaide came along. She's been a godsend."

Diane took in a full breath of the sea air and reveled in this late afternoon moment on the beach with friends. The sun would be setting soon. The light was yellow and came almost horizontal from the horizon. It was her favorite kind of light.

"It's been years since I've picnicked on the beach," Beverly said wistfully. "I'd forgotten how nice it is."

They continued to visit and eat, enjoying each other's company as much as the setting. It seemed that Memorial Day weekend, combined with good weather, had enticed a lot of people to explore the beach this evening. Couples and groups were happily strolling the promenade. Children intent on pushing back their bedtimes played and lingered in the sand. Everyone seemed to be enjoying the last light of day, with even a few swimmers braving the surf.

"What a great beginning of the season," Diane said as they began putting their picnic things away. "I think this is going to be a perfectly lovely summer."

"I wish I could be here for all of it," Beverly said, again sounding wistful. "Sometimes I think if I could find a decent job in Marble Cove, even if it didn't pay as well, I might just go for it."

Shelley looked surprised. "You'd leave the city and move here full-time?"

"I think I would." Beverly shook the sand out of a blanket. "And I know my father would appreciate it. I'm convinced he needs me more than he's letting on."

"Maybe you should look into it." Margaret dropped a folded blanket onto the picnic basket. "Allan and I were even younger than you when we made the transition, and we've never regretted it once."

Beverly nodded as if considering this.

Diane tucked a flashlight into her jacket pocket and checked the inside pocket to make sure her cell phone was still there. "Are we ready?" She leashed up Rocky.

"Ready when you are," Margaret said.

"All right, troops," Diane said. "We're off to solve the mystery of the lighthouse."

Shelley did a mock salute, and Beverly clicked her heels together.

"But don't forget, we are *incognito*," Diane reminded them. "Just act normal. We're simply four friends out having fun."

"So Diane," Shelley said, "you hear about the big-city boy who came out to Maine and got lost?"

Diane knew she was being set up. "I'll bite. Tell me about the big-city boy who came out to Maine and got lost."

"Well, he stops at a gas station and says, 'Where's this road go?'"

"Okay ..."

"Now, help me out with this, ladies," Shelley said. "So the Mainer at the gas station said ..."

"Don't go nowhere," Shelley, Margaret, and Beverly said together. "It stays right here."

Diane groaned. "Tell me you don't have a whole list of Mainer jokes I have to learn now."

"Girl," Margaret said, "if you don't know Mainer jokes, people will think you're dumber than a hake."

They laughed, evidently at her expense.

And so they went down the beach laughing, visiting, and joking as they made their way toward the lighthouse. By the time they got there, the sun was just setting, but the colors reflecting on the ocean were rich and warm, scrumptious shades of peach, amber, and coral. Margaret had brought her camera along in case they discovered evidence, but now she used it to catch some scenic shots, as well as some pics of her friends and Rocky in front of the lighthouse.

"Would you mind taking a photo of all of us together?" Margaret asked an older couple who were just leaving the lighthouse. The man complied and the four friends all hammed it up for the camera.

"Family reunion?" the woman asked them.

"Of sorts." Margaret thanked them as they returned her camera. "We're related in a miraculous sort of way."

After that couple left, they were the only ones remaining near the lighthouse. The four of them walked around the structure. Diane examined the heavy wooden doors, knocking on them, testing to see if they were unlocked. They ran their hands over the cool stucco walls, covered in layers and layers of white paint. Shelley even climbed onto the footing as she tried to peer into a thick window, but after years of weather and salt, it was impossible to see through the frosty-looking glass. They looked around in the shrubs and bushes to see if anything seemed amiss or if any clues or evidence of foul play had been left behind. Diane even encouraged Rocky to sniff around, as if she expected him to turn into a bloodhound and make some important discovery.

"There's no point in looking for suspicious footprints," Diane said as they looked at the sandy trail running around the lighthouse. "So many people have tramped around here, we'd never know."

"The locks all appear secure," Margaret said. "If corroded locks can be secure."

"There does seem to be a trail through the brush back there," Beverly said, pointing. "But it could be from animals. That's not so unusual."

Diane let out a long sigh. "I guess I should be thankful. I mean, I really didn't like the idea of a smuggler having taken over our sweet lighthouse. But for some reason I feel a bit let down."

"I'd hoped to find something of interest here too," Margaret said. "But maybe just to show that Detective Little ..."

"At least we had fun," Shelley said. "I'm actually relieved, you know? I love being able to bring the kids to the beach, but if I thought there was something dangerous down here, well, it would just ruin everything."

"But what about the flashing lights?" Beverly asked.

"What if it actually was a raised truck?" Diane said.

"Oh yes ..." Beverly nodded. "I forgot."

Diane looked around. "It's getting dark fast. Maybe we should head back."

"Are you terribly disappointed?" Margaret asked her as they walked back along the beach. Because the moon hadn't come up yet, they used their flashlights to illuminate the way.

"I guess I should be relieved," Diane said as she gave a tug on Rocky's leash.

For some reason, the dog seemed drawn to the ocean tonight, but there was no way she was letting him swim after dark. Suddenly he began barking and lunging toward the water's edge as though there was something out there he wanted.

"It's like he wants to chase a cat," Diane said as she pulled his leash. "Come on, Rock—"

"Look at that!" Shelley cried, pointing toward the ocean.

They all looked, and just as on Friday night, there was a flash of light. It seemed to originate from the lighthouse and then streak out over the ocean. But it was what Diane saw out in the ocean, lit up by the flash of light, that caught her attention.

"What is *that?*"

Chapter Twenty-Six

S omeone's in trouble!" Diane screamed. She directed her flashlight out to the spot where she'd seen the splashing illuminated by the lighthouse beam. Now she could see what appeared to be a person with arms flailing in the waves.

"*Help!*" came a muffled cry. "Help me!"

"That's a person!" Beverly yelled.

"And he needs help!" Margaret flopped down on the sand and yanked off her shoes. "I'm going in!"

"Not by yourself." Diane ripped off her jacket, peeled off her Bogs boots, and handed Shelley her cell phone. "Call 911."

"I'm coming with you," Beverly said.

"No." Diane handed Beverly her flashlight and the end of Rocky's leash. "You keep the light directed on us and hold on to my dog!" Margaret was already running straight into the surf. "I have to help Margaret."

"Oh!" Shelley said, pacing the sand. "Hurry!"

With her heart pounding like a jackhammer, Diane sprinted after Margaret. She kept her knees high to leap over a couple of short waves before plunging into a waist-high wave directly behind where Margaret was swimming, trying to keep her eyes focused on the splashing up ahead.

As she swam through the bone-chilling water, Diane silently begged God to help them—help them both and help the person in trouble. She could hear Rocky barking back on shore as well as the hoarse voice of the swimmer crying for help. It sounded like a man's voice. Keeping her head above water and trying to avoid swallowing the splashes of the rolling waves, Diane did the front crawl as fast as her arms could propel her.

"Hold on," Margaret yelled at the man. "We're coming!"

The moon was just rising now and the pale light made it easier to see the flailing arms and splashing water. Diane felt as though she couldn't get there fast enough. She pushed on with all her might, though a corner of her mind told her to save some for the swim back.

Margaret was still a couple of strokes ahead and not easy to catch. But as she swam closer, Diane remembered something—a drowning victim could be dangerous to his rescuers. As she swam, trying to catch up with Margaret, she tried to recall the proper technique she'd learned long ago in a college lifesaving class.

"Margaret!" she gasped when she reached her side. "We need to do this rescue *carefully.*"

"I know!" Margaret shot back. "We'll get him from behind. Do *not* let him grab on to you. We hold on to him. Got it?"

"Yes!"

"If he does get you, just swim down deep as hard as you can. He'll let go. He wants to go up, not down."

"Help! Help!" The man's cries grew louder as they got closer, and Diane could see the expression of pure terror on his chalk-white face. His eyes were wide with fear and his face twisted, as if in pain.

"Hang on." She hoped it wasn't a shark attack. "We're coming."

As soon as they reached him, Margaret took control. She began to tread water just outside his reach. "Do not grab on to us," she commanded like an army sergeant. "We'll help you." She swam sideways to circle around behind him.

Diane was attempting to imitate Margaret, going for the other side, but somehow the man managed to grab on to her arm.

He pulled her to him and clung to her. Diane took a quick breath and went under, pulling him along because he was still clinging to her. Beneath the water, she fought to get free of his grasp, peeling his hands away and pushing him. Finally, she got free and kicked him in the direction of the surface. She reached the top, gasping for air.

Then in one swift movement, Margaret grabbed the man from behind and wrapped her arm around his chest and neck like a wrestler. "Now hold still!" she shouted to him. "Relax! I've got you. But you have to stop fighting me."

Immediately he went limp. "Okay," he said, sounding hoarse. "I'm sorry. I'll try."

"I'm going to swim you to shore now," Margaret said, still speaking in her authoritative voice. She turned herself and the swimmer around and began the rescue stroke toward shore.

Diane knew better than to try to "help" Margaret or double up the rescue hold. So she determined to swim beside and behind Margaret, synchronizing her strokes with hers and nudging her each time. She hoped this would transfer some of her strength to Margaret and help Margaret conserve her strength. In this way they inched toward shore, mostly helped by the incoming waves.

Water splashed over them and into the swimmer's face, and suddenly he began struggling again.

"You need to relax!" Diane yelled directly into the man's ear. She could now see that he was a young man, probably not much older than her own children. His dark hair was long and his eyes were filled with fear. "You're making this harder for everyone."

He gasped and continued to squirm.

"Don't make us knock you out," Margaret screamed at him. "I can do it!"

Fortunately that seemed to help and he settled down again.

As they got closer to shore, their feet finally touched bottom, and they were able to stand him to his feet. Several people came bounding into the surf to assist. A couple of strong-looking young men took over, lifting the drowning victim from them and walking to dry land.

Diane and Margaret collapsed on to their knees in the shallow water. Diane flung her arms around Margaret. Laughing and crying at the same time, she hugged her friend tightly. "I can't believe we just did that."

"Oh my!" Margaret was sobbing too.

Rocky bounded out to them, barking and licking their faces. Beverly and Shelley ran toward them.

"Do you need help?" Beverly yelled as she pointed the flashlight on them.

"We're fine," Diane called back.

"That was amazing!" Shelley cried from the shore.

"Come on." Diane helped Margaret to stand. "Let's get out of here."

Holding hands, the two exhausted women made their way through the ankle-deep waves, Rocky bounding beside them. Beverly and Shelley slapped them on their backs and congratulated them for their heroic rescue.

"Let's go see how he's doing," Diane said between heavy breaths.

So the foursome went over to where a small crowd was now gathered around the man, who was sitting up on the sand.

"Doesn't look like he needs CPR," Margaret whispered to Diane.

Still somewhat breathless, Diane peered down at him. He looked to be about the same age as her son. The two young men were fifty yards away but approaching, carrying an ice chest between them. Maybe a cold drink would do them all good right about now.

"Are you okay?" Margaret asked the swimmer.

He nodded, still panting. "My legs cramped," he explained between breaths. "My muscles froze up. I sank like a stone. I would've drowned."

"These are the women who saved your life," Beverly said as she pointed at Diane and Margaret.

"Thank you." He nodded. "I'm sorry I—I struggled like that. I just panicked. But *thank you!*" Now he actually began to cry.

Down the beach, Diane saw flashing red and blue lights coming toward them.

*   *   *

The next morning, Diane went to see the Memorial Day festivities in town.

As usual, the parade started with the high school marching band, and just as when she was a child, the big bass drum reverberated inside of her and nearly brought tears to her eyes. Next came a float built to look like a boat. It was filled with Boy Scouts dressed as sailors and throwing candy to the crowd. They were followed by baton twirlers from toddlers to teens, with only a few miss-tossed batons. On it went, with fire engines and horses and even a trained cat on a skateboard. Finally she watched the last float, decorated in red, white, and blue, with war veterans in their uniforms and the "Star Spangled Banner" playing loudly.

After the parade, Diane went to The Cove, where she and Margaret met with some reporters. Word of the miraculous Marble Cove rescue had spread swiftly, and Diane and Margaret had agreed to answer some questions from a local news reporter, as well as someone from the TV station.

"Margaret Hoskins is my hero," Diane proudly said into the camera. "When I grow up, I want to be just like her."

Naturally, Margaret just laughed and claimed she couldn't have done the rescue without Diane's help.

"Our other two friends were crucial to the rescue as well." Diane told the reporters. "They called 911 and shined the flashlights out on the water so we could see." She also pointed out how the paramedics and some bystanders were helpful at the end of the rescue.

"Diane and I couldn't have done it without everyone's help."

Then Diane told the reporters about how she'd prayed in desperation. "So God deserves the credit too. Because it really was miraculous."

"I must agree," Margaret said. "It did seem miraculous."

"And we believe in miracles." Diane winked at Margaret, and she winked back.

"Sounds like it took a real group effort," the reporter said.

"Even my dog deserves some credit." Diane recalled how Rocky had barked. "He was the first one to notice something was amiss out in the ocean. He alerted us to the swimmer."

With the interviews finished, Margaret and Diane made their way to the back of the coffee shop, where Beverly and Shelley were waiting.

"You two should've participated in that too," Margaret said as she sat down.

"No, thank you," Beverly said firmly.

"And not with Emma in tow." Shelley shook her head as she bounced the baby on her knee. "Besides, from the looks of it, you two did just fine."

"I'm glad it's over," Diane said.

"Wow, what a night we had last night." Shelley grinned at them. "I told Dan I want to go out with you women at least once a week now. Kind of a girls' night out."

"Last night's act will be a tough one to follow," Margaret said dryly.

"You don't think we can make the newspaper *every* week?" Beverly teased.

"It's fun being the local heroes," Shelley said. "Well, Margaret and Diane are heroes, anyway. But it's still fun being involved."

"We were all heroes last night." Diane tickled Emma's chin. "I think we should design some kind of superhero costume with a cape and the works. Only, on our chests we can wear a big M for *Miracle*. And we could dress up every time we have girls' night out."

They all laughed, making more jokes about the fun they might have this summer and beyond.

"I wish I didn't have to leave today." Beverly set her cup down sadly. "I agree with Shelley's idea. If I lived here full-time, I'd vote for a weekly girls' night out too." She grinned at Diane. "But I'd have to just say no to your costume idea."

"Maybe for Halloween," Diane teased.

"Just keep coming back every weekend," Shelley told Beverly. "That way you won't miss out on much."

"That's true," Diane said. "And you mentioned how your dad needs you more now—so you really should come to Marble Cove every time you get the chance."

Beverly nodded. "Yes, I plan to do that. But the trip does get a little wearing."

"Then start looking for a job in Marble Cove," Shelley said eagerly. "Just don't look for one at the shipping company; Dan's pretty sure they're going down."

"Shelley," Diane said seriously, "it's great that you'll be getting more regular nights out with the girls. But you have to make sure Dan gets his night out with the boys too. You both need it."

Shelley sighed. "Sure, sure."

Margaret glanced at her watch now. "I hate to break this up, girls, but I told Allan I'd take over the gallery at noon."

"And I better scram too." Shelley stood with Emma. "Before this little girl starts singing for her supper."

"I should go too." Beverly picked up her purse. "I promised to fix my father some lunch before I leave."

They stood and exchanged hugs. Then Margaret headed down the street toward the gallery, Shelley and Beverly went back home together, and Diane walked over to the grocery store. She had a short errands list today. Just pick up a few staples—fruit and milk and eggs. Then she'd stop by the Pet Place to get a new collar for Rocky. He'd put on enough weight that his first collar was already getting tight.

As she waited to cross Main Street, Diane didn't even mind that the town was much busier than usual today. They'd just had a parade, after all. And this was the way she remembered Marble Cove from summers of her youth ... as well as from her visits here with Eric and the kids every year in late August. The touristy-hectic-busy pace simply felt familiar and normal. At least it was the old normal. Because, as she crossed the street, Diane realized that something was different this summer. She was no longer a tourist here. And that felt good.

She smiled as she entered the Pet Place. The smell of animals and pet food was surprisingly comforting, a small town sort of thing. She took her time selecting what she hoped was the perfect collar for Rocky, getting him a new chew toy as well.

"Thanks, Diane," Lee Waters handed her the receipt. "This turquoise color will look good against Rocky's coat." He glanced over to the front door. "Why didn't you bring Rocky along today?"

She chuckled as she tucked the new collar into her shopping bag. "I would've, but I wasn't sure how he'd handle the parade. You know how the sirens and horses and noises can be for a dog."

"Yes, that was probably smart." Lee's eyes lit up now. "Hey, is it true what I heard this morning? Did you and some other women rescue a drowning swimmer last night?"

She smiled and nodded.

"Wow!"

She laughed. "Yes, I suppose so." She thanked him and left.

She paused on Main Street, admiring the flags lining the street and all waving in the ocean breeze like a choreographed dance. She lingered there for a moment, listening to tidbits of conversations, kids begging their parents for an ice cream before lunch, a mom trying to find a shop that carried rubber flip-flops, a man who wanted to buy some fish bait. It all seemed so familiar ... so *at home*. Smiling to herself, she turned down Newport Avenue.

Before she reached her door, Mrs. Peabody came out all a-flutter and begged Diane to recap the adventurous ordeal from last night. Diane told her a nutshell version and then patted her shopping bag, saying she'd better get the dairy products into the fridge.

As she walked past the Hoskins' house, last night's rescue seemed far away and slightly surreal. Diane knew she'd done her part to help, but she had to give Margaret the bulk of the credit for having the cool head and self-control to keep the three of them from drowning, and she hoped she'd conveyed that to the reporters this morning. Diane had no desire to be portrayed as a hero.

It wasn't until Diane was on her porch that she realized that both she and Margaret had left out one very important piece of the story. Neither of them had remembered to mention the part the lighthouse had played in the rescue. They forgot to tell the reporters about the flash of light that had illuminated the drowning swimmer and gotten their attention.

As Diane went into the house, she considered calling the reporters and adding this one last bit of information. Reporters were used to that sort of thing—people often recalled something else later on. It was perfectly acceptable to let a reporter know. She picked up the phone and thought for a moment. How was she going to explain the mysterious light without sounding nutty? And what about what Detective Little had said about the raised pickup trucks?

Besides, how did one really explain a miracle?

For now, even though she felt certain the lighthouse had many stories to tell, she would leave it at that. The role of the lighthouse would be their secret. After all, whether the whole world knew it or not, a miracle was still a miracle. And the four of them had all agreed that last night's rescue was nothing short of a miracle. Whether or not the lighthouse had actually played a part would have to remain a mystery for now.

And Diane knew in her heart that the most miraculous thing about Marble Cove, the best part of living here now, was experiencing the sweet bonds of friendship with Beverly, Shelley, and Margaret.

Author Bio

Melody Carlson is one of the most prolific novelists of our time. With some two hundred books published and sales topping five million, Melody writes primarily for women and teens. She's won numerous honors and awards, including the Rita and Gold Medallion, and some of her books are being considered for TV movies. Melody has two grown sons and makes her home in the Pacific Northwest with her husband. When not writing, Melody likes to travel, bike, camp, garden, and walk her yellow Labrador in the great outdoors. Visit Melody online at www.melodycarlson.com.

A CONVERSATION WITH MELODY CARLSON

Q. What was your favorite part of writing The View from the Lighthouse?

A. I enjoy getting to know a new cast of characters. It's hard to learn everything about them in the opening book and some characters, like Beverly, are a bit elusive. I also enjoy creating the setting, deciding what colors to paint a house or what kinds of shrubbery grow there. Most of all I love seeing the characters interacting with each other, building friendships, and helping each other.

Q. How did the story take shape? How long did it take you to write it?

A. I'm not usually one to outline books, but in a series like this, outlines are a must. So that's really where the story begins. After that, I feel a bit like Diane because I'm exploring a new neighborhood, setting up housekeeping, getting acquainted with my new "friends." Writing, for me, is like a journey—I know I'm going from point A to point B, but I don't know everything that's along the way. Also, I'm a very fast writer and usually complete a novel within a month. For some reason that's just the way my brain likes to work.

Q. What kind of research did you do for this story?

A. First I read up a bit on Maine, things like wildlife, weather, geography, and even about the way people talk and think. I had no idea that Mainers were so independent or that they sometimes consider themselves a separate country. As far as understanding the beach and lighthouse elements, I live on the other coast and have a beach cabin (strangely similar to Diane's) as well as a beautiful lighthouse on our beach—so that part of the "research" was easy.

Q. How did you first become a writer?

A. I think I've always been a writer, but I didn't figure out it was possible to get published, beyond school newspapers, until I was in my early thirties. For some reason I suddenly felt like I needed to write or explode. I was pumping out stories, then books, and a few years later my books began to sell. That was more than two hundred books ago.

Q. Tell us about your writing process—where and when do you write? Do you listen to a certain type of music? Do you work from outlines?

A. I have a writing studio at my home in Central Oregon that's separate from our house. I sometimes listen to music though not usually. I also write at the beach and sometimes in our motor-home when we're on the road. I try to write during "normal" workday hours and consider writing my job—thankfully it's a fun job. And as I said before, I don't usually work from outlines— mostly because I like the adventure of discovery and being surprised.

Q. *What's your favorite part of writing fiction?*

A. I love that fiction can be fairly true-to-life—and yet the writer has control of the outcome. I can put characters through some tough times, and I often do, and yet they emerge stronger and wiser in the end.

Q. *What are some of your other hobbies?*

A. I like being outdoors—walking, biking, camping, gardening. I also enjoy reading and cooking and home décor.

Q. *What was your favorite book growing up?*

A. I loved a lot of stories, including *The Diary of Anne Frank*, *To Kill a Mockingbird*, and *The Pearl*.

Q. *What are you currently reading?*

A. Right now I'm reading a Christmas novella that I'm considering for an endorsement—I can't say the title because I haven't decided if I'm endorsing it or not, but so far I'm liking it.

Baking with Shelley

Here's a simple and delicious recipe for a zesty summer treat!

Lemon Squares

1 cup flour

1/4 cup powdered sugar

1 stick margarine or butter, softened

2 eggs

1/2 teaspoon baking powder

1 cup sugar

2 tablespoons fresh lemon juice

1 tablespoon powdered sugar

Heat oven to 350 degrees. Oil 8 x 8-inch pan. Sift flour and 1/4 cup powdered sugar into two-quart bowl. Using a slotted spoon, cream in margarine or butter. Pat mixture evenly into bottom of pan. Bake for twenty minutes. In separate bowl whisk together eggs, baking powder, sugar, and fresh lemon juice. Remove pan from oven and pour mixture over baked crust. Bake for twenty minutes. Remove pan from oven and let stand till cool. Sprinkle one tablespoon powdered sugar over top. Cut into nine squares.

FROM THE
GUIDEPOSTS ARCHIVES

This story by Cathy Slack of Glendale, Arizona,
as told to Skip Westphal, originally appeared in
the May 1987 issue of *Guideposts*.

S tay away from the pool, Danny," I told my three-year-old as he headed for the backyard to ride his Big Wheel. "Yes, Mom," he said.

Listening to the sound of his plastic tricycle, I returned to the kitchen, sighing. It was not easy being a widow, and raising two children on my own was often a strain. I busied myself about the house until something made me stop dead still. I cocked my ear. No sounds of Danny's tricycle.

I rushed to the kitchen window and looked out at the swimming pool. Danny's Big Wheel was bobbing in the water, and there, floating face down, was Danny. Desperately I pulled Danny out of the water and tried to administer CPR, but his body was cold and his face was gray. Siren lights swirled as the paramedics arrived, and the helicopter soon whisked Danny off to the hospital, where he lay in a coma. After my long, prayerful vigil, Danny opened his eyes, and soon he was well again, back home playing as usual. But somehow he seemed changed.

One day he said, "Mom, I want to see a picture of my daddy." I hadn't realized I'd never shown him a picture of his father, who had died before Danny was born. The first photograph I brought out showed my husband and his baseball team. Danny looked at it for a few moments. Then he pointed to one of the coaches.

"That's my daddy," he said.

"How do you know?" I asked.

"He talked to me in the hospital before I woke up. He said, 'You must go home now. Mommy needs you.'"

I looked at the man he'd pointed to; it was the father he had never seen.

Read on for a sneak peek at the next exciting book in
Miracles of Marble Cove!

What exactly is going on at the old lighthouse?

Finding Grace
by Anne Marie Rodgers

Dawn was breaking in Marble Cove, Maine. Long ribbons of pink and lavender clouds hovered above the horizon as a half circle of golden rays shot its beams into the sky. From the rocking chair on her porch, Shelley Bauer smiled and cradled her hot coffee mug in both hands. She treasured the few seconds of peace she stole in these early morning moments before her day began.

She gathered her bulky cable-knit fisherman's cardigan around her, curling her toes more deeply into the fleece lining of her slippers. It might be June, but Maine was reluctant to declare summer's arrival.

As she watched, the sun inched higher. Golden fingers reached across the restless Atlantic. The ocean began to gently reveal more blue than black hues, although the weather-rounded boulders and rocks along the coastline were still dark, shrouded in wisps of low-lying fog and mystery.

The Orlean Point lighthouse was almost a cut-out shape against the rich glow of the sky. She knew the old structure to be a white tower spearing into the sky, but it was little more than a dark image, lightening moment by moment as the sun rose.

A rustling sound coming from the baby monitor she'd set on the table beside her was a signal that Emma, her eight-month-old daughter, would soon be waking.

Shelley stood and stretched, but a muscle in her back protested the movement. Wincing, she took a deep breath, as the memory of her recent car accident rushed back into her mind, and once again, she sent a small prayer heavenward. *Thank you, Lord, for your divine intervention.*

She still marveled at the chain of events that day. She never, *ever* left her children with anyone except Dan. But when her new neighbor Diane had offered, for some reason, one she now realized had been prompted by a heavenly directive, she had left the children at home—and saved their lives when the back half of her car was completely demolished by a speeding semi. Any other day, her two most precious gifts in the entire world would have been sitting in that back seat. The idea of it could still make her hands shake and her pulse race. She took another deep, calming breath.

The first discontented squeak warned her that she'd better hustle if she wanted to get Emma out of her crib before the baby's noise woke her older brother Aiden.

Shelley's husband Dan came into the kitchen just as she set a plate of French toast at his place at the table. He paused to chuckle at Emma's activity, and then he crossed the room.

"Morning." He dipped his head and kissed her. "*Mm-mmm.* Looks good. I have an early shift today, so I have to get going."

Dan plowed his way through his breakfast. He glanced up once and caught her looking at him fondly. "What?"

"I just enjoy watching you enjoy my food."

He grinned. "What's not to enjoy? You're a great cook." As he rose from his seat, though, he frowned. "This chair seems a little wobbly to me."

Shelley nodded. "I meant to mention it yesterday, but I forgot. Is there some way we can brace it without damaging the chair itself?" Their antique mission oak table and four chairs had once belonged to Shelley's maternal grandparents. Although they both had passed away when she was young, some of her fondest childhood memories involved them, and she treasured the dining set.

"I'll look at it when I get a chance. I'm sure I can fix it up." Dan picked up his keys and gave her and Emma good-bye kisses. "Hope you have a good day with the kids, honey."

She nodded. "You have a good day too."

Dan flashed the same grin that had won her heart the first time they'd met. "See you later." And then he was gone.

Shelley smiled as she washed up their breakfast dishes. The strain that shadowed so many of their conversations these days seemed to be gone this morning. Perhaps things were looking up at Dan's workplace, but he didn't want to say anything just yet.

More than an hour passed. Shelley cleaned up the early breakfast dishes and made some pumpernickel bread dough. After she set it to rise on the warm corner of the counter beside the refrigerator, she sat down and began folding a basket of the kids' clothes.

A few minutes after eight, her three-year-old son Aiden came stumbling into the kitchen, rubbing his eyes.

Shelley opened her arms and caught him in a bear hug as she lifted him into her lap. "Good morning, my sweet boy. How are you?"

Aiden laid his head on her shoulder and snuggled in without speaking. Shelley rocked back and forth slightly, treasuring the moment. Her son was growing up, and most of the time he was far too lively and squirmy to want to sit in Mommy's lap.

"Want to count lighthouses?" she asked. Aiden shook his head. Sometimes he liked to count the strip of lighthouses that ran along the wallpaper border at chair rail height in her kitchen.

Painted white above and a rich red below the border, the walls were accented by other lighthouses that decorated every conceivable surface: the calendar, magnets on the refrigerator, the placemats at the table, even the clock on the wall and a cookie jar. She loved that unique cookie jar; she'd never seen another one like it. The main gallery ran around the top of the jar, and the lid was composed of the entire tower, the watchroom, and the lens.

Shelley got Aiden started on his cereal and then picked up Emma, who had been happily gnawing on a toy in her playpen. Strapping the infant into her high chair, Shelley began to feed her some fruit that she'd run through the fruit processor. Dry Cheerios and formula were fine, but Emma needed more to eat now.

"Mommy?" Aiden banged his spoon on a glossy newspaper advertisement, spraying milk from his cereal across the table. "I want this!"

"Aiden!" With one hand, Shelley whisked the paper away from the table and grabbed a dishcloth to mop up the mess. She winced as the quick motion irritated a muscle in her back that was still tender after the accident. "You have better manners than that, and I expect you to use them."

"But I want that." Aiden's voice was defiant. *That* was a Lego set he'd seen in the ad.

"You'll have to ask Santa next Christmas. You already had your birthday, remember?" Shelley turned back to the table to feed Emma another bite. The eight-month-old opened her mouth like a baby bird, making Shelley chuckle. "That's my sweet girl. What a good eater you are."

Emma grinned, a fat drop of drool rushing down her chin to drip onto the bib she wore. Shelley smiled back. "Mama?" she said. "Emma, can you say 'mama?'"

"I—want—that!" Aiden shouted, each word punctuated by a bang of his spoon.

"*Ah-da-da-da-DA!*" Apparently Emma was inspired by her brother.

Sighing inwardly, Shelley did her best to hang on to her temper. She was the grown-up, she reminded herself, and her son needed consistency and guidance, not a swat across the bottom. "Aiden, if you bang your spoon again, you will sit in time-out." She kept her voice calm and matter-of-fact, as she'd read in the childrearing book she had bought last week … and hoped her son couldn't tell that she was gritting her teeth.

Aiden, who had been hearing such words and seeing his mother follow through for a week now, finally seemed to be getting the message that tantrum-throwing didn't get him anywhere, and he subsided. "But Mommy," he said reasonably, "I *like* dose Legos."

"I know, sweetie." Shelley smiled, wishing their budget wasn't so strained, wishing she could give Aiden all the Legos he wanted. "I see things all the time that I like, but we can't buy them all."

Aiden, clearly seeing he wasn't going to win this round, squirmed in his seat and changed direction with his demands. "I want to get down."

"May I please get down?" Shelley said automatically.

"Yeah. Me too." Aiden squirmed again, totally missing the manners cue.

Shelley had to laugh. *One thing at a time,* she reminded herself. Aiden was realizing that there were consequences for misbehavior. They could worry about manners at another meal. She checked his bowl. Satisfied that he had eaten enough, she said, "All right, you may get down. You were a good eater today."

She unbuckled the strap on his booster seat with her free hand, and Aiden wriggled down by himself. "I want to play in the yard until Adelaide comes," he announced.

The Hoskins' Down syndrome daughter Adelaide came over several mornings a week to play with Aiden, a recent arrangement upon which Shelley had come to depend. Those two hours without her son dogging her footsteps seeking interaction and entertainment were so helpful. There was nothing wrong, she reminded herself, with needing a break from your child for a couple of hours.

"That's fine. Put your bowl in the dishwasher first."

Aiden picked up the plastic bowl and carried it to the counter, tugging open the dishwasher door and putting his bowl on the top rack like she had taught him.

"Good job!" she said. "Now you may go outside."

"See you." Her son's nonchalant phrase made her smile.

"See you," she said.

Aiden clomped off the porch, sounding more like a moose than a small boy, and Shelley continued her breakfast clean-up.

Emma squealed. "*Ay-day-day-day.*"

"Aiden went outside. He'll be back in a little while," Shelley told her, smiling. She set Emma in her playpen with her post-breakfast bottle of formula, where the baby immediately reached for the pink blanket with the silky edge that one of Dan's sisters had given her when she was born. Emma had developed quite an attachment to it, and Shelley tried not to be secretly delighted that she preferred it to the crocheted baby blanket her mother-in-law had made.

The screen door banged open. "Mommy!"

"Yes, Aiden?" Now what?

"I want a new swing. An' a new sliding board, an' a new sandbox—"

"The ones you have now are just fine," Shelley said firmly. "But if you really don't like them, I can ask Daddy to take them away."

"No!" Alarm lit her son's blue eyes, and he vanished from the doorway.

She chuckled to herself as she finished clearing the table and started wiping off the counters. She finally seemed to be getting the hang of handling her son since he'd stopped being mommy's boy and had started pursuing independence.

She winced as she walked into what looked vaguely like her living room buried beneath several layers of toys, laundry, newspapers, and magazines, and Dan's jacket, which never seemed able to find its home in the closet. She'd been a great housekeeper before Emma was born, but even with Adelaide's helpful visits, handling two small children seemed to eat up minutes faster than she could use them. True, things had been improving lately, but some days ... She sighed.

She picked up Dan's jacket and hung it in the closet, smoothing a frayed spot along one cuff. She might be able to do a satin stitch or darn over it, but soon he was going to need a replacement. And where would that money come from?

If only Dan hadn't spent all the money he earned renovating for Diane on a new big screen TV and Blu-Ray player. What had he been thinking? Then again, if only she'd gone to college when she'd graduated from high school ten years ago ... What had *she* been thinking?

She sighed again, and stared out toward the lighthouse, her solace when she was feeling especially overwhelmed. As she began to bend to pick up a rogue Lego, movement down near the base of the lighthouse arrested her in midmotion. What was that? She slowly stood upright, as she strained to see. There definitely had been something moving out there—something a lot bigger than a dog. Something like a person. What on earth would a person be doing around the lighthouse at this time of day? The lighthouse has been decommissioned for years.

She couldn't help but wonder if it had anything to do with the mysterious lights that she and her neighbors had seen. Lights they were certain meant something, even though they had been dismissed outright by Detective Fred Little. "The lighthouse must still be hooked up with the electric company," he said. He'd informed several other curious people around town of the same thing, and the matter had been put to rest for them. But Shelley, Diane, Margaret, and Beverly all felt the lights *meant* something.

She stood a moment longer, hoping for a better look, but whatever—*whoever*—it was appeared to be gone.

To read *Finding Grace* in its entirety, you can order by mail:
Guideposts, PO Box 5815, Harlan, Iowa 51593
by phone: (800) 932-2145
or online: ShopGuideposts.com

A Note from the Editors

Your purchase of *Miracles of Marble Cove* makes a difference! Every time you buy a product from Guideposts, you help fund our many nonprofit outreach and ministry programs, which include distributing Comfort Kits to hospitalized children, supplying our servicemen and women with uplifting booklets and magazines, and rallying prayer volunteers. To learn more about our programs and how you can get involved, please visit GuidepostsFoundation.org.

Thank you for your continued support!